A Postcard from

Hamburg

A World War 2 Spy Thriller

by

JJ Toner

First published as an eBook 2 April 2015

This paperback edition published 30 September, 2016 by JJ Toner Publishers PO Box 25, Greystones, Co Wicklow, Ireland

ISBN 978-1-908519-30-6

Other books by JJ Toner

The Black Orchestra, ISBN 978-1-908519-17-7

The Wings of the Eagle, ISBN 978-1-908519-18-4

eBooks:

The Black Orchestra, ISBN 978-1-908519-14-6

The Wings of the Eagle, ISBN 978-1-908519-15-3

The Serpent's Egg, ISBN 978-1-908519-30-6

Zugzwang, a short story, ISBN 978-1-908519-23-8

Ovolution and Other Stories, a collection of fun SF stories,
ISBN 978-1-908519-00-9

Houdini's Handcuffs (first published as *St Patrick's Day Special*), a
police thriller featuring DI Ben Jordan, ISBN 978-1-908519-24-5

Find Emily, The second DI Jordan thriller, ISBN 978-1-908519-11-5

JJ Toner lives in Co Wicklow, Ireland.

http://www.JJToner.net/

DEDICATION

For Pam

ACKNOWLEDGEMENTS

Sincere thanks to Lucille Redmond for her editing skills and her endless patience, to Anya Kelleye for another marvellous cover, to Karen Perkins of LionheART Publishing House for formatting the book for print, and to Pam, Dave, and Marion Kummerow for proofreading the book.

Special thanks to Bill Simpson and my friends on the Absolute Write Water Cooler Forum who gave me flying lessons: alleycat, cbenoi1, Aerial, ClareGreen, Deb Kinnard, and, especially, Prophetsnake.

A Postcard from

Hamburg

Part 1 – Camp Twenty

Chapter 1

June, 1943
Secret Intelligence Services HQ,
Broadway Buildings, Whitehall, London

Kurt Müller ran his eyes over the contract before signing it. By this simple act he was transformed from an Oberleutnant in the Abwehr – the military intelligence service of the Third Reich – to a humble foot soldier in the British army, his pay 2 shillings per day.

Colonel Underwood handed him a second single-page document, headed 'Official Secrets'. Kurt read it quickly, signed it, and handed it back.

"You are now an enlisted member of the Intelligence Corps in the service of His Majesty George VI. Congratulations," said the colonel. He stood, holding out his hand.

Kurt stood, shook the colonel's hand, and they both resumed their seats. "Could we talk about leave, Colonel? I was hoping to visit my girlfriend in Ireland. Her daughter's birthday is in a few days."

"Not possible, Müller, we have a most urgent mission for you. It shouldn't take long, and after that you may have a few days' leave."

Kurt bit his tongue. He dearly wanted to make it back to Dublin for Anna's tenth birthday, but there was no point arguing with the British army. He said, "I hope you're not expecting me to return to Germany again, sir. I doubt that I'd make it out of there alive a third time."

The colonel shook his head. "Nothing like that, Kurt. Our

colleagues in counterintelligence have requested your assistance with their investigations. They run ah… an establishment not far from here where they interrogate subversives and suspected German spies…" He paused in mid-sentence, took off his spectacles and polished them with a handkerchief.

Bright sunlight pouring in through the high window behind the colonel made it impossible to read his expression. "What's this establishment called?" Kurt asked.

"They call it Camp Twenty. It's run by a Lieutenant Colonel Stephens."

Kurt was not familiar with either name.

Underwood put his glasses back on his nose, tucking the metal arms behind his ears, one by one. "Unearthing Nazi spies is an uncertain business. Stephens needs our help – your help – to decide whether certain individuals who claim to be innocent civilians may actually be enemy agents. The hope is that you will be able to identify some of these from your time with the Abwehr."

"But it's a year since I worked in the Abwehr."

"Quite. The colonel knows that, which is why he wants you to pose as a suspect and…"

"He wants me to spy on the other prisoners?"

"Not to put a fine point on it, yes. The plan is to send you in there as a suspect, let you mix with your countrymen, shake the bushes, so to speak, and see what comes tumbling out."

"How long will I have to stay in there?"

Colonel Underwood lifted a bony shoulder. "Colonel Stephens will decide when to let you go." He waved a dismissive hand and turned his attention to the papers on his desk. "Talk to Major Faulkner about an alias and a cover story."

#

Kurt found Erika Cleasby, his companion from their last mission, nursing a cup of tea in the empty canteen. She'd had her hair cut short, almost like a man's, and swept away from her face. It was an extraordinary transformation that accentuated her hazel eyes and full lips.

He took a cup of ersatz coffee to the table and sat beside her.

"You look great, Erika. That's an interesting new hair style." He took a sip of his drink and pulled a face.

"Hello, Kurt. Do you like it?" She patted her hair. "It's the latest fashion in Paris, so I'm told."

"It's beautiful. When are you leaving?" He'd heard a rumour that she was to be posted to France. Half-Swedish, half-Canadian, Erika was fluent in at least four languages that he knew of, including French.

"Any day now. What about you?"

"I've been given a short assignment in London. Colonel Underwood has promised me some leave when it's finished. I'm hoping to get home to my family."

"How is Gudrun? Have you heard from her? Where is she?"

"She's still in Dublin with my mother. She doesn't know where I am."

"And Anna? How old is she now?"

"She's nearly ten."

"I thought your mother had a telephone."

"She does but it doesn't seem to be working anymore."

"You should write her a letter."

Kurt made no reply to that. He had been meaning to write, but somehow never found the time.

He asked Erika where she was billeted. There were no women residents at SIS headquarters.

"A small hotel on Bayswater Road, for another week anyhow – until I leave for France," she replied.

#

"This is your cover story, Kurt. Read it, memorise it and throw it away."

Major Faulkner handed over a folder. Kurt flipped it open. "So I'll be posing as this… Aldus Drexler?"

"Aldus Drexler is your alias. You will arrive at Camp Twenty with an obviously false identity card and nothing else. For the purposes of this exercise, Aldus Drexler is the only name you will admit to for the duration of the exercise."

"Even among the prisoners?"

"Even among the prisoners you are Aldus Drexler, unless someone recognises you."

"Then what?"

"Improvise. Get into the mental state of an Abwehr agent behind enemy lines, and behave accordingly."

"Like an actor."

"No, this is not acting. You need to believe that you are an Abwehr agent, concealing vital information from your jailers. And be warned..." Major Faulkner writhed in his seat. Kurt had never seen him so unnerved. "...Lieutenant Colonel Stephens has a certain reputation..."

Kurt knew what that meant. His innards churned. "What if I refuse?"

The major fixed him with his gaze. "That's not an option, Kurt. As a member of His Majesty's armed forces you are obliged to follow a direct order."

Chapter 2

Wearing handcuffs and escorted by an armed Tommy, Kurt was delivered in an army truck to Camp Twenty in Latchmere Road, 40 minutes bone-shaking drive from SIS headquarters. He was instantly dismayed by the sight of the building, a dilapidated three-storey mansion standing in its own grounds, surrounded on all sides by two rings of cheerless 10-foot high barbed-wire fence. A sentry guarded the only entrance. The Tommy marched Kurt inside, released him to a look-alike and departed.

Two guards frogmarched him into a room with bare floorboards and no furniture. The place had the disinfectant reek of a hospital overlaid with a sinister layer of body odours. They removed the handcuffs and ordered him to strip. Kurt removed his clothes.

One of the guards clicked his fingers. "And the watch."

Kurt removed his watch and handed it over. The guards gave him a threadbare shirt in duck-egg blue, a matching pair of wafer thin trousers and light shoes with no laces.

"What about underwear?" he asked.

"No talking," said one guard.

"*Sprechen verboten!*" said the other one in a comic German accent, spraying Kurt's face with spittle.

Kurt put on the clothes. The pants barely reached his shins.

They led him down a bare corridor to another room, opened the door without knocking, and pushed him inside. A stern-faced man in the uniform of an officer sat behind a desk. Kurt assumed this must be Lieutenant Colonel Stephens. The guard stood at the door. Kurt remained standing. There was nowhere to sit.

"Herr Aldus Drexler. Where do you come from?" Stephens spoke in flawless German, his accent difficult to place.

Kurt replied in German. "I'm from Munich." His stomach growled; he hadn't eaten since breakfast, 8 hours earlier.

Stephens peered at him through a monocle that appeared welded to his right eye.

"When and why did you arrive on British soil?"

"I have been here since early 1939. I was on a student exchange when the war broke out. I couldn't get home."

The colonel's lip curled in a sneer. "Ah, the student exchange! If I had a pfenning for every time I've heard that yarn, I would be a very rich man. You'd be well advised to come up with something more original than that when you speak to my men."

Kurt watched as Stephens's jaw moved. He was grinding his molars. Either that or he had saved some titbits from his last meal. Kurt did his best to suppress a smile.

"You find something amusing?"

Kurt shook his head. "Nothing. It was a passing thought."

"Share it with us."

Kurt assembled a plausible story as he spoke. "You remind me of an uncle of mine, a shoemaker from Wiesbaden."

"How do I remind you of him?" Stephens glared at Kurt.

"He wore an eyeglass like yours."

"You find my eyeglass amusing?"

"Not at all, sir," said Kurt, his stomach disagreeing with him loudly.

The Tommy by the door cleared his throat.

"Leave us," said the colonel, and the guard left the room.

Stephens waited until the door was closed, then continued in a moderated tone, "I hope Colonel Underwood has explained your purpose here. The prisoners in Camp Twenty are all known or suspected enemy agents. Our task is to extract the maximum amount of information from them in the minimum time. We are particularly interested in their methods of communicating with their handlers in Germany. Your job is to infiltrate and gather information. If you recognise anyone you must let me know immediately. Do you understand?"

"Yes, sir."

"It will be vital to maintain the fiction," said Stephens. "As long as the prisoners think of you as one of their own, they will be unguarded in what they say in your presence. If the prisoners suspect for a moment that you're working for us, you will learn nothing and it's quite possible they may kill you. For this reason none of my men have been told who you really are. As far as they know you are just another enemy agent and you will be treated accordingly. Is that clear?"

Kurt shivered. "Yes, Colonel."

"We shall talk again." Stephens strode to the door up and opened it. "Guard! Bring this prisoner to his dormitory."

The guard came in and escorted Kurt from the colonel's office.

Kurt wasn't certain what he had expected, but the short interview had been a strange, surreal experience. The colonel's message was clear: he was in for a rough passage.

His guard took him to the top floor. As they climbed the stairs Kurt caught distant echoing sounds, sounds of muffled screams and men shouting. The guard unlocked a door and bundled him inside. Kurt stumbled forward and found himself in a foul smelling room with three prisoners, all three seated on their cots. The door slammed shut and the key turned in the lock.

The window was boarded up, and the air in the room was foul. A naked bulb hanging from the ceiling provided the only light. Kurt quickly identified an open bucket in a corner behind the door as the origin of the stench.

"Welcome to Camp Twenty. I'm Hubert," said the man to his left in guttural German.

"What time is it?" said the man to his right.

"I arrived at about 2:00 pm. It must be close to three," Kurt replied.

"What news from the War?" said the third prisoner.

Kurt replied, "We lost Tunisia last month. And the Luftwaffe shot down a civilian airliner over the Bay of Biscay. There was a rumour that Winston Churchill was on board…"

"But he wasn't?"

Kurt said, "He spoke on the radio a couple of days later."

"A pity," said the third man. "I'm Boris. This is Simon."

Kurt nodded to each man. "I'm Aldus."

"Have you met Tin-eye yet?" said Hubert.

"Tin-eye?"

"Oberstleutnant Stephens." He made a circle with his fingers and placed it over one eye.

"Briefly," said Kurt. "He seemed like a typical British tinpot dictator, all bluster and no steel."

Boris laughed. "That's Tin-eye. He's not the worst of them."

"Watch out for Cartwright. Be careful what you say to him. He's a tricky bastard," said Simon.

"How will I know him?" said Kurt.

Boris said, "You'll know him when you meet him. He's short and fat."

"Look for a beer cask on legs," said Hubert.

"He's a bastard," Simon repeated, shaking his head.

"When do we get fed?" said Kurt.

The three men laughed in unison. "After dark if we're lucky."

Chapter 3

'After dark' was an amorphous concept. With no daylight to measure the passage of time, it dragged by. Kurt attempted conversation with his fellow prisoners. Other than providing their birth places, the names of their wives and ages of their children, their responses were short and uninformative, and he soon gave up. Mindful of his mission, he examined their faces. He recognised none of them. All three looked older than their years, pale-faced and suffering from varying degrees of hair loss. They all had poor teeth and Kurt was alarmed by how thin they were, with legs like sticks and fingers like gnarled twigs. Hubert was tall – Kurt estimated 1.94m. Boris was the youngest and had more hair than the others. Simon had a permanent runny nose.

Simon stood up, shuffled across the cell, dropped his trousers and squatted over the bucket. "Forgive me." He said, sniffing loudly.

When he had finished he returned to his place.

#

With a rattle of key in lock, the door swung open and they all got to their feet. Two Tommies led them to a large open room on the ground floor with rough wooden tables and benches occupied by a ragtag collection of prisoners, all dressed in the standard uniform. The first thing that struck Kurt was the lack of noise; nobody spoke. It was like the refectory of a silent monastic order. Obviously, speaking was 'verboten' here. He counted 23 men including the three he'd spent the afternoon with. Running his eyes over the faces he could see, he spotted one that was vaguely familiar, a man in his early fifties with the physique of an aging prize-fighter, close-shaved hair and pale blond eyebrows. Kurt couldn't put a name to the face, nor recall where he had seen him before.

They sat at one of the tables and every man in the room was given a spoon, a bowl of broth and a thin slice of bread. Kurt tucked in. The broth was lukewarm. It tasted of cabbage with traces of onion. As he reached the bottom of the bowl, he found hard lumps the size of nail clippings that might have been pieces of carrot or turnip. They might have been nail clippings. He used his bread to mop up every morsel. When he'd finished he looked up to discover that few of the other prisoners had finished eating.

He ran his eyes over the prisoners again, but recognised no one else. Through the windows he could see that it was well after dark. Being midsummer, it must have been 11:00 pm or later. Late in the day for a meal. The soup was a passable first course, although a bit watery. Kurt wondered what the main course would be. Mutton, probably.

A shout from one of the guards, echoed around the room. *"Raus!"*

Everyone stood and moved toward the door.

"Is that all we get?" Kurt whispered to his tall companion.

"That's it," Hubert replied.

"Silence. *Sprechen verboten!*" a guard roared. There was nothing comical about that accent.

The next stop was a washroom equipped with four urinals and six filthy toilets, with no partitions between the toilet pans. The men were given 15 minutes to use the toilets and wash in cold water. After that they were marched upstairs. Kurt and his three companions were ushered into their sleeping quarters. The guard closed the door and locked it.

Without a word the three men collapsed onto their cots. Kurt did the same, pulled the thin blanket across his shoulders and fell asleep.

Chapter 4

Day 2 began with breakfast in the mess. Cold grey porridge was served with lukewarm tea, cheese and bread. A murmur of voices told Kurt that the men were permitted to speak. He sat beside the one man in the room that he had thought he recognised.

He introduced himself. "Aldus Drexler."

"This is not your table," said the man. He was much like the rest of the prisoners, thin, pasty-faced and balding. His biceps were impressive, but his stomach muscles had begun to sag with age. There was something about the turn of his mouth that Kurt found tantalisingly familiar.

"I'm sorry," said Kurt, "I thought I knew you."

"You were mistaken," said the man. "This is not your table."

"I'm sure we've met before – in Berlin, perhaps?"

The man resumed his conversation with the prisoner across the table. Kurt racked his brain, trying to imagine what the man would have looked like in his prime and dressed in a Wehrmacht uniform. The man's voice was familiar, too.

Kurt said, "Perhaps we met on basic training. Where did you do your initial training?"

The man turned to Kurt. He lowered his voice. "Go back to your own table, Müller. We are not acquainted."

Carrying his food, Kurt returned to the three men of his 'set', a ripple of adrenalin running through his body. The man knew his real name! As he ate he continued to search his brain for a memory of where they had met. All he came up with was a vague thought that the man's family name was something short beginning with the letter 'B', something like 'Beck'. Baum? Bach... not likely!

#

After breakfast Kurt was taken to an interview room for interrogation. The questions were delivered in German by a lanky individual dressed as a corporal, sitting behind a plain wooden table, while an armed soldier stood guard by the door.

Kurt was forced to stand.

The interrogator took him through his cover story. When he was asked where he had been living Kurt gave the address given to him by Faulkner at SIS headquarters. "17 Hampton Gardens, Wimbledon. But the house was bombed in 1942. I've been living rough since then."

"On the streets?"

"Yes, and in the underground."

"How did you wash and keep your clothes clean?"

Kurt answered as best he could. The interrogator's face gave no clue of belief or disbelief.

"What was the name of your landlord in Hampton Gardens?"

"Mrs. Lydia Evans. She was killed in the bombing."

"Is there anyone who can verify that you lived there?"

"Afraid not."

The three people in the room felt like a crowd. The ceiling was high, but there was barely large enough floor space for the furniture. The absence of windows and the heat emanating from the uniformed soldier created a stifling atmosphere. Kurt could smell the corporal's sweat.

"Is your transmitter still functioning?" This question was delivered in the same calm tone of voice as all the others. It would have been easy for a weary prisoner to reply "yes" or "no" without thinking.

"What? I don't have a transmitter."

The lanky interrogator never blinked. "Tell me about the student exchange. What were you studying?"

"Mathematics. I had planned to do a postgraduate course and research in Exeter University, but I never got the chance."

"The subject of your research?"

"Algebraic Topologies and Riemannian Geometry Constructs."

"Riemannian…?"

"It's an active field among contemporary mathematicians."

"I see. But the War broke out before you could get started?"

"Exactly."

"What was the name of your professor at Exeter?"

"Gareth Rees." The first morsel of truth in the whole sorry fabrication.

"Why did you not choose one of the many fine universities in Germany for your studies?"

"I got to know Rees's work in Dublin where I obtained my primary degree." A second morsel of truth.

"And the name of you professor in Dublin?"

"Stephan Hirsch."

"Your father's name?"

"Walter Müller."

Shit!

After a long pause the interrogator said, "So your name is Aldus Müller?"

"Aldus Müller Drexler. I prefer Aldus Drexler," said Kurt, making the most of a bad mess. "My mother married again after my father died, and my stepfather gave me his name."

The questioning continued through the day in one-hour sessions with short breaks in between. Kurt was provided with water and biscuits and allowed toilet breaks whenever he requested them. His lanky interrogator never raised his voice and remained polite at all times, although the questioning was repetitive, covering the same ground over and over again with the occasional 'rogue' question tossed in every so often in an attempt to trip him up.

In the afternoon the prisoners were permitted 30 minutes in an exercise yard in groups of 10. Kurt checked the faces of the men in the yard, but 'Beck' or 'Baum' or whatever his name, was not among them and he recognised no one else.

Once the exercise period was over, Kurt was taken back to the interview room to face a further battery of questions about his parents and his childhood. They broke for the evening meal – more watery vegetable broth – and resumed again immediately afterwards.

By the time he was allowed to rest Kurt was like a wet rag. He fell onto his cot and slept.

Chapter 5

"On your feet, Drexler. *Raus! Raus!*" Kurt awoke from a deep sleep, a Tommy shaking him by the shoulder. His first thought was that the building was on fire. He had been asleep for less than an hour.

He rubbed his eyes. "What's happening? What time is it?"

"Get up. *Schnell!*"

Kurt swung his legs off the cot and got to his feet shakily.

Two Tommies grabbed him by the arms and dragged him from the room, barefoot.

"My shoes—"

They marched him down the stairs and into a cell where another two Tommies were waiting, a beefy one sitting behind a rough wooden table, the other by the door. The room was badly lit, a single naked bulb dangling overhead, its light intensified by the thick blackout curtains. Kurt stood, swaying, trying to collect his wits.

"Name?" said Beefy.

"Aldus Drexler." Kurt was still half asleep. His innards groaned.

"I will ask you again. What is your name?"

"Drexler. Aldus Drexler."

"When were you born?"

"July first, 1913." The truth.

"We have information that you are an agent of the Abwehr."

Kurt repeated his cover story for the hundredth time. "I was on a student exchange. I got stranded when the war started."

"You expect us to believe that cock-and-bull story?"

"It's the truth," said Kurt, inserting a squeak of outrage into his voice.

"We know you were sent here to spy for the Third Reich. We shoot spies."

Beefy paused. This must be Cartwright. The man was less than 1.7 metres tall, his physique exactly like a beer cask with legs, and with nothing but a few miserable strands of hair on his head. "You mentioned an uncle when you spoke with the colonel. Tell me more about this uncle. Where does he live?"

"In Wiesbaden."

"Is he still living there?"

"Yes, I believe so. I haven't seen him in several years."

"How many years?"

Kurt was fully awake now, but his brain was addled from fatigue.

"I think I last saw him before I moved to England."

"When was that?"

"In July 1939."

"You're sure about that?" Cartwright's eyes glinted in the half-light.

Kurt nodded. He was busy storing away these details in his head.

"What was his name, this uncle of yours?"

"Heinrich. Uncle Heinrich. He was my father's brother." Close to the truth.

"Was? Didn't you say he was alive?"

"To the best of my knowledge," said Kurt, "but my father is dead."

"When did he die?"

"In July 1934." The truth.

Cartwright switched to English suddenly. "Tell me about your mother."

"She is Irish."

"You learnt your English from her? Shouldn't you have an Irish accent?"

Kurt gave a small laugh. "I do have an Irish accent."

Cartwright grunted. "What did your father do?"

"He worked in local government, in urban planning."

"And your stepfather? This… Drexler?"

Kurt's mind went blank. The lanky interrogator had covered all this, but he couldn't recall what he'd said his fictional stepfather did for a living. He said, "Yes, his name was Drexler."

Luckily, Cartwright changed tack.

"You say you were a postgraduate student when the war started. What were you studying and in what university?"

"Mathematics," True. "In Exeter." A lie

"Your professor?"

Kurt was stumped by this question. He remembered answering it when the lanky interrogator asked that question, but he was rocking with sleep. "I'm sorry, I can't recall his name."

"Why not?"

"I'm tired. I've been questioned for hours and I've had no sleep."

"Tell me about your uncle again. What was his name?"

"Heinrich Drexler."

The interrogator paused. "Heinrich Drexler? Shouldn't that be Heinrich Müller? You did say your father's name was Walter Müller."

Shit.

"Yes, sorry. You're right of course. Heinrich Müller was his name."

"What sort of shoes did he make?"

"Boots, I think. I'm not sure."

"He was your favourite uncle, a shoemaker. Are you telling me he never made you a pair of shoes?"

"Never."

"That is strange. How far is Wiesbaden from Munich?"

"I'm not sure. 200 kilometres? We hardly ever visited him. Never."

"And yet you remember his eyeglass."

Kurt's innards growled again. "Look, I was a child…"

"You say you studied in Exeter University," said Cartwright.

"I intended to do postgraduate work and research there, but I never enrolled." Kurt was sure that was his cover story, but he couldn't recall why he'd never enrolled.

"And yet you cannot recall the name of the professor there?"

"His name escapes me. I'm exhausted…"

An hour later, after continuous questioning, Cartwright switched back to German. His voice rose a semitone.

"I believe your name is Müller. Aldus Drexler is clearly an alias. What is your given name?"

"My name is Aldus. Aldus Müller Drexler." Cold sweat trickled under Kurt's arms.

"This student exchange story is a load of horsefeathers," said Cartwright. "Admit it and we can all go and get some sleep."

Kurt shook his head. "I can't admit what's not true."

"Tell us who your handler is, give us the names of all your fellow agents, show us where you have hidden your transmitter, and we may let you live."

"I have no handler and no transmitter. How can I convince you?"

"Give us the names of every Abwehr agent you know of in Britain."

Kurt shook his head. "I am no spy. I told you. I know nothing of spies or the Abwehr."

Cartwright stood up abruptly and left the room. Another soldier replaced him, and the new man started from the beginning. What is your real name? How and when did you enter the country? Where have you hidden your transmitter? And so on, the questioning continuing right through the night.

#

The interrogations continued through the third day and night and on into day four with breaks only for meals, to use the toilet, and the afternoon 30-minute exercise period. He was allowed to go to bed each night, but then woken again cruelly after a short time for more questioning. The most severe interrogation was conducted by Cartwright, his bullish intimidating attitude full of supressed violence.

By day 5 Kurt was beginning to hallucinate. A grotesque effigy of Tin-eye Stephens's head appeared on the wall behind his interrogator, grinning mindlessly. Then the head transformed into a horned demon with red, burning eyes and laughed at him.

Chapter 6

He was allowed to sleep for six glorious hours that night. In the morning, while all the other prisoners were at breakfast, Kurt was taken to the colonel's office.

"Report," barked the colonel.

Kurt shrugged "I have nothing."

The colonel glared at him through his monocle. "You've been here four days and you have found out nothing?"

"I have been denied sleep and interrogated non-stop since I arrived. I have scarcely had time to get to know any of the prisoners. Frankly, Colonel, I think the whole exercise is a total waste of time."

"Have you seen anyone you know?"

"No one."

"Why are you lying to me? Colonel Underwood assured me you were to be trusted."

"I'm not lying. I recognised no one."

"What about the man you spoke to in the mess hall?"

"I thought his face was familiar, but I was mistaken."

"And yet he knew your real name."

Kurt was astonished. The man had spoken *sotto voce* when he used the name 'Müller'. How had the British picked that up?

"I'm sorry, Colonel, if he used my real name, he may have mistaken me for someone else. I don't know this man."

"You are dismissed," said the colonel. "Get me something concrete before we meet again."

"But Colonel, this whole exercise is pointless."

"Dismissed!" Colonel Stephens snapped. A Tommy opened the door and took Kurt back to the mess.

#

Kurt spooned up the porridge. It was stone cold, but tasted pretty good. The man he thought of as 'Beck' was in his usual place. There was something about his manner, something comical that Kurt couldn't define. He remembered seeing the man standing up, delivering a speech – no, not a speech – a lecture in a classroom.

And then it came to him. Kurt had met the man in the training unit in Brandenburg, near Berlin. He was an Abwehr trainer with responsibility for training future agents in the subtleties of the English language and familiarising them with English and Irish customs.

He was not good at his job, as poor as any instructor Kurt had ever met. He recalled moments of hilarious schoolboy howlers in the classroom. He racked his brain and came up with the man's name, at last. It was van Beuhl, Hauptmann van Beuhl. He drew a grateful sigh.

The two Tommies were waiting for him as the prisoners filed out of the mess. They singled him out and took him back to the interview room.

Cartwright looked well fed and rested, his few strands of hair damp from his morning ablutions. He began the session with an appeal to Kurt's common sense. It was time to come clean and tell the truth, to reveal what he knew about Abwehr operations in Britain.

Kurt crossed his arms and refused to cooperate. "I've told you a thousand times that I know nothing about the Abwehr. Why don't you try your questions on someone else?"

Cartwright's eyes narrowed. The interrogation intensified, and went on through the day without a break. As nightfall approached Kurt was beyond exhaustion. His back was in spasm after hours on his feet. He would have admitted anything he was accused of, signed any confession they placed in front of him, betrayed any friend, if only they allowed him to sit, or – impossible happiness – to sleep.

Cartwright seemed nearly as tired as Kurt by then. He sprayed out a final tirade – Kurt was a worthless worm, his mission a hopeless failure. He deserved to be treated like the useless scum that he was. Every word carried a cargo of spittle.

Kurt fixed his eyes on a point in the middle distance behind Cartwright's right ear and let the abuse stream by him.

"Take him away," snorted Cartwright.

To his joy, he was returned to his sleeping quarters. Weak and trembling from the hunger, his back in agony, he collapsed onto his cot.

Moments later he found himself pinned down by two of his roommates, one sitting on his legs, another holding his arms above his head, while Hubert, the tall one, stood over him holding a makeshift knife.

"Traitor!" he hissed.

Chapter 7

"**B**ritish spy!" Hubert snarled, testing the blade along his thumb.

"I am no spy," said Kurt, gasping from the pain in his back. "For Christ's sake release my arms."

"You were seen talking to Tin-eye Stephens in his office," said Boris.

"The colonel is a pigdog," snarled Kurt. "These British are weak, decadent people. They will all be enslaved when the Reich prevails."

Hubert put the knife to Kurt's throat. "What did Tin-eye say to you? What did you tell him?"

Kurt pushed back against the thin mattress to avoid the blade. "He threatened to have me shot."

"And you told him what?" Hubert pressed the blade harder into Kurt's throat.

"I told him nothing! I have been tortured, starved and deprived of sleep. I have told them nothing. I have no fear of these fools and their threats. For the sake of the Reich, leave me in peace and let me sleep."

Simon, tugging his arms, leaned into his face, his breath rank. "Then tell us why you have received special treatment."

Kurt would have laughed, but for the pain in his back and the knife pressing into the skin at his jugular vein. "What special treatment? I have been forced to stand while they interrogated me for four days and nights without sleep."

"Have you been beaten senseless?" said Hubert. "Or forced to scrub the floors with a rag and cold water?"

"Have they broken your fingers and toes with a hammer?" said Simon.

"Have they threatened to remove your appendix with a rusty knife?" said Boris.

Hubert responded to Kurt's wide-eyed look of astonishment with a nod. "So far, the British have handled you with kid gloves, my friend."

Hubert removed the knife and nodded to the others to release him. "Tell us your story."

Kurt moved to relieve the pain in his back before wearily starting to go through his cover story.

Hubert waved a warning finger at him. "Tell us your real story."

Kurt cobbled together a version of his real life. He was born in Ulm, studied Mathematics and now lived in Berlin. He admitted membership of the Abwehr, his mission to gather intelligence for Operation Sealion, the invasion of Britain. Since 1940 when that plan was abandoned, his task had been to gather information about the RAF – the location of air bases, numbers and types of aircraft and so on. He had a transmitter hidden in a secret location to the north of London.

"Your rank?" said Hubert.

"Oberleutnant, first class."

They asked him if he was a member of the NSDAP. This was a tricky question. Kurt had never been a member of the Party. He hated everything about it, everything it stood for. As a member of the Black Orchestra, he had dedicated his life to the party's destruction. But how to answer the question? Kurt had discovered secret opposition to the Nazis among Germans everywhere, but given the wide popularity of the Führer he chose the safer option.

Getting to his feet shakily, he stood to attention and gave the Roman salute. "For Führer and Fatherland!"

All three of his roommates stood to attention and repeated the phrase. Then all four shared the Hitler salute with cries of "Sieg Heil!"

Kurt's back went into spasm again.

#

Kurt looked for Hauptmann van Beuhl at breakfast, but he was missing. He asked his companions where he might be and Hubert replied, "They shot him."

The scowl on his roommate's face told Kurt that he was serious. A wave of dizziness swept over him. He pushed his plate away.

"Aren't you going to eat that?" said Simon.

Kurt said, "I'm not hungry." Simon grabbed the bread and cheese from Kurt's plate.

"You should never have gone near him," said Boris.

Three more hours of intense questioning followed. Once again Cartwright went through his cover story in fine detail, cross-questioning him, returning to questions previously answered, probing for weaknesses and inconsistencies, inserting lies into Kurt's earlier answers. Kurt was too tired and too devastated by the news about van Beuhl to care. He began to make mistakes. His mythical uncle Heinrich, the shoemaker from Wiesbaden, developed an over-fondness for schnapps, before becoming an addictive gambler from Baden Baden.

"At last, we're getting somewhere," said Cartwright, clearly buoyed by his successes. "Now tell us your real name."

"Aldus Müller Drexler."

"What is your mission?"

"I have none."

"Where have you hidden your transmitter?"

"This is pointless," said Kurt. "I have rights as a German non-combattant."

Cartwright observed him with an amused expression on his face. "And what rights do you think you Nazi swine grant to Jewish people? What rights do they have – men women and children – that the Nazis can ship them to Polish death camps and exterminate them in their thousands in gas chambers?"

Kurt was aware of persistent rumours of death camps in Poland, but he'd never believed them. He hadn't heard the term 'gas chambers' before. It sent a shiver down his spine.

Cartwright nodded to the guard in the room. "Give us a moment."

The Tommy left the room. Cartwright stood up. "Turn around. Face the wall."

Kurt did so. Cartwright handcuffed Kurt's wrists, and forced him to his knees. Then Kurt felt the barrel of a gun touch the back of his skull.

"Your true name." Cartwright's voice had risen an octave.

"I've told you, my name is Aldus Müller Drexler." The icy barrel touched his neck, longing to spit a bullet through his spine.

"You've told us your transmitter is hidden somewhere north of London. Now tell me what is your mission."

"I have no mission." Kurt began to sweat. He was sure he hadn't said anything to Cartwright about a mission. That was a yarn he'd spun for his roommates.

"For the last time," said Cartwright. "Who are you and what is your mission?" He increased the pressure of the gun barrel, pushing Kurt's head forward.

"I have no mission. I've told you I am a student. You can't shoot me."

And then Kurt couldn't breathe. A wave of nausea swept over him. He tried to beg for his life, but he couldn't speak. Amid all the panic one clear thought emerged: He had never admitted having a transmitter to any of his interrogators. This was a story he'd told his roommates. One of them must have passed this information on. One of them must be an informant like him.

Cartwright cocked the gun, pulling back the hammer with a loud, final click.

"Last chance," he said.

Chapter 8

The door flew open, and a Tommy charged in.

"Colonel Stephens wants to speak to the prisoner Drexler."

Cartwright removed the gun from Kurt's head. "Now?"

"I'm to fetch him immediately."

Cartwright holstered his gun. "You have the luck of the devil, my friend. We'll continue this discussion later."

Kurt gulped air into his lungs. The Tommy helped him to his feet and Cartwright removed the handcuffs. Kurt forced his trembling legs to carry him around the table. The Tommy took him down the corridor, deposited him in the colonel's office and closed the door.

The colonel was alone. The expression on his face suggested that he was severely inconvenienced by something.

Kurt said, "Are your interrogators permitted to shoot your prisoners?"

Colonel Stephens frowned. "Why do you ask that?"

"Two minutes ago I had a gun to my head. I swear if you hadn't sent for me your man Cartwright would have shot me."

"He was probably bluffing."

Kurt said, "I don't think so."

The colonel paused before replying. "We are at war, and all of the prisoners here are presumed to be enemy spies. We are perfectly within our rights to do with them whatever we have to in order to encourage them to talk. Sometimes there are accidents…"

"Shouldn't I have special protection? I am here to help you."

"As I've already explained to you, we have to treat you the same as all the others. If we don't your cover will be blown and you will be of no use to me."

"And what use will I be if your men shoot me? I am not an enemy agent."

"So you say." The colonel waved a hand to close the discussion. "In any event you were in no real danger."

"It felt very real to me."

"And yet here you are, safe and well." The colonel's face was blank.

Kurt realised then that there must have been a microphone in the interview room that allowed the colonel to hear the exchange between Kurt and Cartwright. The colonel had sent a man to intervene before Cartwright could pull the trigger. He'd left it awfully late. Another few seconds and Kurt's brains would have been decorating the interview room floor.

Colonel Stephens rapped his desk. "Report!"

Kurt replied, "I looked for that man in the mess hall, the one I thought I knew. I couldn't see him."

"You have his name?"

"Yes, but tell me where he is. Is it true that you shot him?"

The colonel hesitated before replying, "He was an Abwehr spy. Give me his name."

"Why do you need his name if you've already shot him?"

"For our records." The colonel broke eye contact. He picked up a pen and wrote something down.

So it was true!

Every bone in Kurt's body stiffened. He stared at the top of the colonel's head, struggling to suppress the urge to shout and scream at the man. The words filled his mind. *How could you shoot a prisoner simply because he knew my name?*

He took a deep breath and said, "His name was Hauptmann van Beuhl. He was an Abwehr training officer, based in Brandenburg."

Colonel Stephens wrote the name down. Without looking up, he said, "That information is useful, thank you. And last night's demonstration of Nazi Party jingoism was helpful, too."

Kurt knew then for certain that the whole building was wired with listening devices and recording equipment that could pick up and record every conversation in every room. This was how the colonel knew that van Beuhl had used Kurt's family name, and how Cartwright knew about the mythical transmitter hidden somewhere north of London.

He said, "I'd like to be relieved from this exercise, Colonel – "

The colonel raised a hand. "Before you say another word, I have decided to call a halt to your mission here. I believe there is nothing more of substance that you can achieve at Camp Twenty."

Kurt was surprised. He had expected continued resistance from the colonel.

Colonel Stephens stood. "Colonel Underwood has asked us to release you. He has a new mission for you. But take a look at this." He unfolded a crumpled piece of paper and handed it to Kurt.

A finger of ice ran up Kurt's spine at the sight of his own face staring back at him from a torn fragment of a Gestapo notice. A reward of RM 1,000 was offered for information leading to the arrest of Kurt Müller for subversion against the Fatherland.

"Where did you get this?"

"Come with me," said the colonel, striding to the door.

First, they returned his clothes and his watch. When he was dressed, the colonel and a guard led Kurt along a corridor and down a staircase to the basement. The air temperature dropped three degrees with each step. The guard unlocked a door and they entered a room that was unnaturally cold and smelled strongly of formaldehyde.

The colonel waved a hand at a naked body lying on one of five tables. "Tell me if you recognise this man."

Kurt examined the corpse. The man had been middle aged, with an extended belly and thick, soft hands. His fingers were stained with nicotine, his fingernails well manicured. The skin had lost all of its colour. Four neat bullet holes in the chest and one in the forehead told him how the man had died.

"Well?" said the colonel. "Do you know him?"

Kurt looked at the face again. He tried to imagine what the man would have looked like alive and with his eyes open. There was something familiar about him, the bulbous nose was distinctive, but Kurt couldn't recall where he'd seen the face before.

He said, "Do you have his name?"

The guard replied, "He called himself Harry Crum, but his papers are false. He was driving a stolen taxi cab."

"And he was carrying the Gestapo notice? That suggests he was really stupid – or careless. What happened?"

"He was spotted by the police when he refused one too many fares," said the guard. "They called us. We challenged him and he resisted arrest. We found the notice inside his boot."

The guard took the lid off a cardboard box and tipped the contents onto a second table.

"These are all his personal effects," said the colonel. "Take a look through them and see if anything rings any bells."

Kurt went through the contents of the box. There wasn't much. A crumpled suit, a pair of boots, size 14, with holes in the soles, a toothbrush and hand towel, an identity card, cab license and ration book in the name Harry Crum with an address in St Albans, a comb, a pair of scissors, a box of matches, a used train ticket St Albans to London return, a half-empty packet of Lucky Strikes, a map of London. At the bottom of the box Kurt found three dog-eared photographs. The first showed a middle aged woman, the second an elderly man. The third turned Kurt's blood to ice.

It was a photograph of Gudrun.

Part 2 – The Postcard

Chapter 9

Ðe examined the picture quickly. It had been taken in Dublin close to his mother's apartment in Wicklow Street. Gudrun's clothes and hairstyle suggested it had been taken recently – certainly since he'd last seen her.

Kurt looked at the photograph on Harry Crum's identity card. Again, he knew he'd seen the man before, but where? Whoever the dead man was, he had been close enough to Gudrun in Dublin to take her photograph.

He turned to the colonel. "I don't know this man."

As Kurt shovelled the personal effects back into the box he slipped Gudrun's picture up his sleeve.

"He knew who you were. Are you sure you can't give us his name?"

"I'm certain, Colonel. Those Gestapo notices are printed in the thousands. I've never seen him before."

They released him from Camp Twenty.

He waved down a cab in Latchmere Road and asked to be taken to Broadway.

As the cab moved through the traffic he took out the photograph and examined it again. Wearing a light summer dress, her dark hair tied in a ponytail, Gudrun looked as beautiful as the first day he'd met her. The heavy grain of the photograph accentuated her features, her broad nose, her wide mouth, big eyes and slightly square chin. She was looking away from the camera, obviously unaware that she was being photographed. That tilt of her head was familiar, the hint of a smile suggesting that something amusing had caught her eye. He tried to imagine what she had been doing when the picture was taken, but nothing came to mind. She was outside the flat, coming or going, he couldn't guess which.

The thought of where the picture had come from turned his stomach. The Nazis had taken it, and whatever their motive, Gudrun was in serious danger.

He rapped on the glass partition. "Driver, take me to Bayswater Road."

He stopped the cab at Fortnum and Mason's on Oxford Street, paid him off, and stepped inside a public telephone box. He dialled the operator, and asked for his mother's number in Dublin.

"Have six pence ready, caller," said the operator. Then, "I'm sorry, caller, that number seems to be disconnected."

He made his way on foot to the Bayswater Road. Erika had said she was billeted in a hotel there. If he could find her she would help him. He cursed himself for not asking her the name of her hotel, but how many hotels could there be on the road?

Enquiries at a newsagents told him that two hotels still operated on the Bayswater Road: the South Downs and the Fillimore.

A light rain was falling as he left the newsagents. He took shelter behind a half-demolished wall in a bombed house where he had a clear view of both hotels. The ruin was home to no one apart from a grey, dishevelled pigeon huddled on a high ledge. A massive slab of plaster swung in the breeze over Kurt's head, only a scrap of torn wallpaper preventing it from falling on him.

As the day turned to dusk the pigeon flew off with a clatter of wings. People emerged from the tube stations in ever increasing numbers. Kurt watched their grim faces and smiled, marvelling at the stupidity and blind optimism that drove the Nazis to wage war against these indomitable people. Since the entry of the USA into the conflict in December, 1941, the war was effectively over, but everybody knew that the Nazis would fight on to the last man, the last bullet.

He was there two hours before he spotted Erika and intercepted her on the street. "I'm on the run," he said. "Take me to your room and I'll explain everything."

"Go round the back of the hotel Fillimore and take the fire escape to the second floor. I'll meet you there," she said.

He slipped to the rear of the hotel and climbed the metal fire escape to the second floor. Erika opened a fire door and let him in.

Her room, room 203, was hardly much bigger than a broom closet, but it had a bed, an easy chair, and a kettle of water boiling on a gas ring.

She made a pot of tea. "I hope you like it black," she said. "I don't have any milk."

Whoever had chosen the décor must have had a death wish. The curtains and counterpane were brown, and so was the wallpaper. The room had the strange, toxic smell of stale tobacco fumes.

He showed Erika the picture of Gudrun and told her where it had come from. "I wish they hadn't shot this Harry Crum. I could have asked him why he took this picture."

"You should call Gudrun, make sure she's safe."

"I tried but Mother's telephone is still out of order." He sipped his tea. "Do you have any food? I haven't eaten anything for hours."

She set about warming some beans. "I take it you haven't been given leave?"

"No."

"You can stay here for a few days. I'll unlock the door to the fire escape so that you can get in and out. Give me your ration card."

"I don't have it," said Kurt. "It's in my locker at headquarters."

"Right, I'll get that tomorrow."

"I don't have the key, Erika, but if you can get into the locker my Irish passport's in there. I'm going to need that."

Chapter 10

Kurt left the hotel in the morning, using the fire escape. The sky was overcast, threatening rain. He hurried back to the public telephone box in Oxford Street and lifted the receiver.

"Number please," said the operator.

"I'd like you to get me a number in Ireland," he said. "I wish to speak to Trinity College, Dublin University."

"Hold the line, caller. I'll see if I can connect you. You will need six pence. Have your money ready."

Kurt knew his request was a challenge. Since the blitz, in 1940 and 1941, the London telephone network was held together with string and chewing gum.

While he waited he read the notes that people had scribbled on the walls. A series of clicks and some distant voices that he took to be operator to operator, suggested that something was happening. And then, magically, "Enter six pence, caller."

Kurt pushed six pennies into the box, hearing them clang in one after the other.

"Go ahead, caller. Press button A."

Kurt pressed the button.

"Hello, this is Dublin University, Trinity College."

The sound of an Irish accent gave Kurt a ripple of goose bumps.

"Professor Stephan Hirsch in the Department of Mathematics, please."

"Hold the line. I'll see if he's there."

Kurt held the line and his breath. The informal Irish way of doing things made him utterly homesick. Ireland was only across the sea, but Dublin was a world away from London. He prayed that the professor was there to take his call.

"Hello, this is Professor Hirsch. Who's calling?"

Relief washed over Kurt at the sound of his friend's voice.

"Professor, it's Kurt Müller. I'm calling from London."

"Kurt, you dog. Good to hear your voice. What can I do for you?"

"I need to contact my mother, urgently. Her telephone is out of order. Could you get a message to her, ask her to call this number…" Kurt read out the number of the telephone box. "…in exactly two hours?" He checked the time on Fortnum and Masons clock. It was 10:30 am. He gave the professor his mother's address, adding, "She goes by her maiden name, Mary O'Reilly."

"Got it," said the professor.

"Sorry to bother you with this, Professor."

"No problem, Kurt. How's the war going over there?"

"Great. It should be over by Christmas. How's your world?"

"Very dull and boring compared to yours."

The London operator came on the line. "Please enter another three pence, caller."

"That's all right, operator," said Kurt. "We're nearly finished. Professor, thank you for your help."

"You're welcome, Kurt. Look after yourself, and look me up after the war."

He stepped out of the telephone box into a rainstorm. A westerly wind snatched the door from his hand and drove slanting rain into his face as he hurried back to the hotel.

Chapter 11

Erika spent the morning at the Special Operations Executive building in Baker Street. The Operations Director of the Free French in London was a tall, thin man with a pencil moustache and an unruly mop of tawny hair. Erika knew him only as Capitaine Z.

He offered her a packet of NAAFI Ardath straight cut cigarettes, and when she pulled a face he produced an unopened pack of Chesterfields from his desk. They lit up together like lovers and he began the briefing.

"One of SIS's top agents has been captured by the enemy. He must be freed and returned to London." He handed her a photograph of a man in civilian clothes. "This picture is a couple of years old. His hair has turned completely white since then. He's a tall man, 1.9 metres. He was posing as an RAF flying officer by the name of Jason Jones when he was captured, so the chances are he's been interned in a prisoner of war camp somewhere in France. Take a good look at the face. Commit it to memory."

"When was he captured?" she asked.

"Two weeks ago."

Erika looked at the picture again. Jones looked confident, smartly dressed, carrying a briefcase. "You don't know where he is?"

The Frenchman straightened his back. "No. He was discovered in a farmhouse near Rheims, so he is most likely to be in one of the camps in the north of the country, but he could be anywhere. The information that this man has is vital to the war effort. It may even influence the outcome of the war. He must be found and brought back to England as quickly as possible. Your mission is to persuade the Free French first to locate him, and then to free him. When you find him, tell him you come from Fenchurch Street. He will know then that you are with the SOE. Whitehall will arrange to send a trawler to Nice from Gibraltar to pick him up. You must ask the French to transmit this message when you have him." He handed her a piece of paper.

It read: 'The parcel for Aunt Muriel is ready for collection.'

"Who dreams up these messages?" she said.

"Commit it to memory. The trawler will set sail when they receive that signal, and will arrive at Nice three days later. You must meet that trawler and get Jones on board."

"And if that proves impossible?"

"If that case you must get him to give you the information and bring it back here yourself."

"Leaving the agent behind?"

Capitaine Z pointed a finger at her face. "He must not be left in enemy hands. They must never discover the information he carries."

"When am I flying out?"

Capitaine Z leant forward on his desk. "The RAF has let us down, I'm afraid. We've arranged passage to France for you aboard a fishing trawler."

#

Erika emerged from SOE headquarters to an overcast sky. A storm front was building from the west. She couldn't find a cab, so she ran for the underground as the rain started. When she emerged at Westminster the rain was teeming down. She ran, but by the time she reached SIS headquarters she was wet through, water streaming from her hair and across her face. The Tommy who opened the door gawped at her. Her light cotton dress must have seemed invisible, clinging to her body, revealing her underwear.

"Close your mouth and let me in, soldier," she snapped.

She made a beeline for the rear of the building, thanking her stars that the War Office had the foresight to install a separate toilet for women in the building, even though the women in the place were vastly outnumbered by the men.

She dried her hair and face before stripping off her dress and wringing it out over a hand basin. Then she put it on again, pulling and smoothing where it clung damply to her. She removed and reapplied her lipstick, combed her hair. When she reached into her handbag for her cigarettes, her fingers encountered a puddle of water. She swore quietly, emptied the bag, poured out the water, dried the interior as best she could, and put everything back.

She emerged from the ladies toilet holding a damp cigarette, and was greeted by a group of grinning soldiers who gave her a good-natured round of applause. One of them offered her a fresh cigarette and lit it for her. The others cheered as she took a drag deep into her lungs and let it out again.

Tossing them a smile, she hurried to Colonel Underwood's office. She found the colonel sitting at his desk, sipping tea.

He nodded to her. "Come in, Erika, take a seat."

Erika sat.

"I need to ask you a question, and I need a truthful answer," he said solemnly, dragging his eyes from her clinging dress.

"Shoot." Erika crossed her legs.

"Have you seen Kurt in the last 24 hours?"

She frowned. "I can't say I have. I met him in the canteen a week ago. He said he had a small job to do in London, and then he was going on leave. Why?"

"I suspect he may be absent without leave. He should have reported here yesterday, but we haven't seen him."

"That's not like Kurt. Perhaps he's in trouble." She tried to look convincingly anxious.

"What do you mean?"

"He's a wanted man in Germany. Maybe the Gestapo have taken him."

The colonel shook his head. "From central London? I think not."

"Where d'you think he is, Colonel?"

"We thought he might be trying to get back to Dublin."

"And you think he went AWOL to go home? That doesn't sound like Kurt."

"Yes, well, if you do come across him, tell him to return to base."

"Sorry I can't help you," said Erika. "I hope you find him."

"How are you getting on with that lot in Baker Street?" He made a face as if someone had broken wind in his office. She already knew what he thought of 'the Baker Street Irregulars'.

"Fine, Colonel. They have a mission lined up for me. It's due to start in a couple of days. I came by to get a few things from my locker and to collect my wages."

The colonel opened a file on his desk, withdrew two pay packets and handed them over.

"I don't suppose you can tell me much about your mission? Overseas, is it?"

"Actually, there's not much to tell. I'm still a bit unclear about the details myself."

"I understand," said the colonel. "Good luck with it. Be sure to drop in and visit us when you get back to London."

"Count on it, Colonel," she said.

Erika opened her locker and fossicked about in there until everyone had left and she had the locker room to herself. Kurt's locker was secured by a padlock. Hunting in her own locker for something to break the padlock, she found nothing stronger than a nail file. Closing her locker, she lit a cigarette and sat down to wait for help to arrive.

Within five minutes a young Tommy came into the room and opened his locker. He nodded to Erika.

"Oh, hello, soldier," said Erika, "I'm so glad you're here. I've forgotten my key, and I absolutely have to open my locker today. Can you help?"

The young soldier examined the padlock on Kurt's locker. "Do you want me to break the lock? If I do that you won't be able to use it again."

"Do you think you could manage it? You look strong enough."

The young man hesitated. The tops of his ears blushed red.

She put a sob in her voice. "Oh dear, I simply have to get my things. I'm going on leave in the morning and I've lost my key…"

"I don't know…"

Erika batted her eyelashes. "I'm sure you can do it if you put your muscles into it, soldier."

Two minutes later he had sprung the padlock on Kurt's locker and was smiling proudly at her.

"Oh thank you," said Erika.

"Would you, er, care for a cup of tea, Miss?" He was blushing right down to his collar now.

"Oh, rather! But I simply can't – I must get my things. My train is in an hour…"

He stumbled sadly from the room, and Erika got to work. She extracted Kurt's Irish passport and his ration book, closed the locker, and left the building.

Chapter 12

Sheltering under an old umbrella of Erika's, Kurt hurried back to the telephone box to receive his scheduled call from Ireland. The Fortnum and Masons clock showed he had three minutes to spare when he arrived, but the box was occupied by a woman in a feathered hat. Continually checking his watch, he paced up and down outside the box in the teeming rain. At 12:30 he tapped on the glass. The woman glared at him and turned her back. He went around the other side of the box and rapped on the glass again. He gesticulated, pointing to his watch. Again, the woman turned her back. He hammered on the glass.

At 12:35 the woman finally completed her call. She put the telephone onto its cradle, but made no move to leave.

Kurt opened the door, holding on tight against the wind. "I need this telephone. I'm expecting a call."

She rummaged in her bag. "I was here first. I have just one more call to make. You can wait."

"I'm sorry, Madam, my call is urgent."

"So is mine. Please leave and close the door."

This close to the woman Kurt could see the layers of make up, her badly applied lipstick. She was a lot older than she appeared from a distance. The smell of powder in the confined space made his eyes water.

"Listen, Madam," he said. "My call is a matter of national security."

She looked down her long, pointed nose at him. "You're not wearing a uniform. You'll just have to wait your turn." She lifted the telephone and began to dial. Kurt let the door close and continued pacing.

Three minutes later the woman completed her call. Kurt opened the door. She scowled at him, and began searching her bag for change.

"I won't be much longer," she said. "I need to make one more short call. Do you have any change?"

Kurt was contemplating murder when the telephone rang.

She picked it up. "Hello?"

"That's my call," said Kurt. He wrestled the handset from the woman, and she squeezed past him. Kurt stepped into the box. The door slammed closed behind him.

"Hello, Kurt. Is that you?"

"Yes, It's me, Mother. Let me speak with Gudrun."

"I'm sorry, Kurt, Gudrun's not here. She's missing. She failed to collect Anna from school three days ago and we haven't seen her since."

Kurt swore under his breath. He was too late.

His mother said, "We have received a postcard from her."

Kurt's heartbeat increased. "Where was it posted from?"

"Germany. There's a picture of Hitler on the stamp."

His heartbeat doubled. How was that possible?

"Are you sure it's from Gudrun?"

"Yes, I'm certain. It's her handwriting."

"What does it say?"

"It says: 'Wish you were here, Gudrun.' "

"Is that all?"

"Anna wants to speak to you."

"Hello, Papa."

"Hello Anna. How are you?"

"Please find Mama and send her home."

"I will, Anna, I promise. Let me talk to Nana again. Love you."

"I love you too, Papa."

A loud insistent banging on the telephone box forced Kurt to turn and peer out through the rain. He found himself face to face with a London bobby, waving his truncheon. He waved back and mouthed the words 'two minutes'.

"Listen, mother, I have to go. Put the postcard into an envelope and send it to me. Have you got a pencil?"

"Yes, go ahead."

The bobby opened the door of the telephone box. "This lady has made a complaint. She says you forced her out of the box…"

The woman stood there holding her hat against the wind, a miserable pouting expression on her face.

"Just one moment, officer," said Kurt, then into the telephone, "Address it to Erika Cleasby, Room 203, Hotel Fillimore, Bayswater Road, London."

"Erika Cleasby?"

"Yes."

"What was the hotel called again?"

"Fillimore."

"Can you spell that?" said his mother.

"Never mind the spelling. It's on the Bayswater Road. Have you got that?"

"Bayswater…"

"Road. Yes. Bayswater Road."

"I've got that. Erika Cleasby, Hotel Fillimore, Bayswater Road…"

The bobby seized the telephone and replaced it on its cradle. "Step out of the box."

Snorting in triumph or disgust, the woman squeezed between Kurt and the bobby and took possession of the box.

"Show me your leave pass or discharge papers," the bobby shouted above the wind.

"I don't have anything like that," said Kurt.

The bobby grabbed Kurt by the arm. "Right, my son, you're coming with me down to the station."

"I'm Irish," said Kurt. "I'm not in any army, I'm just looking for a bit of work."

The policeman pursed his lips and gripped Kurt's arm a little tighter. "Irish is it? Show me your papers."

"I don't have them with me. Sure why would I be carrying my papers, everyone knows me."

"Name?"

"Kevin O'Reilly."

"That lady said you received an incoming call on the telephone. Who was it from?"

"My mother in Ireland. Look, officer, let go of my arm, I have to get back to my digs." Kurt twisted his arm from the bobby's grip and darted across the street to Fortnums department store. The bobby followed. Moving at a pace that surprised Kurt, given his age and physical condition, he caught up with Kurt at the door.

"I want to see you down at the station tomorrow morning with your full identification. D'you hear me?"

"I do, sir, I do. Can I go now?" Kurt went into the shop and slid away among the displays of exotic teas and candles, before leaving through a rear entrance.

Chapter 13

Ðe took a train to St Albans. Listening to the rhythmical clickety-clack of the wagon wheels on the rails, Kurt ran through the telephone call in his head, he wondered if his mother had caught enough of the address. Would she work out how to spell the name of the hotel, and would it matter if she got it wrong?

Next, his mind turned to Gudrun. Could she have left Ireland and travelled to Germany of her own volition for some pressing reason? Could one of her parents be ill? The message on the postcard made no sense, though, unless she had lost her mind. He wrestled with the puzzle until there was only one thought left, the one that he had banished to the back of his mind. Now it screamed for his attention. Could the Gestapo have something to do with her disappearance?

#

Harry Crum's house in St Albans was easy to find. The yellow police tape around the entrance was visible from the end of the street.

Kurt walked back and forth past the two-up two-down a couple of times to satisfy himself that there were no police on duty. Then he darted across the street and slipped around the back of the property.

Gaining access was easy. It took little effort to remove a pane of glass from a rotten window frame and climb inside.

The kitchen was derelict. He found one of everything, one chair, one plate, one fork, one knife, one cup, and one battered saucepan. The pantry held nothing but scraps of vegetables, stale bread and mouldy cheese.

Apart from a crucifix hanging over the door, the living room walls were bare. Peeling wallpaper with a bamboo motif did little to lift the gloom. In the bedroom upstairs he found nothing but a single bed with a bare mattress. The bathroom contained a badly stained bath, a filthy WC, and a cracked washbasin. No soap and no towels.

He went back to the living room. Short of lifting floorboards, he could think of nowhere else he could search. The police had stripped the place bare – apart from the crucifix over the door.

Standing on the rickety kitchen chair he removed the crucifix from its hook. It was a rough wooden artefact of a type common in Germany, a hand-carved souvenir from Oberammergau. Whatever else Harry Crum may have been, he must have been a religious man.

Kurt turned the crucifix over and found a handwritten inscription on the back: 'To Erhart from Ingrid, Farm Helmhof, Hamburg, 1934'.

Chapter 14

When Erika arrived in the evening she had news.

"My mission starts the day after tomorrow. I have an evening rendezvous in Ramsgate with a trawler captain called Dawkins." She showed him her French papers. Her alias was Michelle Médard, Paris resident.

She prepared a meal.

"You're not parachuting in?"

"There's been a change of plan. The RAF wouldn't give us a plane. Did you make contact with Gudrun?"

Kurt told her about his telephone call, the woman and the policeman, and what his mother had said.

"So, Gudrun's in Germany?"

"Yes, but I won't know where in Germany until I get the postcard."

"You should have asked her when you had the chance."

"I would have if that pesky woman hadn't called a bobby and the bobby had given me time to finish the call."

"How long will it take for the postcard to arrive? Is there even a postal service between Ireland and Britain?"

"I don't know, but there are mail boat sailings every day."

"Okay. When I leave I won't check out. You can keep the room for a few days. It's paid to the middle of next week."

"Thanks, Erika."

What was the message on the postcard, again?" she said.

"'Wish you were here'. It was signed, 'Gudrun'."

"And your mother is certain it was in Gudrun's handwriting?"

"Yes, she was positive about that."

Erika was silent for two minutes. Then she said quietly, "It's got to be a trap."

"I know that, Erika, but I have to try to reach her. Gudrun means everything to me. She means everything to Anna."

"You probably won't survive the attempt. It's you the Gestapo are really after."

He said, "I'm hoping if I surrender to them they'll release Gudrun."

"You realise they'll probably kill both of you."

Kurt said nothing.

While Erika prepared a meal he told her about his trip to St Albans and the Oberammergau crucifix he'd found in the dead agent's house.

"You think Gudrun might be on that farm in Hamburg?"

"It's the only lead I have."

Erika put a bowl of beans and carrots and two plates on the table, and Kurt made a face. "Beans again? I thought you were going to use my ration book to buy some meat."

"There wasn't any meat," she said. "Eat your vegetables and tell me how you're going to get into Germany."

"I thought Colonel Underwood might help."

She snorted. "Colonel Underwood will lock you up as soon as he sees you. You're AWOL, remember."

After the meal, Kurt made tea. They had powdered milk.

Erika lit a cigarette. "You could come with me."

"To France?"

"Why not? France to Germany shouldn't be too difficult."

Kurt thought about that. She was probably right about Colonel Underwood. Maybe with Erika's help he might make it from France to Germany, although he was sure she was underestimating the level of difficulty. It was a plan he could think about. But would the postcard arrive in the next couple of days? That seemed unlikely.

Chapter 15

Gudrun had been on her way to pick up Anna from school, halfway down a narrow laneway behind Christchurch Cathedral when the man appeared from nowhere and blocked her path.

A tall, bulky man in dark clothes, he spoke to her in German. She placed him as a Saxon from his accent, a rough diamond from his speech patterns.

He had said very little.

"You will come with me. If you obey my instructions Anna will be safe. If you do not, Anna will die."

Her first thought was to make a dash for safety, to run away and seek out a policeman. She might have called to the passers-by for help. She might even have tussled with the stranger. But when he showed her those photographs of Anna all the fight went out of her.

She asked for permission to say goodbye to Anna, but he refused. He took her by the arm and led her away.

His name was Toby and he was acting for someone else. That was all Gudrun discovered as she meekly accompanied the heavy man to the ferry terminal.

He had false papers that allowed them to travel as an Irish married couple. She had tried to get more information from him during their passage to Wales on the mail boat, but he refused to answer any of her questions.

Now, as they sat in the rail train on their way toward London, Gudrun ran through what had happened over and over in her head. She considered making a desperate dash for freedom or declaring to a ticket inspector that she was being held captive, but she couldn't risk what might happen to Anna.

She hated what was happening to her.

She hated this man and his employers, whoever they were. She dreaded how her absence would affect Anna. Kurt was the real target of this man and his employers – she knew that. And she hated that there was nothing she could do to change what was happening.

She would play this out to the end and pray that Kurt would rescue her.

Chapter 16

Two days went by. Erika checked for incoming post every morning and evening, but nothing arrived from Ireland. On the morning of the third day she finished her packing. She wore a light blue pleated skirt, a white blouse and a red scarf around her head. She looked like a schoolgirl wrapped in a French flag.

Kurt stood by the window watching out for the postman.

"Any sign of him?" she said.

"Not yet."

"Don't look so glum," said Erika. "I bet he'll deliver your postcard this morning."

"Only if he flies in on the back of a pig."

She looked at her watch. "I'll wait as long as I can, but I have to leave soon, I have a train to catch."

He spotted the postman's bicycle heading up the street. "Here he comes now." She left the room to collect the post, and returned empty-handed.

"I'm sorry, Kurt. Maybe you'll get it tomorrow." She handed him a £5 note. "This might help."

"Thanks, Erika. I'll pay you back as soon as I can. Good luck with your mission. And thanks for waiting."

She gave him a quick hug. "Just find Gudrun."

She slipped on a short blue overcoat and picked up her bag. As she stepped onto the fire escape a gust of wind nearly blew her away. Kurt watched her hurry down the steps, turn the corner and disappear into the city under a darkening sky.

The next day, the storm returned and settled over the city like a malevolent spectre. Gale force winds whipped the Thames into a frenzy and tore down trees. The newspaper headlines said whole sections of the Home Counties were without power. Low-lying areas of the city were flooded, and rivers burst their banks all along the south coast. Many Londoners, hardened by the blitz, were shaken by the intensity of the storm.

In the early evening he ran out of food and went out through the fire escape to buy provisions. When he returned to the hotel, battling his way through high winds, a military police car was parked at the hotel entrance.

Turning up his lapels he hurried to the nearest tube station at Queens Road where he spent the night wrapped in a borrowed blanket, in the company of a dozen displaced persons or homeless families.

Sleep was an elusive commodity. The trains rattled in and out of the station until late, and the lights remained on all night. Hordes of restless children ran up and down the platform long after midnight, long after they should have been sleeping. Nobody complained to the parents. It seemed an accepted fact that unruly, overactive children were a natural consequence of war in a big city.

#

He emerged from the tube station in the early morning in time to see the postman entering the hotel. The military police car was still on station outside the entrance. The policemen were probably inside having breakfast.

Kurt dashed across the road, climbed the fire escape as quickly and quietly as he could, opened the fire door on the second floor and stepped inside. He took the stairs down to the ground floor, where he remained hidden. The owner of the hotel was at his usual place behind the reception desk; most of the hotel guests were in the dining room having breakfast.

Kurt set off the fire alarm. The throbbing klaxon sounded. A red light flashed over the front entrance.

The owner of the hotel rushed into the dining room to evacuate the guests. Seizing his chance, Kurt slipped behind the desk and removed a letter from pigeonhole number 203. Then he left by the front door, mingling with the guests.

Kurt walked a mile along Oxford Street through wind and rain, before stepping into a shop doorway to examine the envelope. It bore an Irish stamp and was addressed to Erika Cleasby in his mother's handwriting. Tearing open the envelope he pulled out the postcard.

He read the message: 'Wish you were here, Gudrun'. At first glance he was sure the handwriting was Gudrun's. He checked the postmark. It had been posted from Hamburg.

Part 3 – Passage

Chapter 17

Ꝺe stowed the envelope in an inside jacket pocket and set off in an easterly direction toward St Pancras Station, clutching his lapels. Driven by the mounting wind, the rain funnelled in waves between the buildings and poured from the rooftops. Kurt shared the slippery pavements with a few unfortunate Londoners, soldiers, and civil defence workers caught without shelter in the storm.

Within minutes the clock tower of St Pancras emerged through the teeming rain. Kurt ran inside the station and shook the water from his hair.

The front concourse was deserted. It should have been teeming with people buying tickets and running to catch trains. There were no trains on the tracks. Instead, a locomotive lay on its side straddling the rails, pieces of shattered railway carriages littered the abandoned platforms, and a river of rain poured through a massive hole in the roof.

The absence of bodies or ambulances told Kurt that this bomb had fallen at least a day earlier. His mind turned to Erika.

He stopped a railway engineer and asked, "When did this happen?"

"Three days ago," the man replied in a Scots accent. "It was an unexploded bomb."

Kurt swallowed. That was the day when Erika set out. She could be lying in a hospital somewhere, injured. She could be dead.

"Were there people killed?"

"Aye, there were, and many injured. The bomb exploded in the morning rush hour."

Kurt asked the railway worker where he could catch a train to Ramsgate.

"You need to take a tube to Victoria. You can catch trains to the coast from there. There are no tube trains running from this station, today." He pointed to the south. "Follow that road to Russell Square. It's not far."

It was a relief to get out of the rain and wind at Russell Square tube station. A wooden escalator led downward to the platforms, but it wasn't running. Everyone used it as a staircase. When he reached the platform he was disappointed to find that the trains weren't running. The electric power had been disconnected. All along the platforms people sat on the ground or lay wrapped in blankets on makeshift beds, some reading newspapers by candlelight or brewing tea on portable primus stoves. Whole families were living here, plumes of water vapour rising from them, filling the air. The look on their faces told Kurt that some of them had been here a while.

He found a space to sit against a wall. He was wet through, but his precious envelope was safe and dry against his chest. He took it out, dried his hands on his shirt, opened the envelope and pulled out the postcard.

It was postmarked Hamburg Central. Hamburg, where the dead agent, Harry Crum's farm was located.

He checked the handwriting and signature again. They were Gudrun's – no question. The message: 'Wish you were here' was a clear cry for help. He flipped the card over. The reverse side showed a colour picture of a classical German Schloss – a medieval castle, complete with towers, turrets and crenelated walls, and surrounded by forest.

"What you got there?" said a stranger, sitting down beside him.

"It's nothing, a letter from my girl," said Kurt. Returning the postcard to the envelope, he tucked it back in his jacket pocket.

"Give us a look."

"It's private." Kurt could imagine what might happen if he showed these people a stamp with Hitler's picture on it.

"You're not from around here, are you?" said the man.

Kurt got to his feet.

"Don't go. Here, I have cigarettes." The man searched his pockets.

"Thank you, but I don't smoke," said Kurt and he moved away down the platform.

Gudrun was in Germany. She could have been in China for all the chance he had of reaching her. He had no hope now of getting to Ramsgate in time to catch up with Erika, and without her help making it to France could be impossible. He gritted his teeth. He wasn't going to give up. If he could get to the south coast he would find some way of crossing the Channel on his own.

He found himself close to a family. A small girl in pigtails looked up at her mother and said, "Mummy, why is Adolf Hitler trying to kill us? Why does he hate us so much?"

The girl's mother replied, "Heaven only knows, poppet."

He moved on.

"Hold this," said a woman wearing navy blue. She handed him a rubber hot water bottle. Kurt held the bottle while the woman poured hot water into it from a kettle, careful not to splash his hands. She wore a badge on her chest that read 'WVS Civil Defence'.

When the bottle was full, she asked him to put the lid on and tighten it. "I can't do it because of my arthritis," she said.

Kurt tightened it and handed it back. "The hot water bottle should help with that."

She gave him a strange look. "You're not from around here, are you? It's not for me. It's for the old man." She pointed to a pair of boots sticking out from under a blanket.

He found another space and sat against the wall. A different WVS volunteer offered him a blanket and he took it gratefully. His clothes were still damp.

He dozed. The mass of steaming bodies brought a little warmth to the cold tube station. He fell asleep.

#

He woke with a start. The crowds had thinned and the overhead lights were shining. A warm breeze swept along the platform, accompanied by the roar of a tube train rushing into the station. It drew to a halt at the platform, and Kurt jumped on board.

He left the underground at Victoria and bought a Southern Railway ticket for Ramsgate. A half hour later he was on his way south, his eyelids drooping again under the rhythm of the wheels on the tracks.

The train rolled into Bromley South and ground to a halt, blowing steam. Five minutes later it hadn't moved. Kurt opened the window and stuck his head out.

"What's happening?" he asked a passing railway worker.

"There's some problem down the line," the railwayman replied. "There should be an announcement soon."

A whine from the public address system signalled the announcement.

"Due to damage to the track, the train will terminate here. The Southern Railway regrets any inconvenience…"

Kurt swore. He opened the carriage door, stepped down from the train and headed for the station exit.

The rain had stopped, but the high wind still blew. He closed all the buttons on his jacket and set off on foot in a southerly direction.

After 30 minutes of brisk walking he stopped for a rest and found himself outside a bakery, breathing in the intoxicating aroma of fresh bread. Instantly he was transported back to Berlin and the early mornings outside his local bakery in Horst Wessel Platz.

A bread van drew up, a gas balloon like a small dirigible strapped to the roof, rippling and wobbling in the wind. The driver climbed down, opened the back doors, slid out an empty wooden tray and took it into the shop, leaving the engine running. The driver returned with a tray laden with bread, took a second empty tray from the van and went back into the shop.

Acting on an impulse, Kurt closed the van doors, jumped into the driver's seat, found a forward gear and accelerated away, the engine whining, and the bakery deliveryman in his rear view mirror, shouting and shaking his fist after him.

Chapter 18

Kurt drove east and took what he hoped was the road to Kent. Handling the van proved difficult. He was unaccustomed to driving on the left hand side of the road and having to change gear with his left hand. The gas balloon on the roof shifted the van's centre of gravity, making it unstable in the high wind. He had to drive slowly to keep it from tipping over onto its side.

He reached Rochester and caught sight of a moving train, but decided to drive on in the van. The wind continued to buffet the van, but it became easier to handle as he used up the fuel and the gas balloon grew smaller.

Soon, he was in open country, driving under heavy dark clouds through tranquil farmland that reminded him of home.

As he drove, he watched for signs of the bombing. He saw craters here and there in the fields, but to a casual observer this part of England could have been at peace. There were sheep and cattle grazing happily, crops growing in the fields, fruit ripening in orchards. The war was an abomination, created by the twisted will of a madman. As that little girl in the tube station had said, it made no sense to the vast majority of the people on both sides. The ordinary people of England were really no different from the ordinary people of Germany.

He had just passed through Herne Bay when a police car dashed past going back the way he'd come. It was time to abandon the bread van. He watched in his rear view mirror until the police car was out of sight around a bend in the road before pulling over. Then he stuffed his pockets with bread rolls and continued on foot.

Within minutes he heard the police car racing back, and hid behind a hedge at the side of the road. After that, he took to the fields. Marching double-time, he covered the first seven miles in 43 minutes. By the end of the next hour, marching briskly in swirling winds, he was within a mile of his destination, sweating, out of breath and with an aching back. He made a mental note to take more regular exercise to improve his physical fitness.

He found Ramsgate harbour a mile further on from the town, with two rows of brightly coloured trawlers moored side by side. Even within the harbour walls the trawlers bobbed about restlessly at their moorings, like battery hens at a feeding trough. Beyond the sheltering arms of the two piers the sea was running high with white horses streaking the water. Huge waves washed over the east pier wall.

Kurt checked his watch. It was 3:30 pm. He knew he had missed Erika by at least a day, and the weather had closed in. It could be days before any of these trawlers would be putting to sea again.

The rain started again, accompanied by lightning over the sea and distant rolling thunder. He ran for the nearest bar and ducked inside. He ordered a glass of cider.

"Kent or Dorset?" said the barmaid.

"Kent," Kurt replied. He had no idea that they made cider locally or what the difference might be.

The drink reminded him of the bitter, refreshing cider from Munich that few people knew – Munich's Helles beer was so famous it had eclipsed the cider industry for centuries.

"I was hoping to meet Captain Dawkins here," he said to the barmaid.

She busied herself at the pumps. "A friend of yours is he?"

"A friend of a friend."

"He's not here. He might be in later," she said, giving Kurt a close inspection under her hooded eyelids.

Kurt said, "Do you do food?"

"Yes, but you're a bit late for lunch." She handed him a greasy menu.

Kurt handed over his ration card and ordered a Cornish pasty.

He found a dark corner with an empty table. He was tucking in to his pasty and had started on a glass of 'Old Kirton' Dorset cider – dry and sharp – when he received a tap on the shoulder. He turned to find a smiling, bearded man with a weather-beaten face. "You were looking for Dickie Dawkins?"

"Captain Dawkins, yes. How do you do," said Kurt.

"I'm not Dawkins, but I have a boat. Maybe I can help you."

The barmaid arrived with a pint of ale for the stranger. Kurt said, "Let me pay for that." He tossed a shilling on the barmaid's tray.

"That's uncommon civil. Cheers," said the stranger. He downed half the drink in one long gulp before wiping his mouth on his sleeve.

He introduced himself as Selwyn Green. He had a small pleasure craft used for jaunts along the coast that had been idle since the outbreak of the war.

"Not interested," said Kurt.

"Please yourself," said Green. He finished his drink, wiped his mouth again, plonked the empty glass on the table, and stalked away.

Kurt tried four more varieties of south coast cider. By 6:00 pm he couldn't feel his toes, and his eyes were glazing over. The other patrons in the bar had begun to appear like amorphous shapes moving in and out of the shadows. His eyelids drooped. He struggled to stay awake.

A navy-clad figure filled his field of vision and sat opposite him at the table. "I hear you're looking for a boat."

Not another one, thought Kurt.

This stranger was wearing a skipper's peaked cap, and he had brought his own glass, fully charged.

"I'm looking for Captain Dawkins," said Kurt.

"I'm Dawkins," said the stranger. "Who are you and what can I do you for?"

Kurt's mood lifted slightly. He peered at the man facing him. Dawkins was clean-shaven with a square chin and an amused look on his face. "My name's Kevin. Michelle Médard gave me your name. She said you could take me across the Channel."

"Keep your voice down," said Dawkins, casting his gaze around the room. "Do you have money?"

Kurt nodded. "Not on me, but I have access to money."

Dawkins downed his pint in one long swallow. "I'll be making the run tomorrow morning. Where are you staying?"

"I haven't found anywhere yet."

"Right, drink up and come with me."

Kurt stood on shaky legs, downed his cider, and followed Captain Dawkins out of the bar.

Dawkins led him to another tavern – the Chamberlain – a few steps along the sea front. "They do rooms here. I'll meet you in the docks at 5:00 am sharp. Look for the *Hasty Jane* in Portsmouth FC colours. Bring the money."

"How much?"

"Six hundred pounds." Dawkins walked away.

Kurt checked in. He asked to be woken at 4:30 am, and took the stairs to his room, thinking: Where am I going to get £600 by 5:00 am tomorrow morning? Too tired to worry about it, he collapsed onto the bed and fell into a deep sleep.

#

He woke in darkness, fully dressed from the night before. He had drunk too much, but for some reason that he couldn't even guess at, he had no headache.

He was startled by an urgent rat-a-tat on his door, and realised that was what had woken him. Had the military police found him?

"Who's there?" he said, standing behind the door.

"It's me. Let me in."

He threw open the door, grabbed Erika by the shoulders, and planted a serious kiss on her lips.

She pulled away from him, wiping her mouth. "What was that for?"

"I'm sorry. I was just so glad to see you." He beamed at her.

Erika said, "Next time, please brush your teeth before sticking your tongue down my throat. Or better still, just give me a brotherly hug."

Chapter 19

Kurt stood aside. "Tell me why you're not in France already."

She stepped in and he closed the door. "The skipper of the trawler has been waiting for a break in the weather. He's hoping we might set out this morning."

"You mean you haven't even tried to make the passage yet?"

"We've tried, but it was too rough. Boy, was it rough!" She looked at him gloomily.

"What's the weather like now? And what time is it?"

She checked her watch. "It's 4:15. The forecast is for better weather this morning."

The wind sounded as bad as ever, howling down the chimney.

He excused himself, searched the corridor outside until he found a toilet. Returning to his room he removed his jacket and did his best to smooth out the wrinkles and creases.

"Captain Dawkins wants £600 to ferry me across to France," he said.

She pursed her lips. "Does he, indeed! Just leave Captain Dawkins to me."

He showed her the postcard. She read the message and checked the stamp. "Hamburg is an awfully big city, Kurt."

"Remember the farm address on the back of the Oberammergau crucifix, the one I found in St Albans?"

"You think that's where she's being held?"

"I'm certain of it."

Erika said, "I have a contact in the area who might be able to help you. He's a keeper in Hamburg zoo and a committed anti-Nazi. His name's Peter Wolfe."

"An old flame?" he asked.

"Nothing like that. He's a useful contact, a committed Resistance worker."

Kurt said, "I wondered if you had a beau in London, whether my presence in the hotel room might have been awkward."

She frowned. "I've lost all interest in sex. This war's too serious. Maybe when it ends I might look for someone again."

#

At 4:50 am they left the tavern. For the first time in a week, the sky was clear and a rosy dawn light filled the streets. The wind was still too blustery for comfort, though, the tips of the waves painted gold in the light of the rising sun.

Kurt ran his eyes over the trawlers on their moorings. They bobbed about, jostling one another as they had before, but now they reminded him of dogs excited at the prospect of a walk on the leash. Several of the trawlers had their engines running with plumes of grey smoke rising from exhaust pipes sticking up like chimneys from the wheelhouses.

"There she is," said Erika, approaching a broad boat newly painted in royal blue. The wheelhouse sported a crest with a crescent moon on it, and the prow of the boat carried the name *Hasty Jane*.

A flash of movement behind them made Kurt look back toward the town. An army car sped along the esplanade and drew up outside the Chamberlain. Two military policemen jumped out and ran into the tavern.

Captain Dawkins stuck his head out of the wheelhouse. "Cast off and come aboard."

Erika loosed one rope from a bollard and Kurt the other one. They threw them on board and leapt across the widening gap onto the deck.

"Have you brought the money?" said the skipper to Kurt.

"He's with me," said Erika. "If you really think you can squeeze a few extra bob out of His Majesty's intelligence service, send them a bill."

Captain Dawkins turned the engine down. "I agreed to transport one person, not two. Have you any idea the risks I'm running taking even one of you across the Channel?"

"Take it up with Whitehall," she said. "Now let's get moving or we'll find someone else to do the job."

"No one else would touch it," said the skipper.

The policemen ran from the tavern, jumped into their car, and sped toward the pier.

Kurt said, "Captain Green would, for one."

The skipper laughed, "Have you seen Selwyn's boat? You'd be lucky to make it out of the harbour."

"We don't have time for this," said Erika. "What does it matter whether you're carrying one passenger or two? You won't be leaving British waters. We need to get started. Let me remind you you'll get nothing if you miss the rendezvous."

The skipper handed Kurt the mooring rope. "Hold on tight to this, and don't let go, no matter what."

Erika slipped under cover of the wheelhouse with the skipper.

The military car screeched to a halt on the pier as the skipper pointed the bow at the mouth of the harbour and opened the throttle.

One of the soldiers pulled a loudhailer from the car and bellowed across the waves, "Return to the pier."

Kurt glanced back. Both soldiers were waving their handguns.

The skipper turned the wheel to the left, but Erika turned it back firmly, and the shouts of the gesticulating policemen were drowned out by the trawler's engine as it headed out of the harbour.

Chapter 20

As soon as they hit the open sea the small boat struggled against the tide. The skipper kept her bow pointing directly into the wind. This reduced lateral drift, but meant that the trawler crawled along, progressing in a series of bone-rattling impacts as they met the crest of each wave, followed by equally violent crashes into the wave trough. Kurt clutched the mooring rope in one hand and the gunwale with the other. His stomach heaved. He choked back vomit, terrified of plunging overboard if he leant over the side to get sick.

Each downward crash doused the deck with salt spray. Sheltered by the wheelhouse, Erika and the skipper avoided most of it, but Kurt took a soaking each time.

The dead German's pasty face wandered into Kurt's mind. Where had he seen that bulbous nose before? Suddenly, Kurt remembered. He was SS-Sturmbannführer Necker's driver. Necker's figure came to mind: a tall man with grey hair cut in the military style, a duelling scar on his cheek. Manfred Necker was Kurt's arch-enemy, the man who had pursued Kurt from one end of Germany to the other, the monster who had killed one of Kurt's closest friends.

Snippets of half-remembered conversations with Necker came to mind. The man was the embodiment of an SS officer, a committed member of Hitler's elite. If Necker was behind Gudrun's abduction then she was in great peril.

The guilt that Kurt felt then threatened to overwhelm him. Gudrun had played no part in his dealings with Necker; she had been in Dublin all during that episode. If Necker's actions were motivated by revenge, as seemed likely, then Gudrun's fate was entirely of Kurt's making. It was his fault that she was in this mess. He set his jaw. He was going to have to find her and get her out of it.

The trip seemed to last for an eternity. Then at last he saw a second boat directly ahead, coming toward them. It took a few minutes to reach them, and then the two boats were too close, in real danger of being thrown against each other by the roiling sea.

The French trawler was painted red. It had no name. The only identification it had was the legend 'F17' painted on its wheelhouse.

With great skill the two skippers steered the boats until they were side by side, the two boats moving with the waves more or less in unison.

Kurt went first. Once he had both feet on the deck of the French vessel, he held out a hand and hauled Erika across. As soon as she was safely aboard the *Hasty Jane* turned for home.

The French trawler was heavier and sat lower in the water, making the second half of the journey easier and shorter than the first. Erika and the French skipper were able to bellow short sentences to one another in the wheelhouse. Kurt found himself a secure spot at the back of the wheelhouse close to the engine well, surrounded by heavy ropes and fishing nets.

A portly seagull that had made its home in the stern of the vessel kept a wary, unblinking eye on Kurt the whole way in to port.

They entered Boulogne with the engine puttering quietly. The skipper secured the vessel at its moorings and they prepared to leave the boat. At that moment a two-man German patrol walked by on the pier. The seagull gave a loud, raucous cry and the soldiers came over to investigate.

Kurt and Erika ducked down inside the wheelhouse. The skipper closed the wheelhouse door and spoke with the soldiers. Kurt held his breath. Dressed in his dark pants and jacket he might have passed for a French fisherman – a mute, perhaps – but they would never have been able to explain Erika's presence if they were discovered.

After what seemed an age, the soldiers laughed and moved on.

"You can come out now," said the skipper.

Kurt and Erika disembarked quickly. The skipper led them to a house overlooking the harbour, opened the door and ushered them inside. "This is my home. You can rest here. I apologise for the behaviour of my pet seagull. She must have taken a dislike to you."

Kurt laughed. "She's a pet? The bird is obviously an enemy agent."

The skipper took them to a bedroom upstairs, adding some more information as they climbed. "The Free French will be here to meet you in a couple of hours. I am not with them, but they use my boat from time to time." He opened a closet. "This clothing belongs to them."

The closet was equipped with lots of clothes for men and women. They found winter clothing, summer clothing, clothing for small people and outsized people of both sexes, and every size and shape of frame in between.

Erika chose a couple of blouses and a pair of shoes. Kurt stuck with the clothes he had.

"It's a pity they don't have any weapons," he said. "I feel naked without a gun or a knife. Even a boy scout's penknife would feel good at this moment."

Before Erika could reply, the bedroom door burst open and three scowling Frenchmen entered.

Chapter 21

Erika ran her eyes over the three men. All three looked like seamen from their dress, but one of them stood out. He was tall, muscular, and exuded an aura of self-assurance that the others lacked, the obvious leader of the group.

This tall Frenchmen spoke through gritted teeth, "Where is Uncle Silas?"

"At Blenheim Castle," Erika replied.

Where did the SOE get these routines?

"You are Michelle Médard? Who is this?"

Erika replied in quiet French. "I am Médard. This is Kevin O'Reilly. He's from Ireland, and he works for British Intelligence."

"London said nothing about any Irishman. Why didn't they warn us that he was coming?"

"Because London didn't know. I helped Kevin because he's a good friend. I've known him for a year."

"You trust him?"

"With my life." Erika spoke with passion, remembering the number of times Kurt had saved her life on their last mission together.

The leader of the Free Frenchmen waved to the others and they relaxed. "Why is he here? How is it possible that Special Operations know nothing about him?"

"He is on a personal mission. His girlfriend left him. He came with me to find her and persuade her to return to him."

"Ah! An affair of the heart," said the leader. "But does he not know there is a war on?"

"He was desolated by the loss," replied Erika.

"Never chase after a woman, my friend," said the leader to Kurt, and when Kurt failed to respond, he said to Erika, "Really? He speaks no French?"

Erika shook her head. "Not a word."

The leader cupped his chin between thumb and forefinger. "Are all Irishmen fools? How does he expect to find his lover if he speaks no French? And, if by some miracle he does find her, how is he going to return her to Ireland?"

"He lives in London."

The Frenchman shrugged. "That makes little difference. Explain to your friend that he must remain with us until we are satisfied that he is not a German spy. If his story can be verified we may help with his foolish quest."

"What should I call you?" she said.

"My name is Roger. They call me Roger the Legionnaire."

Speaking quickly, Erika said to Kurt, "They are very nervous of you. I've explained why you're here to their leader. His name is Roger. They intend to check your story."

Kurt said, "Can they help to get me into Germany?"

The two shorter the men pulled out handguns and pointed them at Kurt, accompanied by a lot of French chatter about "Allemagne" and "Les Boches".

Roger told them to be calm and they lowered their weapons.

Erika explained that Kevin's girlfriend was not in France, but in Germany. He would need help crossing the border.

All three Frenchmen burst into derisive laughter at this. Roger the Legionnaire said to Erika, "Come with us, both of you. We must take you to a safe house where we can talk about your mission and when and where the weapons will be dropped."

Erika returned his earnest look with a sickly smile. Her London briefing had mentioned nothing about any weapons drop.

Avoiding a German patrol, Roger took them to another house in the town. Kurt was bundled into a basement room and locked in. Erika was taken to a parlour at the rear of the house where a man and a woman were seated at a table.

Roger made the introductions. Lacosse a small, frowning man who looked like an accountant, wearing a pince-nez, starched collar and cuffs and a flamboyant bowtie, and sitting beside him, a petite woman called Loulou. Roger joined them at the table. Lacosse waved a hand to indicate to Erika that she had the floor.

"I bring you good news from London," she began, stringing the words together as she spoke. "London has asked me to convey to you their great pleasure at the work you have done so far to interrupt the free passage of enemy war supplies through France to the southern ports and to the east. Your work has shortened the war and brought forward the glorious day when France will once again be free of the invader."

She paused for breath and looked for a response from her audience. There was none.

"Congratulations too on the success of your escape routes. London is pleased and grateful for the remarkable number of Allied pilots and escaped prisoners of war that have made the journey home."

"Please tell us about your mission," said Lacosse. "We are fully aware of London's opinions about us."

Erika took a seat at the table. "I am here to ask you to locate and free one particular RAF pilot and use your escape routes to transport him to the south coast."

The response to this announcement was stunned silence. Roger and Lacosse turned to Loulou.

She said, "The escape lines we use are many and varied. Each operation consists of several segments chosen from many possible segments. Our fastest route to England is through Boulogne by trawler. All our other routes are across the Pyrenees and through Spain. Another of our lines evacuated airmen by sea from the south coast, but that line has been broken and the route hasn't been used since."

Roger asked, "Who is this man? Why is this particular pilot so important?"

Erika had anticipated this question. She had a story prepared. "His name is Flying Officer Jones. He is the RAF's top flight instructor. He was on a training mission over northern France in the first week of this month when he was shot down. London would very much like him back." The look on the faces of her audience told Erika that they didn't believe her. She couldn't blame them; the story was on the thin side of threadbare. "The British will send a trawler from Gibraltar to pick him up from Nice. All we have to do is send an agreed signal to London and the trawler will rendezvous at Nice three days later."

"And if we can't get him there on that date?" said Lacosse.

"The trawler will wait a few days if necessary, depending on the level of enemy activity in the area."

"Why ask us to carry out this mission? Are there not British commandos that could rescue this flying officer?" asked Roger.

Erika replied, "London believes that only the Free French can carry out this mission. Yours is the only group that can find out where he is being held, and yours is the only group on the ground with the necessary level of manpower and expertise to complete a successful rescue mission."

The murmur that greeted this statement was less a murmur of satisfaction, more one of bewilderment.

Lacosse said, "We have men, it is true, but we have few weapons and almost no explosives. What arrangements have been made for the RAF to drop supplies to us?"

Erika took a deep breath and replied, "There are no such arrangements in place, as far as I know."

Her last few words were drowned out by curses from Roger and Loulou. Lacosse held up a hand for silence. Obviously, he was the most senior of the three.

He spoke quietly. "London has set us many tasks since the Free French was formed as a fighting unit. Many of these tasks made no sense to us, but we have attempted to carry them out to the best of our ability and with few weapons at our disposal, often against our better judgment. The action you are suggesting bears all the signs of another crazy idea dreamt up in some office in Whitehall. It carries with it great risk. Understand that I speak not only of the risk to my men; much greater is the risk of retaliation by the Boches on the general population. And for what? For a pilot trainer?" Lacosse stood, followed by the others. "No, I'm sorry, Mademoiselle, the whole idea is badly thought out. Unfortunately, you have had a wasted journey. I cannot commit Free French forces to this madness."

Chapter 22

Kurt was once more in a locked room. At least this one had some furniture – a table, a settee and an old armchair – and he could switch the light on and off, but it was still a prison of sorts, the window barred on the outside. He had every faith in Erika's ability to explain his presence to the French, but could she persuade them to help him? And how long would that take?

Gudrun was in the hands of the Gestapo – he was sure of that now. They had abducted her and forced her to write the postcard. As a known member of the infamous Black Orchestra, they wanted Kurt back in Germany where they could extract the names of the leaders of the German Resistance from him.

The door opened and Erika came in. The door closed again and he heard the key turn in the lock. Erika was shaking with emotion. Kurt had never seen her so upset. She was so furious she was on the point of tears. Kurt had only ever seen her cry once before. Erika was as tough as a Pickelhaube, and just as spikey.

"What happened, Erika?"

She turned her face away. Kurt placed a hand on her shoulder. She shrugged it off.

"Tell me what happened. Did they hurt you?"

She shook her head and said, "They flatly refused to do what I asked. They said the whole plan was madness dreamt up in an ivory tower in London. They said it was too risky."

"Maybe you didn't explain it to them clearly."

Erika's eyes flashed anger at that. She turned to face him. "I explained it perfectly well, Kurt. They said they haven't enough weapons or explosives, and…"

"And what?"

"There was something I couldn't tell them…"

"Tell me the whole story. Leave nothing out," said Kurt.

Erika explained what her mission was. She was to persuade the Free French to locate one particular Flying Officer and pass him to one of the escape lines who would smuggle him to the south of France.

"Could we rescue this pilot without the help of the Free French?" Kurt asked. He knew it was a stupid question before he'd reached the end of the sentence.

"How? I don't even know where he is. He could be anywhere in France."

"Why is this pilot so important? There must be hundreds of RAF pilots in prisoner of war camps. Why rescue this one?"

Erika hesitated.

"You know you can trust me," said Kurt.

She looked at him, her eyes red-rimmed, and took a deep breath. "That's where my cover story fell down. I told them that he is a top flight instructor for the RAF."

"But that's not true?"

"No. He's an important SOE agent. He's not even a pilot. He carries vital intelligence in his head that London needs."

"You couldn't tell the French that?"

"I must keep that information from them. The risk to the agent would be too great."

Kurt gave the problem a few moments' thought. Then he said, "You're just going to have to tell them."

"I can't!"

"If it means saving the whole mission, I think you have to, Erika."

"Maybe I could come up with a more convincing cover story, something strong enough for the French to take it on, but not the whole truth."

Kurt shook his head. "I would tell them the truth."

#

Two hours later the door opened. Roger the Legionnaire came in carrying a tray of food and placed it on the table.

Kurt was asleep in the armchair. Roger went across and woke him before sitting beside Erika. "I'm sorry that Lacosse refused to help you, Michelle." His English was excellent.

Kurt pitched in to the food. There was cheese and bread and reconstituted dried eggs, and red wine in an unlabelled bottle.

Erika said, "I don't know what to do. I cannot return to London without completing my mission."

Roger replied, "Lacosse is not an unreasonable man. He would gladly help you recover this Flying Officer Jones, but there's a limit to what he can ask his men to do. You must give him a stronger reason."

"What would you suggest?"

"I think this is no ordinary pilot, much more than the RAF's top training officer. Am I right?"

Erika said, "I must protect—"

He held up his hand. "I understand. You don't have to say another word. What you need is something to inspire the men to carry out the mission. How about telling Lacosse that this Flying Officer Jones is a war hero."

"And King George wants to pin a big medal on his chest," said Kurt through a mouthful of bread and cheese.

Erika said, "The DSO. He rescued four crew members from a burning Lancaster."

Roger smiled. "Nothing fires the French heart more than a war hero." He stood. Looking up at him, Erika was reminded of her father, a tall, muscular Canadian with a heart as big as a mountain and a smile that would charm the birds from the trees. "I'll leave you to finish your meal. I'll ask Lacosse to pay you a visit before he leaves for Paris."

When Roger was gone, Kurt said, "It might be better if General de Gaulle was to present Jones with the *Croix de Guerre*."

"Why not both?"

"Of course! Two of the men he pulled from the burning wreck were Frenchmen, after all."

Erika laughed. "What a hero! Pass me those eggs, Kurt."

While they ate, Kurt had a thought. "Why was Roger so helpful?"

"What do you mean?" said Erika.

"I mean why does he care about your mission?"

Erika shrugged. "Who cares if it works?"

#

When they'd finished their evening meal Kurt and Erika were separated. Erika was placed in a parlour full of stuffed animals and birds in glass display cases and odd pieces of musty, dilapidated furniture that were once someone's prized possessions.

Lacosse entered the room, took a seat on the edge of a chaise longue. Erika spun him the new story about Jones the war hero. "He is to receive *La Croix de Guerre.*"

Lacosse adjusted the spectacles perched on the end of his nose. "Why did you not say so in front of the men?"

He reminded Erika of a dentist she'd known when she was a student in Canada, a creepy little man who'd been locked up for interfering with his female patients. "The information is highly secret," she said. "There is nothing that pleases the Boches more than capturing an Allied war hero. You could tell your men privately, but you must swear them to secrecy."

"Very well, Mademoiselle, I can give no guarantees that the men will undertake this dangerous mission, but I shall do as you ask."

Erika watched Lacosse as he spoke. There was a curious formality in his speech that told her, louder than any words, that he had doubts about the war hero story. But it seemed he was willing to go along with it.

"What about my friend, Kevin?" she said.

Lacosse rolled his eyes. "The Irishman will be interviewed, his story will be checked. You will appreciate that our escape lines are not set up to smuggle people into Germany, but if his story can be confirmed I'm sure the escape people will do what they can for him."

"How long might that take?"

"I cannot say. It could take several weeks or they might find a way to get him across the border in the next few days. Tell him to be patient."

"Kevin is not known for his patience," she said.

When Erika told Kurt that it could be a week or two before the French found a way to smuggle him across the German border, he leapt to his feet, his fists clenched. "A week? Gudrun could be dead by then."

"Calm yourself, Kurt. I'm sure our French friends are doing the best they can to get you into Germany. You're just going to have to be patient."

"Fuck that for a game of soldiers. I'll find my own way into Germany."

"Sit down and listen to what I have to say."

Kurt resumed his seat, but his fists remained tightly closed.

"How far d'you think you'd get on your own without a word of French? You don't even have any French money, do you?"

She gave him 2,000 Francs. Kurt thanked her.

He hated having to wait. But Erika was right, of course: he would never make it into Germany on his own. Perhaps coming to France with Erika had been a mistake. He should have found a more direct way of getting to Hamburg. He consoled himself with the thought that it was him the Gestapo wanted; they would keep Gudrun alive until he presented himself to them.

Chapter 23

Claude Dansey, second-in-command at the Secret Intelligence Service, sipped his scotch and soda contentedly. In a world at war, Boodles, the celebrated London club, was an oasis of calm. Jeremy Wichard of the Foreign Office sat opposite, nursing a brandy.

"The chef outdid himself as usual," said Wichard.

"Best meal in London. I don't know how he does it," Dansey replied.

Dansey had had the Dover sole, Wichard the rack of lamb.

"I hear Gubbins of the SOE has applied for membership," said Dansey.

"He'll be blackballed, naturally," said Wichard.

"Naturally."

Wichard said, "What of Operation Tabletop?"

"The wheels are in motion."

"Baker Street has been briefed, I take it?"

Dansey nodded. "A couple of weeks ago. Their man is already on station, I believe."

"Don't you mean their woman?" said Wichard.

"Quite. We should hear something in another week, two at the latest."

"How much does SOE know?"

Dansey tapped the side of his nose. "Only that Jones carries information vital to the war effort. They'll bust a gut to get him home."

Wichard signaled to the waiter who topped up their glasses. "The Prime Minister is fully informed?"

"Fully," said Dansey. "I briefed his personal private secretary myself."

Both men sipped their drinks.

Wichard said, "What if they succeed?"

"They won't."

"But what if they do?"

Dansey shrugged. "Hopefully the French mole will have broken cover."

"And if they fail?"

"We'll have the French mole, and the enemy will swallow our misinformation. Either way, we lose nothing."

Wichard sipped his scotch. "Apart from the SOE agent."

"Apart from her, obviously."

Part 4 - Action

Chapter 24

The next day Erika was transported to Paris in the cab of an old vegetable lorry. The driver was a young American named Charles with wild, windswept tawny hair.

The smell of rotting vegetation was so strong in the cab that Erika had to breathe through her mouth. "How long have you lived in France, Charles?" she asked.

"Nearly ten years. My father was an engineer during the Great War. He married a Frenchwoman and took her back to his home town in New Hampshire. But she couldn't settle, so they returned to France. I was seventeen then."

That made him 27 now. He looked younger.

"My father runs a pig farm near Rouen."

"And you sell vegetables."

He grinned. "What gave it away? I have a market stall in Rennes. Anything I can't sell on the stall we feed to his pigs, and he sells pig manure to the farmers who supply my vegetables. It's a sweet deal all round."

"You have no problem getting fuel for your lorry?"

"Bessie likes her gasoline." He patted the steering wheel affectionately. "It can be difficult sometimes, but the Germans like their food almost as much as the French do."

Erika told him a little about her childhood in Sweden and Germany.

"Where did you pick up your French?"

"I studied Physics in the University of Montréal."

"I thought there was something about your accent," he said, looking at her with an amused glint in his eye.

"You can't talk about strange accents, Cowboy. Just keep your eyes on the road." Actually, Erika was impressed by his accent. It had a hint of the country *paysant* about it. She was sure it would fool any German. It would fool most Frenchmen.

"You're not married, I take it?" he said later, without looking at her.

"Not anymore," she replied. "How about you?"

She knew the answer before he spoke. What woman would marry a man with half the acreage of Normandy under his fingernails!

"Still searching for the right woman." He turned his head and grinned at her.

"Keep your eyes on the road, Charles," she said.

They were stopped at three checkpoints before reaching the streets of Paris. Two were Gendarmerie checkpoints, the third a German patrol. Their papers passed muster with no problem, and no one inspected the smelly load in the back of the lorry. The soldier at the German checkpoint asked Charles who *la nana* was.

"She's my cousin from Paris."

The soldier leered at her through the window, sucking air through his monumental teeth. Erika gave him a weak smile.

When they were moving again, the American laughed and said in English, "That pig fancied you. You shouldn't have thrown him a smile. He'll be watching out for you on the way back."

She shuddered. "Did you see those teeth? He looked like a horse."

Charles parked the lorry in a backstreet in the Sorbonne area and led Erika to a four-storey house. The American cast his gaze around before opening the door. They slipped inside.

Erika looked around the house. It was sparsely furnished with utilitarian items, tables, wooden chairs, a few dilapidated soft chairs. There were five bedrooms, all packed with beds and with extra mattresses on the floors. She found a room on the top floor that was completely empty apart from a massive carved oak farmhouse *garde-robe* up against one wall, full of what looked like theatrical costumes.

"The house is used as student accommodation during term time.

During the summer months it's empty, and we can use it," said Charles.

"The Sorbonne is operating as normal during the Occupation?"

He gave a Gallic shrug. "It's operating. I'm not sure how normally."

In the bathroom she found an eighteenth century toilet that was no more than a hole in the floor over a foul-smelling sewer.

#

Erika picked out a bed with the least disreputable-looking mattress, and found some blankets in an airing cupboard. Charles hung around watching Erika prepare her bed until she told him to "take a hike". Charles shrugged and took a mattress to a room on the ground floor.

In the morning, Charles went out in search of breakfast. Erika had to make do with cold water for washing and a vigorous rub with a finger on her teeth. Squatting over the ancient toilet was by far the worst of these experiences.

Charles returned with dry croissants and black ersatz coffee which they devoured in silence.

Later, Charles answered a knock on the front door and admitted a short, slight man in a black beret.

He introduced himself as "Favier", opened a brown envelope and pulled out a handful of photographs. Each picture showed a man behind barbed wire. The men varied in looks and ages. They were all wearing uniforms. Most of the pictures were of poor quality. Some had been taken from distance with zoom lenses. Erika looked through them all and shook her head. "Jones is not here."

"These men are all called Jones," said the minuscule stranger through rabbit's teeth. "Please look again."

Erika checked them again and handed the pictures back. "No, I'm sorry, Monsieur, he's not here."

The stranger gathered up the pictures, dropped them into the fireplace and set them alight.

Erika spoke in English to the American. "That was a total waste of time. Is that the best they could do in three days?"

"Credit where credit's due, Michelle. Think of the resources they had to call on to identify those airmen and the risks they took photographing them."

Erika was suitably chastened by Charles's words. "I understand that, but at the rate we're going it'll be Christmas and the war will be over before…"

Charles signalled for her to stop talking. He touched his ear and they all listened.

Erika heard feet marching in the street outside, coming closer, closer. Charles got to his feet and signalled for Erika to do the same. Favier went to a window at the front of the building. The marching stopped, and someone began hammering on the door.

"Six of them," said Favier.

Charles said, "Follow me." He led Erika and Favier upstairs to the empty room as the front door shattered. Heavy boots ran inside and pounded up the stairs. Orders were shouted in German.

Charles placed his hand between two high shelves inside the oak wardrobe. There was a click, and the back of the wardrobe swung forward to reveal a small door. All three ducked through the door and emerged in the adjoining house.

Chapter 25

In the late morning of his second day in captivity, Kurt was interviewed by a Frenchman with good English spoken in an atrocious accent. He told his story once more.

"How do we know you're not a Gestapo agent?" said the Frenchman.

"I hate the Nazis."

"Of course. But how can I be sure you're not lying?"

Kurt showed the Frenchman his Irish passport.

"What is your date of birth?"

"July the first, 1913," said Kurt. It was only then that he realised his thirtieth birthday had passed unnoticed a couple of days earlier.

He showed the Frenchman the postcard from Gudrun and the photograph removed from the dead German agent in London. "She has been taken by the Gestapo. I fear for her life."

"Gudrun is a German name. She is German?"

"Yes."

"She was living with you in Ireland? The Nazis took her from Ireland to Hamburg, you say?"

"I can think of no other reason why she should disappear from her home in Dublin and send me that postcard."

"The handwriting is hers?"

"Without question."

The French interrogator took Kurt's passport, the photograph and the postcard away and returned them a few hours later.

"Your story is good," he said. "As for helping you to get into Germany, this is not something we've ever been asked to do before. But I've never been known to refuse a challenge."

Two days went by. Two days of infuriating idleness, worrying about Gudrun. Outside of mealtimes – they brought him food twice a day – he saw no one. He contemplated breaking out of the house to make his own way across occupied northern France to Hamburg. But of course he knew such an undertaking was bound to fail and could be suicidal. He spoke no French and he was a wanted man with a price on his head in Germany.

Finally, on day 3, the door opened and Roger the muscular Legionnaire came in. "I hear you're looking for transport to northern Germany."

"I need to get to Hamburg as quickly as possible," Kurt replied.

"We have information that a group of 30 merchant seamen are being transported to Bremen to work for the Third Reich. This group was all that was recovered from a merchant vessel torpedoed by a U-boat in the Atlantic. We thought you might join them."

Bremen was roughly 100 km from Hamburg, but if this was the only way of getting into northern Germany then Kurt would take it.

"I would be a prisoner, working for the Reich?" he said.

"Well, yes, that is the only fly in the ointment, so to speak."

"I'm no merchant seaman."

"I am aware of that, but you could act the part, could you not? When you reach Bremen all you have to do is escape and make your way to Hamburg – a distance of only 125 kilometres."

"Is that all?" said Kurt.

"So, what do you say? Do you want to take this offer?"

"If you can offer me nothing better…"

"I forgot to mention, the best part," said Roger. "The ship was carrying an Irish marine flag. These merchant seamen are all Irishmen like you."

#

They waited until dusk before leaving the house. Roger handed Kurt a small canteen of water. "You'll need this on the train," he said.

He led Kurt to a commercial yard and opened the gates to reveal an ancient rust-coloured motorcycle. Grass growing around the wheels told Kurt this machine hadn't been used in a long time.

The Frenchman pulled two pairs of goggles from the saddlebags.

He gave Kurt one. "Put these on. If we're stopped, do nothing. Let me do the talking."

A spider vacated Kurt's goggles before he put them on.

The motorcycle started at the third attempt, belching black smoke. They clambered aboard, and rode east toward Rennes, their nostrils full of the smell of exhaust fumes.

By the time they reached the outskirts of the city the sun had set, yielding a dark night with a tiny sliver of a moon.

Crossing a river, they were stopped at a checkpoint. A gendarme asked for their papers, and the Frenchman handed over his own with a 100-franc note tucked inside.

The gendarme returned the papers, *sans* 100-franc note and waved them on. Once inside the inner city limits, they took a circuitous route through the back streets before coming to a halt. They dismounted, removed their helmets and goggles, and Roger switched off the engine. He propped the machine against a wall overlooking a massive railway marshalling yard.

They clambered over the wall and down a ladder that someone had left there for them.

Trains of every size and type packed the marshalling yard. Kurt counted seven, standing in parallel rows. Roger pointed out the correct train. It was made up of 30 or 40 wooden wagons of the sort used to transport cattle. They approached it from the rear, Roger leading the way, checking the chalk marks on the wagons.

"This is your wagon," he whispered.

They heard laughter from somewhere close by. Roger ducked between two wagons, climbing onto the couplings and Kurt followed. Two German soldiers strolled by armed with automatic weapons. They stopped to light cigarettes. Kurt held his breath until the soldiers moved away.

As soon as the coast was clear Roger slid open the door of the wagon and helped Kurt to climb inside.

"Good luck," said the Frenchman as he closed the wagon door.

Kurt was in almost complete darkness, but he was aware of bodies stirring all around him. Something touched his leg. If he had been in a wagon full of snakes he wouldn't have been any more nervous. Then there were warm bodies all around him.

"Hello?" he said.

The response was a strong arm around his neck and the prick of a knife pressed under his ribs. Someone tore the canteen of water from his hand. Then several pairs of searching hands ran up and down his body, and someone removed his jacket.

"Don't move," said a voice in his ear in a Dublin accent.

Kurt said, "I'm Irish."

"Hold your tongue," said the voice.

Kurt began to make out figures moving around him as his eyes adjusted to the light.

Someone said, "He has money. Not a lot, mind you."

Someone else said, "He's carrying an Irish passport, a photograph of a woman and a letter posted from Dublin. Hold on, hold on, there's a postcard inside. It's from Germany."

The knife under his ribs moved upward a fraction. "Who are you?" said the voice up close.

Chapter 26

"My name's Kevin O'Reilly. I'm from Dublin."

"What are you doing here?"

"I need to get to northern Germany."

This was greeted by a general round of laughter and blasphemous curses.

"Is that where we're going?" said someone.

"Why the fuck d'you want to go to Germany?" said the man with the knife.

"Put away the knife and I'll tell you," said Kurt.

The arm around his neck eased. The knife remained where it was. Kurt could see the shapes of the men around him, now, their eyes shining in the semi-darkness.

"That postcard was sent from a farm in Hamburg by my girlfriend. She's been abducted by the Gestapo and I intend to rescue her."

"Is this your girlfriend?" asked a disembodied voice.

"The girl in the photograph – yes."

"Hamburg? Is that where we're going?" asked another.

"I believe your destination is Bremen," Kurt replied.

"What's in Bremen?" asked another voice.

"No idea, but I expect you'll be put to work for the Third Reich."

"Can they do that to us?" said someone. "We are neutral Irish."

"Tell us about this postcard," said the voice up close. "Your girlfriend has been taken by the Gestapo, you say. Why would they do that?"

Kurt told them a heavily edited version of his story. He had met Gudrun on a holiday in Germany before the war. She had been abducted by the Gestapo from their apartment in Dublin, although he had no idea why. He made no mention of the German Resistance.

The Irishmen listened, throwing an occasional question at him. When he'd finished the knife was removed from his ribs, they gave him back his jacket, his French money, his passport and his letter with the postcard inside. He found a space where he could sit against the wall of the wagon and tried to make himself comfortable.

He never saw his water canteen again.

#

Within a couple of hours the train was moving. The wagon rattled over the tracks shaking the bones of the unfortunate men who lay around in the gloom, lethargic, thirsty, moaning. The contents of Kurt's canteen would have done little to wet a few thirsty throats.

Knotholes in the wagon walls provided a restricted view of their surroundings, and when the train ground to a halt five hours from Rennes, one of the men announced that they had arrived at the German border. After an hour's delay the journey resumed. The train rumbled on through the night. Kurt made friends with some of his fellow passengers and they agreed to create a diversion to help him escape when the train arrived at its destination.

Another four hours passed before they drew to a halt again. The wagon doors slid open and all along the train men staggered out into bright morning sunlight. The train had stopped on an embankment in open country. Beside the train, a dozen army trucks stood on a rough track. Armed soldiers stood about, smoking. Someone had thoughtfully set up a barrel of water, and the men queued to quench their thirst. Kurt joined the queue. He was as dry as he had ever been.

The men were from a dozen countries. Kurt identified Russians, Czechs, Albanians, Greeks, Kurds, Turks. They were given little time to drink their fill, and began to quarrel among themselves. At a signal from one of the Irishmen a fistfight broke out. In the resulting confusion Kurt slid between the wheels of the wagon and lay down on the sleepers under the train. The soldiers broke up the fight, counted the prisoners, loaded them into the trucks, and drove away. Kurt lay quietly under the train, trying not to sneeze.

Two soldiers remained behind, smoking and laughing, walking up and down the length of the train.

Kurt swore. It seemed he would never be able to leave his hiding place. And then the two soldiers split up. One went to the rear of the train, the other to the front. Moving along the track they converged toward the centre, closing the doors of the wagons as they went.

The two soldiers climbed on board the train. It lurched and began to move, and Kurt made himself as flat as he could. The train picked up speed. He lay perfectly still on his back with his arms by his side and his eyes closed until the train had passed him by.

He opened his eyes.

The sky above was cloudless and perfectly blue. He sat up. A warm breeze tousled the hair on his forehead. To his left he saw goats grazing in a field. He turned his head to his right.

In the distance he could see a wide river shining in the bright sunlight, but in the field right beside the railway track, an army camp of some kind, with tents and vehicles and soldiers standing around talking. The smoke from their fires filled his nostrils. The nearest Wehrmacht soldier was no more than 20 metres away.

He lay down again quickly. The railway track embankment was raised above the surrounding countryside, but even so he was sure he would be seen if any of the soldiers turned their eyes in his direction. He needed to get off the track and hide behind the embankment. But would he be seen if he moved? He turned his head to the right. The rail obscured his view; he could see nothing of the camp. He thought about it for three minutes before reaching a decision. Moving crab-like, he positioned his body up against the left-hand rail. Then he took a deep breath and rolled his body over the rail and down the embankment, landing on the dirt path. He lay still and listened, expecting shouted reactions from the camp. There were none. He stood and satisfied himself that the soldiers couldn't see him if he kept his head down.

The dirt path followed the railway track in the space between the fields and the embankment. Kurt followed the path, keeping his head low until he was well out of sight of the camp. Then he straightened his back and marched on, putting as much distance as he could between the army camp and himself.

The dirt track came to a halt in front of a gate leading into a field. Kurt climbed the gate, jumped down and landed on ground sticky with mud and cowpats, riddled with the cows' hoof prints and smelling strongly of urine. There was no way to avoid the quagmire, and by the time Kurt had reached the grass his boots were caked in mud and cattle dung.

He marched on, taking a diagonal route through the field, away from the railway track in an easterly direction He kept up a steady double march pace for the first two hours before stopping to rest, quenching his thirst at a cattle trough.

He marched on, following his own shadow, through open countryside, over small hills, skirting fields of ripening crops and isolated forested areas. This was an ancient landscape unscarred by the war, repudiating utterly the Nazi nightmare.

Careful not to turn an ankle on the uneven ground, he made good progress, taking advantage of any sort of dirt track or small road that he came across.

Eight hours from the railway track, two hours after sunset, he stumbled on an area covered in tents and temporary shelters dotted with small fires. His first impression was of a Hitler Youth camp, but walking through it he soon realised what it was. The camp covered a vast area. The occupants were refugees, tens of thousands of them.

Kurt hurried on. He came upon roads littered with refugees, women, children and elderly people, pushing carts or carrying their meagre possessions on their backs, all moving west, away from the city.

Kurt continued in an easterly direction, moving against the human tide, and soon the city of Hamburg revealed itself. Black smoke rose high into the sky, glowing red from the fires below.

Approaching the outskirts of the city, the extent of the devastation became apparent. He counted plumes of smoke from 12 separate fires, two of them rising hundreds of metres into the sky. Given the number of refugees that he'd seen fleeing the city, he was surprised by the crowds still milling about in the streets. Here and there fire crews worked, their task made more difficult by the warm summer breeze.

Kurt spoke to a fire fighter. "Which way to Farm Helmhof?"

"It's not safe," the man shouted back. "Follow the crowd." He pointed to the west where the refugees were fleeing.

"I have a friend at the farm. I need to find her."

The fireman pointed. "North, about two kilometres."

Kurt returned to the fields and, after two kilometres, a farmhouse appeared on the horizon. Using the available hedgerows as cover he circled the dilapidated farmhouse looking for signs of life.

As he stood looking down from behind the house, now backlit by the glow from the city, a voice said, "What are you doing there?"

He spun around and came face to face with a farmer holding a shotgun.

"This is your land?" said Kurt.

"It is. What do you want?"

"I'm from the Ministry of Supply. I'm looking for Farm Helmhof. Is this it?"

The farmer scratched his bald head. "What business would the Ministry of Supply have with us?"

"So this is Farm Helmhof? I was hoping to talk to Erhart. Is he here?"

The farmer levelled the gun at Kurt's midriff. "Erhart doesn't live here, and if you're from the Ministry of Supply then I'm a Swiss watchmaker. Put your hands up!"

Chapter 27

Kurt placed his hands on his head.

"March," said the farmer.

He took Kurt through the field to the farmhouse and pushed him inside, calling out, "Ingrid, fetch the chain."

"Now look," said Kurt, "There's no need for chains or guns. If you let me explain—"

"Silence! Ingrid, where are you?"

"Coming Papa." A tall, angular woman ran in from another room. She was wearing a filthy full-length smock that might have been blue, a bonnet and wooden clogs. She was carrying a length of chain. She attached a manacle to his wrist and locked it with a small padlock. The other end of the chain she attached to an iron ring set in the wall.

"Now we can talk," said the farmer. "What is your name?"

"Kevin O'Reilly. I'm Irish." There was an armchair within reach. Kurt sat in it.

"I like the look of this one, Father," said Ingrid. "Where did you find him?"

"He was acting suspicious in the bottom field. I asked him who he was and he gave me a cock-and-bull story about the Ministry of Supply."

Ingrid grinned at Kurt, cocking her head to one side like a chicken eyeing a tasty morsel. "He's tall. How tall are you, Kevin Irish?"

Kurt said, "Where is Gudrun? I know she's here. Where are you holding her?"

"What's he saying, Father?" said Ingrid.

The farmer said, "Be silent. There's no one called Gudrun here."

Kurt took out Gudrun's picture waved it at the farmer.

Ingrid snatched it from him. "Who's this, your lover?"

In that moment Kurt knew that he would not find Gudrun on the farm. He prayed that these people would know where he might find her. He rattled the chain. "You can't keep me in chains. There are laws against this."

"He might be hungry," said the farmer. "See if he'll eat something."

The farmer placed his shotgun on a couple of hooks over the door lintel and left the farmhouse.

Ingrid dropped the photograph on the chair beside Kurt. He tucked it away in his pocket with the postcard. "You're a bit skinny, aren't you? But I expect you're strong. Have you worked on a farm before?"

Kurt decided to keep his counsel until he knew what was going on. He had met Gestapo interrogators less frightening than these two.

Ingrid went off to the kitchen to make him something to eat. Kurt stood and tried to reach the shotgun. The chain was too short. He resumed his seat and looked around the room. Over the fireplace, where he expected to see the usual picture of Adolf Hitler, there was a photograph of Pope Pious XII. On the mantelpiece, a plaster statue of the Infant Jesus of Prague, and on the wall over the door a hand-carved crucifix from Oberammergau identical to the one he'd found in the house in St Albans. They were Roman Catholics! The head of the Infant of Prague was askew. It had obviously been broken off at some time in the past and glued back on badly.

Smells of frying meat filled his nostrils and he found himself salivating like one of Pavlov's dogs.

A mirror hung on the wall in the next room, providing him with a limited view of some of the rooms to the left, but not the kitchen, which was to the right.

The chair that he sat on was made of ancient leather. It sagged, and stuffing poked through cracks in the fabric. A sofa on the other side of the room looked every bit as uninviting; Kurt could see the shape of springs within the seat covers. The remnants of a filthy carpet covered the floor, and crawling things moved in dark corners.

Ingrid returned with a steaming plate of ham and eggs. She handed it to Kurt, her grin a permanent fixture on her face, now.

"Tell me about Erhart," he said.

"How do you know him?"

"I met him in England. He had an Oberammergau crucifix like yours on his wall."

She snorted. "Erhart has never been to England. He drives for Baron Necker."

Baron Necker?

"I know Manfred Necker. I didn't know he was a Baron."

"The Baron lives in the castle. Manfred is his son. If you knew Erhart you would know this."

The castle on the postcard! Gudrun must be there.

"Do I get a fork?" said Kurt.

She crossed her arms under her massive bosom. "Use your fingers."

Kurt was starving. He began shovelling the food into his mouth. "How about something to drink, Ingrid?" he said.

"Ingrid is it? You're all friendly, suddenly, now that you want something."

"I'm thirsty."

She left and returned with a glass of water. Kurt swallowed it in two gulps. He finished the food and handed her the plate.

"Enjoy that, did you?" she said.

"Thank you, it was very good," said Kurt. "But I don't enjoy being chained like a dog."

"You'll get used to it, Irishman." She left the room with his plate and glass.

Kurt stood up to stretch his legs. He couldn't go far, but he found a door to a toilet that his chain allowed him to reach.

He tested the chain. It was too heavy to break and the ring was securely bolted to the wall. He examined the manacle on his wrist. The padlock was small, but too strong to break without tools.

Ingrid and her father went about the business of running the farm with barely any further contact with their guest. She fed him once more. When she went to bed he was able to identify her room in the mirror. Darkness fell; he slept in the chair.

#

A loud cockcrow woke him in the early morning. He opened his eyes and caught a hair-raising glimpse of Ingrid in the mirror stepping out of a full-length nightdress.

Dressed in her blue smock, she put her head round the door. "Sleep well, my prince?"

Kurt didn't answer.

She made breakfast – more ham and eggs accompanied by hot, homemade bread rolls with salted butter. The farmer sat on the sofa and polished off his breakfast. He waited until Ingrid had gone out to tend to the animals, then he stood, tucked his thumbs into his braces and addressed Kurt:

"First of all, I need to know if you are married or single."

"I'm not married, but I do have a sweetheart—"

"That's excellent," said the farmer. "Now tell me what religion you are, and don't try to fool me. I can tell an untruth at ten paces."

"I have no religion, but my father was Lutheran."

"A Christian. That's excellent. Ingrid and I are Roman Catholic. You won't mind converting, will you?"

Kurt considered several replies to that question, but none seemed adequate.

"That's good," said the farmer. "I can tell from your hands that you're not a farmer, but you'll soon get used to it. We have two hectares of prime arable land. I keep cattle and a few sheep, but I expect you'll form your own plans in time."

"Now look here—" said Kurt. The farmer ignored him.

"Ingrid likes to keep a few hens for the eggs, and we have a sow that supplies us with bacon. I'm a widower. I'm 73. Ingrid is my only child, so when you marry her you will inherit the whole farm. Any questions?"

"Erhart is not your son?"

"Erhart is my brother's boy."

Kurt had a few other questions, but he was having difficulty sorting them into logical order. He tried, "When are you going to release me from the chain?"

The farmer laughed. "Give it a few weeks of Ingrid's cooking and you'll be as fat as a lord. You won't want to leave."

#

For the evening meal Ingrid provided a feast fit for a king – or a prince that would soon be a king – roast beef with button potatoes, cabbage and turnips smothered in a white parsley sauce. There was beer, fresh pumpernickel and more salted butter. For desert she served stewed plums with raspberries.

For one wild moment Kurt imagined spending the rest of his life on this farm with this woman, far removed from the realities of the war. He would have to clean the place up, bring in new furniture, maybe streamline the farming operation…

After the meal Kurt was presented with an opportunity to speak with Ingrid on her own. He invited her to sit with him. She perched on the sofa with her hands in her lap.

"I can see that you're lonely," he said, "but holding potential husbands in chains is hardly the best way of building a happy marriage."

"You could be happy here, Kevin," she said. "Can't you see how content you could be here – with me?"

"I have a sweetheart, Ingrid. Her name is Gudrun. Here, let me show you." He offered her Gudrun's photograph.

"I've seen it."

He took the postcard out of his pocket and handed it to her. "She sent me this postcard. I was on my way to her when your father found me."

She examined the postcard, turning it over and over.

"Gudrun and I have been together for three years. She has a little girl called Anna."

"How old?"

"Anna is ten. Gudrun is my age."

"How old are you?"

"I'm thirty."

Ingrid's eyes were filling with tears. "I'm older than that. I was hoping to find a husband before… before it's too late, before I'm too old…"

"You still have time, Ingrid. There must be plenty of men in the district that would love to marry you and take over the running of this fine farm."

The tears flowed down her cheeks. "All the men around here have gone to war. Who knows how many will survive and when they will come back."

"The war won't last much longer, Ingrid, and when it does I'm sure you will snare a nice young man to share your future and give your father a grandchild."

Ingrid sprang to her feet, flung the postcard back at Kurt, used the sleeve of her smock to wipe the tears from her eyes, and left the house without another word.

Chapter 28

In the students' house in Paris, Charles swung the wardrobe door and the secret door closed. It was barely visible in the adjoining house, the cracks lining up perfectly with the wallpaper.

He said, "Stand still and remain very quiet."

Erika took a deep breath and held it, listening to the soldiers tramping around in the safe house, smashing furniture, overturning beds, cursing and shouting to each other.

They heard footsteps receding, the front door slamming. Silence.

Erika began to breathe again. "They're gone," she said.

Favier put a finger over her mouth, frowned and shook his head. They stood quietly and waited. Then Erika heard the distinctive sound of a boot scraping on the floor in the room they had just left. A voice said, "*Sie sind nicht hier.*" They are not here.

They heard receding bootsteps on the stairs, maybe three sets. The front door slammed a second time.

Favier nodded. "Now, it is safe to talk."

They waited an hour before Charles went off to recover his precious vegetable lorry. Then Lacosse, the Free French leader arrived and spoke with Favier. When they'd finished, Favier left by the back door.

Lacosse said, "The ferret tells me…"

"The ferret?"

"Favier. Before the war he was a master burglar. His skills have been very useful to us."

"Has he served time in prison?"

"Indeed he has. He was in Fresnes prison when the Nazis

marched into Paris. He was released when the Gestapo emptied the cells for their own use. He tells me that you have rejected every one of the photographs."

Erika said, "None of those men was the man I'm looking for."

"Those were the pictures of every airman called Jones in prisoner of war camps in this part of France." He shrugged. "I don't know what more we can do to help you, Michelle. Unless…"

#

Lacosse led Erika to a narrow street in the heart of the city. He stopped at a plain wooden door between two shop fronts, and knocked.

A female voice called from behind the door, "What are you selling?"

Lacosse replied, "*Poissons et navets,*" Fish and turnips. Erika heard several bolts being drawn and the door swung open to reveal a mountain of flesh dressed in bright colours, topped with a pomaded wig.

She kissed Lacosse on both cheeks as he stepped inside. "Madam, this is Michelle Médard from the west."

"Welcome, child," said the large woman. "You must call me Véronique. Everyone does. Are you hungry?"

"Oh, yes," said Erika. It was close to 3:00 pm, her last meal had been a limp croissant in the early morning, although no thought of food had entered Erika's head since then.

Véronique led them to a kitchen at the rear of the building and began to prepare a meal.

"You have news?" said Lacosse.

"Yes, Monsieur. We can talk later."

"You may speak openly in front of Michelle," said Lacosse.

"I beg your pardon, Mademoiselle," said Véronique. "I never know who might be a friend. We get all sorts here." She turned to Lacosse and said, "There are rumours that the U-boat fleet is to be withdrawn from service. The dockyard in Le Havre is full, and the repair crews have all been given leave."

"Are you sure they haven't been reassigned to active duty – on the Eastern Front, perhaps?"

"Perhaps." She shrugged, creating ripples of flesh that started in her jowls and ran down to her belly. "Who can be sure of anything, nowadays, Monsieur? Many of our customers have been moved west and north to bolster the defences in preparation for invasion from England. I have a colonel-general who is convinced that something will happen before the end of the year."

She offered them coffee or tea.

"Tea, please," said Erika. "That ersatz coffee is not to my taste."

"Did you say ersatz?" said Lacosse. "Madam Véronique has real coffee."

Erika hadn't tasted real coffee for two years. "Oh, how wonderful, Madam! Thank you."

Véronique said, "Babette's young man let slip that the cells in headquarters are filling up with prisoners of war from the camps."

"Any special reason?" said Lacosse.

"No. All I know is that they are all RAF pilots."

Erika said, "Who is Babette and who is her young man?"

Lacosse answered, "Babette is one of Madam Véronique's girls…"

"One of my busiest girls," said Véronique with a fond smile. "Her young man Claus is a member of SS counterintelligence, the SD. He is her best customer."

Lacosse said, "Claus Clanhaus is a very useful contact and supplies us with a lot of solid information."

Erika said, "You trust this Nazi?"

Lacosse shook his head. "No, no, you don't understand. The information Babette collects from him is not so much given as taken. Babette keeps him happy…"

"And he talks to her," said Véronique with a deep rumbling laugh. She put two plates of food on the table in front of her guests. "Eat up while it's hot."

Erika's plate was overflowing. There were carrots, peas, cauliflower, parsnips, butter beans and croquette potatoes, and peeping out from under the pile of vegetables, thickly sliced ham.

Erika took a sip of her coffee. She closed her eyes to savour the long forgotten taste and the rivers of pleasure it created. She sighed and picked up her knife and fork. Lacosse had already devoured a third of his plateful.

"I must leave you for a while," said their hostess.

"Of course, Madam," said Lacosse. "Leave us some paper and a pencil."

Véronique placed the writing materials on the table and left them to their meal.

When Erika was finished eating, she sat back with a satisfied sigh. "How does she do it? Isn't food rationed in France?"

Lacosse answered, "Paris has a thriving black market. If you have enough money you can buy anything here."

Erika said, "This SD man sounds interesting. He may have information about the airman that I'm looking for."

"Undoubtedly. We'll have to get Babette to ask him some key questions. Why not make a start while I go and chat with one or two of the girls?" He pushed the paper and pencil across the table. "Try to frame questions that she could ask without arousing his suspicions." He got to his feet and left the room, belching loudly.

Erika jotted down a few questions and then doodled on the pad sketching a passable picture of Lacosse, complete with horns and a spiked tail.

#

Lacosse returned within 30 minutes. He looked flushed, but content.

"What do you have for me?" he said.

Erika pushed the pad across the table.

Lacosse polished his glasses before peering at what they'd drawn. "These questions are too direct, I think, but I like your friendly looking devil."

Erika stood up. "Can I not meet this Babette?" She sounded petulant, although she hadn't meant to.

Lacosse turned on his heel and left the room. He returned accompanied by one of Madam Véronique's girls, a plump creature in her forties, by Erika's estimation, but made up to look a lot younger. She had a pretty face framed by blond hair and plaits.

"This is Babette," said Lacosse. "Babette, meet Michelle."

Lacosse sat at the table with them, presumably to referee their discourse.

Erika started by complimenting Babette on her clothing – which was revealing and yet somehow appeared demure. Babette returned the compliment.

"Madam Véronique tells me you have a regular customer called Claus from the Sicherheitsdienst. What can you tell me about him?"

"Well," said Babette, "He's a giant, but a gentle giant. He has a scar across his face," she pointed to her own face, indicating a scar that ran from top left across the bridge of her nose to bottom right. "His hands are like dinner plates. His fingers are like my wrists. He's always polite and never rough with me. He always pays his bill, and he gives me small gifts from time to time." She showed them the gemstone bracelet on her wrist.

"How often do you meet him?"

"He comes two times a week, sometimes more."

"You never go to his apartment?"

"Sometimes, on special occasions. On Hitler's birthday we had a party at his room in Avenue Foch."

Erika glanced at Lacosse, who remained impassive.

"What do you talk about with him?"

"He tells me everything. He's a real chatterbox. Sometimes I can't get him to stop talking long enough to let me... you understand."

Lacosse said, "Madam Véronique said Claus told you that airmen have been transferred into 84 Avenue Foch from prisoner of war camps. Michelle seeks information on one airman in particular."

"His name is Jones," said Erika. "Could you ask your Claus Clanhaus where this airman is being held?"

Babette shook her head. "I have never asked him a question like that. I wouldn't know how. He would be suspicious immediately."

"I understand," said Erika. She thanked Babette, and she left.

"What does this Claus Clanhaus do?" said Erika to Lacosse.

"He's an administrator. He has access to all the SD records."

"So he should know where Jones is being held."

"Yes, but Babette cannot ask a direct question. The information we get from this contact is beyond priceless. I wouldn't want her to upset her singular relationship with him."

"I need this information, Monsieur. London needs Jones, and I have to find him." She tapped the table with her fingernails. "Let me take Babette's place for a week. Let me be the one to ask Claus Clanhaus the direct questions."

Lacosse scratched his chin. "If you're sure about this, I could talk to Madam Véronique…"

Chapter 29

Madam Véronique took to the plan with enthusiasm, steering Erika into one of the boudoirs and helping her select an outfit from the girls' wardrobe. "You want something daring but discreet, sexy yet modest, revealing but demure..."

"Sophisticated but sluttish," said Erika.

"Exactly. Adult and youthful at the same time."

"How youthful?" said Erika. "I'm 32."

"Very. Here, remove your underwear and try this on."

The garment on offer was pink taffeta, skimpier than the shortest negligée with chiffon see-through cups.

Erika laughed. "How is that discreet or modest?"

"It's not, it's just the under-layer. Try it on."

Erika slipped out of her underwear and pulled the negligée on. Véronique tied the halter neck at the back.

Erika found a stray strap that seemed to have no purpose. "What's this?"

"That's the release. Pull it down," said Véronique.

Erika did so, and the garment slithered to the floor around her ankles.

By the time she was fully dressed for action, Erika had three layers on, and yet she still felt half-naked. Applying her make up took 45 minutes and the concentrated attentions of several of the girls.

Erika checked her appearance in a cheval mirror. Sexy, daring and sluttish were evident, with little sign of discretion, modesty or sophistication. She looked like a naughty schoolgirl.

The final touch was a spot of Madam Véronique's own perfume, from an expensive bottle that she'd bought before the war.

"What are the commercial arrangements?" asked Erika.

Madam Véronique replied, "The customer pays me in advance. If he has a good time he may slip a little extra to you." She looked at her fob watch. "If he's coming today we should see him in the next 30 minutes."

"What name should I call myself?"

"That's up to you, *ma chérie*," said Véronique. "Angeline, perhaps?"

#

"He's here!" called one of the girls from a window.

Babette hid in Madam Véronique's private rooms. Erika took a last look at herself in the mirror and stubbed out her cigarette.

A knock on the door was answered by Madam Véronique. "What are you selling today, Monsieur?"

"*Poissons et navets*," came the reply. Fish and turnips.

Véronique opened the door and admitted the big man. Waiting in Babette's room, Erika heard a muffled conversation. Babette had gone to visit her mother in the country. Her mother was unwell. She wouldn't be available for a few days. Would the Monsieur care to sample one of the other girls? No? Well how would he like to meet our newest recruit? Her name is Angeline. Clanhaus was not convinced. He was on the point of leaving when 'Angeline' shimmered in and held out a hand.

The SD man took one look, wrapped a fist as big as a snow shovel around her fingers and drew them to his lips. She led him starry-eyed to Babette's room and sat him on the bed.

"What big hands you have," she said "Let's get this off." She removed his tunic. "Oh my, what big muscles you have."

She removed her own outer layer.

Next, she removed his boots. "Oh my, what big feet you have."

She slipped out of her second layer, revealing the skimpy negligée.

He got to his feet while she removed his trousers. The giant stood trembling in his shorts.

"What have you got in there for me? Oh MY!"

She pulled the release strap on her negligée.

#

Clanhaus was back two days later. Erika had spent an hour and a half touching up her make up and selecting a new outer layer of clothing. The addition of ridiculous eyelashes made her look even younger than before.

The city was in one of its regular blackouts. In Babette's room Erika entertained her visitor in the light of sputtering acrid-smelling candles. She forced the SD man to proceed slowly. After 30 minutes of teasing him, she straddled him.

As their bodies merged she said, "It's so thrilling for me to make love with such an important man."

"Yes, I expect it is."

"You are in charge of all the records for the SD in Paris, I think?"

"All of them, yes. But I cannot talk about that."

"Of course, *liebling*, but you are in charge of the records of the prisoners in Fresnes prison?"

"Of course. A little slower, please."

"And the prisoners in Avenue Foch?"

"I cannot discuss – Yes, that's better! – matters of national security."

"Of course not, but I heard on the grapevine that you have had a new intake of prisoners of war into Avenue Foch. Is that correct?"

He spun her round and climbed on top. "The grapevine?"

"Yes, and I heard that many of these are British airmen. Is that true?"

"I cannot discuss those matters," said Clanhaus, his frown corrugating his scar.

"I really like you, Claus, and I thought you liked me."

"I do, but don't ask me questions that I can't answer."

"No more questions then, I promise."

Afterwards, as she dressed, she said, "How would you like to take me out to a restaurant?"

Clanhaus's brow furrowed some more, his mouth drooped. "We are not permitted to use French restaurants. The risks are too great."

"I've seen men in German uniform in restaurants," she said.

"Maybe, but not Sicherheitsdienst men. The Free French are always on the lookout for SD men."

She pouted. "I thought you enjoyed my company."

"I do, *ma cherie liebling*, but what you ask is against regulations. You could visit me in my room in Avenue Foch if you wish."

"When? Tomorrow?"

"Thursday. Many of the officers will be out of the building then."

She beamed at him. "Ooh, that will be so exciting."

Chapter 30

Later that same day, SS-Hauptsturmführer Polhammer, Chief Administration Officer, SD, Paris, received an urgent request for a meeting from one of his men.

He removed every piece of furniture, every fragile object from his office door to his desk before agreeing to see SS-Oberscharführer Claus Clanhaus. Even so, the giant managed to trip over the edge of the carpet on his way in.

Polhammer frowned at Clanhaus. Every time he saw the man he found his mind wrestling with the problem of how to get rid of him. Clanhaus was clearly Aryan, a Teuton to his core. The living embodiment of one of the Nordic gods, he could have passed for Odin except for the hideous scar. Physiologically he was unsuited to deskwork. The man should surely be at the Eastern Front tearing open Russian tanks with his bare hands.

"What is it, Clanhaus? I can only give you a few minutes."

Clanhaus stood with his hands behind his back, giving the impression of a very large recalcitrant schoolboy. "Thank you for seeing me, sir. I know how busy you are."

"Yes, yes. Get on with it."

"Yes, sir. Sorry, sir. You know that I spend time at Madam Véronique's…"

SS- Hauptsturmführer Polhammer was familiar with the establishment. Tuesdays and Thursdays were officer nights.

"Yes?"

"Yes, sir. Well, when I went there today I was introduced to a new girl called Angeline. She asked questions about our recent intake of prisoners of war."

"Did she mention the name Jones at all?"

"No, sir, but she seemed keen to gain access to my private room. So I invited her to visit me here on Thursday next."

"That was very well done, Clanhaus. Dismissed."

SS-Hauptsturmführer Polhammer watched his administrator stumble over the carpet on his way out. He waited until Clanhaus had closed the door before picking up his telephone. "Get me the Sturmbannführer," he barked.

SS-Sturmbannführer Kieffer was having a late afternoon shave in his office. Polhammer could never get used to the sight of the cutthroat razor wielded by a Frenchman. He considered the practice a serious breach of military discipline verging on insanity, but it was more than his job's worth to report the behaviour to Berlin.

Kieffer waved a hand to the barber. "Wait outside."

The barber left, and Kieffer wiped the foam from his face with a hot cloth. "What is it, Polhammer? I trust it's something important."

"Sir," Polhammer clicked his heels. "One of my men has made contact with a probable member of the French Resistance, a woman working in Madam Véronique's salon."

"Do I know this strumpet?"

"I believe not, sir, she is a new addition to the salon. Her name is Angeline."

"Go on."

"She has been asking questions about the airmen recently transferred from the camps. I believe she may have information of value to us."

"Indeed. Pick her up. Let Vogt work on her."

"Sir, she finagled an invitation to my man's room in number 82. I suggest we let her keep that rendezvous, give her the run of the building, and see what she does. If we play our cards right she may identify the British spy for us."

SS-Sturmbannführer Kieffer stroked the damp stubble on his chin. "What you suggest is risky. Foolhardy, even. It might be regarded by some as reckless, but I admire your unorthodox approach, Polhammer. I believe your strategy could be productive and may lead us to a whole nest of underground agitators. You have my permission to proceed. But be warned that it is your head that will roll if your plan backfires, not anyone else's. Send the barber in on your way out."

"Thank you sir, Heil Hitler," said Polhammer, clicking his heels again and saluting smartly.

Polhammer returned to his office and sat down heavily behind his desk. He had Kieffer's permission to let the scene play out, and now that Kieffer had approved the plan there was no way back. Failure would ruin him. His career in the SD would be at an end, as would his membership of the SS. He could even lose his life if the plan went badly wrong. What had he been thinking? He swallowed a couple of headache pills.

Chapter 31

Three days later, Erika pedalled her way on a borrowed bicycle to Avenue Foch in the 16th Arrondissement. In the basket she carried a bottle of Madam Véronique's best wine.

Paris in July – even under occupation – was a magical place of centuries old buildings and generous, wide boulevards. The magnificent city was untouched by the war. The French army had surrendered to the invading tanks rather than making a hopeless stand that would have reduced their city to rubble.

French people bustled about everywhere on foot or on bicycles, with small groups of German soldiers strolling among them or driving by in military vehicles. Apart from the names over the shops and the advertising on the Morris columns, the scene was indistinguishable from any large city in Germany.

She passed the Arc de Triomphe, covered in Nazi flags. Broad and tree-lined, Avenue Foch consisted of five-storey blocks of 18th-century terraces in pale golden stone. It was easy to imagine numbers 82 – 86, the SD headquarters as they must have been: pleasant, luxury apartments, each with a French window and balcony providing an uninterrupted view of the Bois de Boulogne in one direction and the Arc de Triomphe on the other.

Erika parked her bicycle at the railings outside number 82, took the wine from the basket, hid it inside her tunic, and entered the building. Crossing the threshold, an involuntary shiver ran through her body. A pervasive feeling of menace hung over the place. The entrance foyer was fitted out in black marble resembling the inside of a tomb. A few German uniforms rushed about, carrying bundles of paper or briefcases. Erika imagined she could sense the spirits of all the unfortunate members of the French Resistance who had been tortured and killed within these walls.

She felt as out-of-place as she looked, and yet no one gave her a second glance. This gave her the eerie feeling that they all knew exactly who she was and why she was there.

The girl behind the marble desk could have been the receptionist at the entrance to Hades. Erika gave Claus Clanhaus's name and was directed to the staircase. "You want the third floor."

She climbed the staircase to the third floor to find Claus Clanhaus waiting to greet her. He led her along the carpeted corridor to his rooms, ushered her inside and closed the door.

He had three rooms, a small living area, a bedroom and a tiny bathroom. By Paris standards the apartment was the height of luxury. Before the war someone rich and famous would have lived here, paying a monthly rent equivalent to many people's annual wage.

He offered her ersatz coffee. She opened her tunic and handed him the bottle of wine. "A giftt from Madam."

He uncorked the wine and poured some into two teacups, apologising that he had no glasses.

Erika giggled.

Between them they finished the bottle in no time. When Erika pouted at the empty bottle Clanhaus produced a bottle of schnapps from a cupboard.

"I've been saving this for a special occasion," he said. "I think this is a special occasion, don't you, Angeline?"

"Definitely."

"What do you think of the building? Magnificent, isn't it?" he said as they sipped their schnapps.

"It's impressive," said Erika. "Is this where you work?"

"My office is in number 84. I can show you later, if you like."

This unlikely offer set off major warning bells in Erika's mind. She could feel the jaws of an elaborate trap closing around her. But she would take the opportunity on offer and worry about the consequences later.

They finished the schnapps and shared a baguette. With no butter, the bread was dry, but it was fresh. He made coffee. Erika asked for Véronique's 200 franc fee, and the giant paid her. Soon, he was clawing at her clothing, his half-finished coffee congealing in his cup.

She backed away from him and said, "Do you have a prisoner here called Jones?"

"I can't answer questions like that," said Clanhaus.

"I understand, but a cousin of mine is distantly related to a British airman named Jones. I promised her I'd ask as I knew you wouldn't mind telling me."

"No more questions," said Clanhaus, clamping a fist around her arm.

#

Afterwards they shared a cigarette and he watched her with glazed eyes as she dressed. He was a big man and probably well able for alcohol, but Erika could tell from his performance under the sheets that he was inebriated.

"Put your clothes on, Claus," she said.

He snorted. "Why, am I too ugly to look at?"

"You promised to show me where you work, remember?"

He threw his clothes on and went into the bathroom. As soon as he was out of sight, Erika turned the handle on the French window. The door opened without a sound. She stepped out onto an individual wrought iron balcony with a view of the gardens at the rear of the building. A warm breeze welcomed her. She looked left and right. The balconies stood in rows, all empty. Quickly she stepped back inside, and closed the door.

Clanhaus reappeared, buttoning his flies, and took her on a tour. Number 82 was the living quarters for the men, he explained. He showed her where they had installed a door connecting number 82 to number 84.

"Is this the only door to 84?" she asked.

"No, there are interconnecting doors on every floor," he replied.

He took her through to number 84, opened a door and flicked on the light. "This is my office." There was nothing much to see – a desk covered in papers, a chair, a telephone, a filing cabinet, linoleum on the floor.

"Could you check your records while we're here? Please. For my cousin. Just tell me if you have a British airman called Jones in the building."

Clanhaus stood by his filing cabinet. He didn't open it. "You may tell your cousin that we do have a British airman here called Jones. But there must be many airmen called Jones in the RAF."

"Thank you Claus. That's all I need to set my cousin's mind at rest."

They returned to number 82 and continued the tour.

"Why does the staircase only go as far as the third floor?" she asked.

"For security reasons," he replied. "There's a smaller staircase at the end of the corridor that leads to the floors above. The fourth floor is where the boss has his private quarters and offices, and the prisoners are held on the floor above that."

"Can we go up there? Is it permitted?"

"Yes, of course," said the giant SD man.

They took the back stairs to the top floor. On the way along the fifth floor corridor she stopped at a door. "This is the door that leads to number 84?" She tried the handle.

"Yes," he said. "But it's kept locked at all times."

They walked the length of the corridor to a window that he said gave the best view of the Bois de Boulogne. She looked out the window and gasped at the sight. A large portion of the city to the south and west could be seen. He pointed out some of the highlights.

As they descended, she said, "Could I come back another day, Claus? I love the privacy of your rooms. The salon is so public."

"Yes, of course. How about next Thursday?"

"Wednesday is Bastille Day," she said. "We could celebrate together in private. And could we make it later? Around midnight, perhaps?"

"After curfew?"

Foolishly, Erika had forgotten about the 10:00 pm curfew. "I'll bring another bottle of wine," she said, batting her eyelashes at him.

When they reached the foyer, Clanhaus asked the girl at the desk for a pad of forms. He filled in the top form, tore it from the pad and walked Erika outside to her bicycle.

As she mounted her bicycle, he handed her the form. She folded it once and placed it in the basket without looking at it.

"Until Wednesday," he said.

She waited until she was a kilometre from Avenue Foch before stopping to examine the form. It was a temporary *Ausweis* – permission to be out after curfew – made out in the name Michelle Médard for July 14, 1943.

#

"You do realise what you're asking?" said Lacosse. "The building is a fortress. There must be ten SS officers in there, all carrying side arms, as well as guards with rifles. The whole idea is madness."

"Two hours after curfew," added Favier, the master burglar.

"I was hoping the Nazis might have relaxed the curfew for the French National Day of Celebration," she said.

"The Vichy government try that every year," said Favier, "and every year the Boches turn them down."

"Well, hopefully the Germans will all be asleep in their quarters or out celebrating Bastille Day. It's a perfect day for it."

Lacosse said, "You don't think they'll be out on the balconies?"

"Possibly, but I saw no one on any of the balconies at the back of the building. It's pretty dark back there. If you wear black no one will see you."

"How do we get from the third floor of building 82 to the top floor in Building 84?" asked Favier.

"I've told you, the two buildings are connected by doors on every floor. You climb the back stairs to the top floor in 82 and find the door from there to building 84. The door is kept locked, but it should be a simple matter for Monsieur Favier to get through it."

Lacosse chewed his lip while he considered his response. Finally, he said, "All right. We'll do it. We'll aim for 12:30."

Chapter 32

"Excuse me, sir."

SS-Hauptsturmführer Polhammer looked up from the papers on his desk. The giant Clanhaus was standing too close, blotting out the daylight, casting a shadow over the desk.

"What is it, Clanhaus?"

"That new pussy, Angeline, paid me a visit."

"Good. You showed her around? She saw where the prisoners are held?"

Clanhaus shifted his weight from one leg to the other. The effect was like an eclipse of the moon. "Yes, sir. She's coming back on Wednesday."

"Bastille Day? What time?"

"Midnight."

"Very well. Try not to disturb the carpet on your way out."

"There was something else, sir."

"Go on."

"She asked me if we are holding a British airman called Jones."

"Indeed? And how did you respond?"

"I told her we have."

"Well done, Clanhaus. Dismissed."

"Yes, sir. Thank you, sir."

SS-Hauptsturmführer Polhammer lifted the telephone and rang upstairs. SS-Sturmbannführer Kieffer answered on the third ring.

"Yes?"

"It's Polhammer, sir. I have news. Can we meet?"

"I'm tied up at the moment. Tell me over the telephone."

"You recall the doxy that I told you about, the one my man Clanhaus said was interested in our prisoners?"

"Angelique. Yes, I remember." He grunted.

"Angeline, sir. She was admitted and spent some time with Clanhaus. He took her on a guided tour of the building."

"Do you think..." Kieffer grunted again. Then he groaned. " Do you really think that was wise?"

"I thought it was what we agreed, sir."

"Was it? I'm not sure. Did she show any interest in the airmen?"

"Yes, sir. She asked about Jones by name. And she's coming back next Wednesday – Bastille Day."

Kieffer gave a long moan.

"Sir? Are you still there?"

"Something's come up. I have to go," said Kieffer. "Keep me informed."

Polhammer put the telephone down and stared at it for a full minute. Then he picked it up again.

"Get me the Gestapo in Rue des Saussaies. I wish to speak with SS-Obersturmführer Spittbendler."

Chapter 33

Toby shuffled the cards and dealt the two hands. Gudrun had lost count of the number of games they'd played. She'd lost count of the number of days that they had been playing this accursed game, the number of hours she'd had to look at her jailer's ugly face. They'd started the week with a full box of matches each. She was down to her last dozen; Toby's pile had grown.

She played a card, the 10 of acorns. Toby followed suit with the king and snorted.

"You're not very good at this game, are you?"

Gudrun tossed her cards on the table. "Enough, Toby! I've had enough!"

Toby's ugly face transformed into a gargoyle's. "Now why did you do that? I can see your cards. You've spoiled the game."

She swept her cards and matches from the table. "This has gone on long enough."

"Pick up the cards and I'll deal again."

"Let me go, Toby, please. Anna must be out of her mind by now with worry. Please let me go. I will return to Ireland. I promise I will never tell a living soul where I've been. I swear."

"Pick up the cards."

"Don't you have any feelings, Toby? Don't you have a soul? How long do you intend to keep me here?"

"As long as I have to. Now pick up the cards."

Gudrun retrieved the cards from the floor and flung them on the table. Toby assembled the pack, shuffled them, and dealt a new hand. They played the hand in silence.

"I win again," he said, adding three of Gudrun's matches to his mounting pile. He gathered up the cards and shuffled the deck again. "You know in some parts of the Tyrol, where I'm from, they play the game with 36 cards."

"You've told me that, a thousand times," said Gudrun.

"And in other places they use 40."

"Just deal the cards."

By midnight Gudrun couldn't keep her eyes open. Toby yawned. "That's enough fun for one day." He reattached Gudrun's handcuffs to the bedpost. "Sleep well."

Gudrun made herself as comfortable as she could on the bed. She closed her eyes. Before drifting off to sleep she said a silent prayer that Kurt would stay safe, that he would find her and rescue her before it was too late.

Chapter 34

In Farm Helmhof, near Hamburg, the farmer sat down heavily on the sofa opposite Kurt, and lit his pipe.

"I imagine you're still hoping to get away from here. I know that most young men would run several kilometres rather than contemplate marriage to my daughter. But she is sturdy, and she has all the skills of a farmer's wife. You could do a lot worse. This is a good farm – two hectares. It may take a few months or a year, but you will come to accept your destiny in the end, and marry her."

Kurt glanced at the shotgun. He would try again to reach it when he had the chance.

"You are a Christian, so you will understand when I tell you why. I prayed to God to find a husband for my daughter and He answered my prayer. I had a vision sent to me by an angel. In that vision I saw my daughter walking up the aisle dressed in a wedding dress, a young man waiting for her at the altar. I heard a heavenly choir singing and a voice said: 'The bottom field will bear fruit'. I have been watching the bottom field for a twelvemonth. I knew you would appear one day. God has sent you to my daughter. Your destiny is clear."

"How can you be sure your vision was of me and not someone else? There have been others in these chains before me, I think."

"None of them was worthy."

Kurt wondered what happened to all the unsuccessful candidates but he kept the thought to himself. He said, "You may be right, I could be the man in your vision, but no power in heaven or earth will force me to marry a girl I do not know. Release me from the chain and I will spend time with her, alone, to see if she is truly the one that God has chosen for me."

"Hah!" said the farmer. "I've heard that line before. If I take off the chain what's to keep you from running off?"

"I give you my word, I will not leave as long as Ingrid wants me to stay."

The farmer considered Kurt's promise. "Your solemn word? And if Ingrid wants you, do you swear to marry her?"

"On my life, I swear it," said Kurt.

The farmer removed the padlock, releasing Kurt from the chain.

#

He found Ingrid in the farmyard feeding the chickens, scattering seeds, speaking to the birds with strange clucking sounds. Once again Kurt thought she looked like one of them, the way her head tilted and flicked rapidly from side to side.

"We need to talk, Ingrid," he said.

"How did you get free of the chain?"

"Your father set me free."

"And you're still here?"

"Of course. I would like us to talk so that we can get to know one another."

Ingrid blushed deeply. "There's not much to know. I am the daughter of a farmer. I look after the animals. Come."

She took him by the hand and led him to a barn where they made a nest for themselves in the hay. Thirty minutes later, Kurt and Ingrid had exchanged life stories. Her hand rested on Kurt's chest.

Her fingers found the top three buttons on his shirt and popped them open, one by one. "I like you, Kevin. You're not like the others." She threw a leg across his hips.

Easing out from under her embrace, he sat up. She did the same. He took Gudrun's postcard out of its envelope and handed it to Ingrid. "Take another look at the postcard. Read the message."

"It's in English."

Kurt translated it for her: "Wish you were here, Gudrun. Now look at the stamp. See where it was posted."

"Hamburg. So she's in the city having a good time. She'd like it if you were there with her. She loves you."

He shook his head. "No, Ingrid, that's not what the message

means. Gudrun and I are both being hunted by the Gestapo. The last time I saw her she was living happily in Ireland with her daughter, Anna."

"So how did she send the postcard from Hamburg?"

"The Gestapo have taken her. They are holding her. They forced her to write the postcard, hoping that I would try to rescue her. Don't you see? My girlfriend is in serious trouble."

"Maybe she went to Hamburg of her own free will and the message means what it says."

"She disappeared from her home in Ireland one day when she should have collected Anna from school. There can be no doubt that she has been taken."

She gave a sulky cluck. "I'm sorry for Gudrun, but she has a child. I have no one. If you go to Hamburg to find her you could die."

He said, "Would you separate a suckling lamb from its ewe?"

She shook her head, her eyes filling with tears.

"So how can we separate Gudrun from Anna? I can't do that to Anna."

Ingrid wept.

Kurt put an arm around her shoulders. "When the war is over and the men return home, I'm sure you will find your ideal husband. Bringing men to the farmhouse at the point of a gun and chaining them is not the way."

"But Papa's vision…"

"Your father's vision will come true, Ingrid, but not using guns and chains."

"But I like you, Kevin. Of all the men that Papa has brought to me, you are the best."

She leapt up, stamped her foot and pouted. "I will not let you go."

Part 5 - Reaction

Chapter 35

A kilometre from the farm, Kurt met a hyena. Driven wild by the bombing, the creature stood in the centre of the street baring its teeth, but slunk away in fear as Kurt advanced toward it. In the next street he met a couple of alpacas rushing about like headless chickens. They disappeared together down a side street.

The Allied bombing raid had destroyed the walls of the zoo. Kurt stepped over the rubble, avoiding a family of aardvarks that scuttled across his path. Many of the animal enclosures were damaged, and he could hear distressing sounds of large animals in pain. He moved toward the sounds.

An elephant charged past, its trunk swinging from side to side like a huge policeman's truncheon, giving an impression that it was late for an important meeting rather than one of blind panic.

Kurt came across a zookeeper dressed in green, carrying a bear cub. The cub was hanging on for its life. It looked heavy.

Kurt said, "I'm looking for Peter Wolfe."

The keeper nodded with her head. "He's over there. Look in the reptile house."

Kurt hurried in the direction indicated and found a second zookeeper dressed in green attempting to put a 2-metre python into a wooden box. The snake had other plans and had wrapped itself around the keeper's arm.

"Peter Wolfe?" said Kurt.

The keeper pointed to a brightly coloured banded snake, slithering under a tarpaulin. "Do me a favour, will you. Pick up that snake, and pop it into the box."

"I don't think so," said Kurt.

"It's not venomous," said the keeper. "It's distressed, but not dangerous. Pick it up close to the head and it won't bite you."

"I'd really rather not," said Kurt, a tremor running through him from head to feet.

"Okay, take the python. Quickly, the coral is getting away."

Given a choice between the giant python and the coral snake, Kurt made up his mind. He pulled the tarpaulin to one side, leant down and grabbed the coral snake behind its head. Lifting it from the ground, he dropped it into the box, tail first.

The keeper unwrapped the python from his arm, dropped it into the box, and closed the lid. "There's another one over there, under that pile of wood," he said.

Kurt held up both hands. "I've done my bit for the day, my friend. I'm not too comfortable around animals that slither."

"How about animals with legs? There's a 4-metre Nile crocodile around here somewhere…"

Kurt laughed and the keeper slapped him on the back.

"You did well with that coral snake. *Vielen Dank*. What can I do for you?"

"Are you Peter Wolfe?"

"Who're you?"

"My name's Kevin. Erika Cleasby gave me your name. She said you might be able to help me."

"Erika the physicist? How is Erika? I haven't seen her for at least two years. Any friend of Erika's is a friend of mine. How can I help?"

Kurt showed him the postcard. "Do you know this castle?"

Wolfe looked at the picture on the card. "Everyone around here knows it. It's a magnificent castle, dating back to the thirteenth century. The current Baron is in his eighties."

Kurt said, "I need to get inside."

"I take it you don't have an invitation?"

"Can you get me inside?"

Wolfe ran a finger over his impressive moustache. "Most of these old castles are impregnable, but there might be a way. Give me your address."

"I don't have an address," said Kurt. "I just got here from France."

"You can stay with me," said the zookeeper. "You look

exhausted. I'll take you to the castle in the morning. But first, give me a hand with these reptiles."

The walk to Wolfe's apartment in the centre of the town took 15 minutes. The apartment building stood defiantly in a square with three other buildings that had suffered varying degrees of bomb damage. There was no electricity in Wolfe's building and not a scrap of food in his apartment, but he had a few bottles of good quality beer in his larder.

Kurt asked Wolfe how he had avoided conscription.

"I have three brothers, all older than me, all in the army. I was left to help my mother on the family farm."

"You are a farmer, and yet you find time to be a zookeeper?"

"The reptiles are easy to handle. They only have to be fed once or twice a week."

Kurt ran through his story quickly. Wolfe read the message on the postcard and blew a low whistle. "It's almost certainly a trap, you do realise that?"

"Yes. My plan is to free Gudrun at any cost. I may have to sacrifice myself in order to get her out. If that happens it would help to know that she had someone on the outside to help her."

"As I said, any friend of Erika's is a friend of mine. You can rely on me, Kevin."

Halfway through his second bottle of beer, Kurt fell asleep in his chair.

#

The castle was even more intimidating in reality than it looked on the postcard. Surrounded on all sides by oak woodland in its summer foliage, its towers thrust at the blue sky.

Wolfe pointed out a gated sewer outlet low on the castle wall. "That sewer has been moving aristocratic shit for 700 years." He grinned. "It's your way in. All you have to do is get past the gate."

They returned to the zoo. Calm had returned, most of the animals were back in their cages, and only a few thin plumes of smoke rose from the city centre.

"I hope that's the end of the bombing," said Wolfe. "Every year since the start of the war the city has taken a battering, but this year has been the worst, and since late last month the raids have been almost continuous."

He sorted the reptiles into cages and fed them with Kurt's help. Then he left Kurt in the ruins of the reptile house while he scouted out some human food – a basket of fruit and a flagon of water. The fruit was mostly overripe, but Kurt devoured it eagerly.

When he'd eaten his fill he thanked his host.

Wolfe laughed. "Don't thank me. You can thank the monkeys on your way out. Now let's see if we can locate that crocodile…"

#

They approached the castle after dark. Wolfe used a pair of bolt cutters to remove the padlock on the sewer gate. He swung the gate open and it squealed like a banshee, the sound echoing across the tops of the trees.

They waited a few moments for a reaction from inside the castle, but there was none.

"Good luck, my friend." said the zookeeper. "When you find your girlfriend bring her to my apartment and I'll help you to get out of the country." He handed Kurt a knife with a narrow blade. "Take this. You may need it."

Kurt shook his hand. "Thank you, and thanks for all your help. I owe you a big favour."

Wolfe looked him in the eyes. His moustache twitched "You owe me nothing, not after handling that dangerous coral snake for me."

Kurt stared back, but couldn't decide whether Wolfe was serious.

Ducking his head, he stepped into the sewer. A lone rat emerged, jumped over his boot and scampered into the forest.

Chapter 36

Paris, Bastille Day July 14, 1943

Reverting to her original outfit of blue skirt, white blouse and red scarf, Erika set out on the bicycle toward the river. Paris at night – even under Occupation and the dreaded curfew – was alive with nightlife, laughter and song. Every street corner that she passed had its nightwalkers, with gendarmes in their traditional peaked kepis and stylish capes patrolling the streets in pairs.

She turned into Rue de Rivoli and immediately realised her mistake. This street had a heavy German military presence with armed guards and a Panzer tank blocking the street. She turned her bicycle, went back the way she'd come and once more headed for the Seine. Place de la Concorde was crowded with drunken German revellers and French women of the night, celebrating the Republic's historic past. She cycled on along the river, the Eiffel Tower peeping above the buildings to her left. She knew there would be more revellers there. For the French population the city was under curfew, but for the invaders it was open for business, the nightclubs, bars and restaurants were all full of German patrons.

She turned north along Avenue Marceau. The Place de l'Étoile was surprisingly empty with just a few drunken German sailors singing Horst Wessel's anthem and warming themselves on the eternal flame.

Avenue Foch was quiet, its trees in shadow like rows of silent mourners. She parked her bicycle as the bells of Notre Dame – silenced since the Occupation – rang midnight. The bells sounded strangely apologetic, the only concession granted to the Vichy government for Bastille Day.

Entering the marble foyer she ignored the marionette behind the desk and took the stairs to the third floor. She went directly to Clanhaus's room and knocked on the door. He let her in, producing a bottle of Champagne and two glasses with a flourish.

She laughed. "What is this for? It's not New Year."

"We're celebrating France's day of glory. I borrowed the glasses." He filled the two glasses with foaming liquid and handed her one. They touched glasses and drank.

"It feels like I've known you my whole life," said Clanhaus.

"I know that feeling," she replied.

By 12:20 am the Champagne was all gone and they were halfway through Erika's wine. He began to get frisky.

Sidestepping him, she unlocked the door to the French window and stepped onto the balcony. A near full moon lit the scene, but the mass of gardens and trees below were impenetrably dark.

He followed her outside, put an arm across her shoulders, and pulled her to him. They listened to the distant sounds of the street revellers for a few minutes.

Erika looked around. All the other third floor balconies were empty. She checked the balconies on the other floors above and below. They were all deserted. Once again she had that feeling of an elaborate trap encircling her.

"Let's go back in," she said.

They stepped inside and he closed the door. When he turned around she was right behind him. He wrapped her in his arms and kissed her neck.

She ran her hands over the muscles in his back and groaned seductively.

"We could go into the bedroom," he said.

"You go ahead, my love. Give me a moment to prepare. Call me when you're ready."

Clanhaus scurried into the bedroom, leaving the door ajar.

Erika opened the French window again and a shadowy figure entered, dark-clad, masked and wearing galoshes over his shoes.

Clanhaus called from the bedroom, "I'm ready, my sweet."

"Coming, my lover," she replied.

The masked man slipped into the bedroom.

Erika followed moments later to find the giant SD man lying on his back beside the bed, a stiletto protruding from between his ribs. There was very little blood.

The assassin returned to the window and gave a low whistle. Three more figures clambered onto the balcony and in through the window. All four were dressed in black from head to toe and they all wore black ski masks. Erika recognized Favier the ferret. He was the short one with the blue eyes, wearing a length of rope wrapped over his shoulder. One of the men removed his mask. It was Lacosse, without his glasses.

He made eye contact with the assassin in the galoshes. "Tell me you subdued him."

The assassin shook his head and ran a thumb across his throat.

"*Merde*, Marcel! Didn't I tell you I wanted him kept alive?"

Marcel, the assassin, shrugged. "The pig resisted. I had no choice."

"Pity, he was a useful contact," said Lacosse.

Lacosse put his mask back on, and Marcel opened the door to the corridor. The coast was clear.

"Where is everyone?" he said.

Erika pushed past him. "Follow me."

They ran along the carpet to the end of the corridor and climbed the back stairs to the top floor, unopposed. She took them to the interconnecting door.

She said, "This is where we need you, Favier. Get this door open."

Favier stepped forward and tried the door handle. The door swung open.

"I thought you said it was kept locked," said Lacosse.

Erika felt something stirring like a flock of butterflies in her gut. The jaws of the trap were closing tighter. No time to worry about that now, she thought.

Marcel, the assassin in the galoshes, said, "Something's not right."

"Come on," she whispered. "Let's find our man and get out of here."

They entered the fifth floor of 84 Avenue Foch. This was entirely different from the third floor of number 82. The floor was bare, the doors to the individual rooms stout wooden affairs with serious locks and spyholes. The Frenchmen looked to Erika for guidance. She took a position halfway along the corridor and called out: "Jones, identify yourself."

A chorus of voices replied from behind the locked doors.

"In here."

"I'm Jones."

"I'm Flying Officer Jones."

"This is hopeless," said Lacosse.

Erika ignored him. She opened the observation flap on the nearest door and said, "Jones, show yourself."

A man stepped to the flap. "I'm Jones."

"Open this door," said Erika, and Favier got to work.

She tried the next door. "Jones, are you in there?"

A second man showed his face. "My name is Jones."

"And this one," she said.

She moved on to the next door.

"Flying Officer Jones, Show yourself."

Two men stepped forward in the gloom. "And this one." She closed the flap and moved to the next door.

No one replied there.

"This is crazy," said Marcel. "We should leave now while we have the chance."

Erika carried on opening flaps, searching. And then she found him, tall with white hair, the face she had committed to memory.

"Open this door, too," she snapped.

Favier's fingers flew as he worked with his lock picks. Erika watched to make sure he opened the correct doors. The others took up defensive positions at either end of the corridor, although there was still no sign of the Germans.

Erika couldn't believe that the SD had left the fifth floor unprotected. The unlocked interconnecting door was still giving her butterflies in the stomach. And Favier was taking far too long to open the cell doors. He had three of them opened but the fourth was giving him trouble.

"Hurry up, Favier," she whispered.

She got no answer.

Three more minutes went by before Favier called out, "Got it," and the final cell door swung open.

Five prisoners stood in the corridor.

"Which one is our man?" said Lacosse.

"We have to take them all," Erika replied. "Let's go."

They headed for the staircase, Favier and Marcel leading the way. As they turned the corner onto the third floor, a voice called out "Halt! Stand where you are, all of you, or we fire."

Chapter 37

$f$aced by several handguns and a Schmeisser submachine gun, Favier took a step backward. The Germans opened fire, and the assassin, Marcel, collapsed under a hail of bullets.

The five prisoners turned and ran back up the stairs to the fourth floor, followed by Erika, Lacosse, Favier, and the last remaining Frenchman.

A German soldier appeared on the stairs below and levelled a rifle at them. The unidentified Frenchman shot him with his pistol.

"Good shot, Loulou," whispered Lacosse.

Erika glanced again at the masked figure. Now, it seemed obvious from the way she moved and the curve of her hips that this was a woman.

Erika sprinted along the corridor to the interconnecting door. She tried it, but it was locked. No surprise there. She ran on up the staircase. The others followed her, the German gunmen in close pursuit.

Erika had no idea what to do next, and she had a horrible feeling that they were all following her lead. They were soon back on the top floor, once again running along the corridor between the prisoners' cells.

"Stop!" she said, and everyone stopped running. "There's no way out. We're trapped."

"Not necessarily," said Favier. He pointed to a hatch above their heads.

Lacosse lifted Loulou like a doll in his arms. She raised the hatch and climbed through. The others followed, the tallest prisoner boosting each of them through the hatch in turn. Finally the tall prisoner climbed up after them. Erika and the others made their way to a loft window. It was locked. Favier poked an elbow through the glass and they all climbed onto the roof.

"Which way?" said Erika.

Loulou said, "Follow me."

The roof had a steep pitch, but there was a balustrade that they could run along. The whole block consisted of one long terrace. They were soon well beyond the SD buildings. Below them, Erika could see the Bois de Boulogne teeming with revellers.

They reached the last building of the terrace. Favier secured his rope to a chimney. Loulou climbed down and secured the other end to the first floor balcony. Then the others climbed down, one at a time.

Someone smashed the door of the French window and as each one arrived on the balcony Erika pushed them through into the apartment.

They heard a rifle shot.

"Get your heads down!" said Lacosse.

Erika peered into the darkness where the flash of the gunfire had coming from. They were sitting ducks in the moonlight.

Jason Jones was the last man to reach the balcony.

"Hurry up, Jones," she whispered as he dropped from the rope.

More shots and Jones gave a cry of pain.

"I'm hit," he said, clutching his thigh.

"Shit!" said Erika, bundling him through the door and throwing herself in after him.

She got to her feet and turned to Lacosse. "What do we do now?"

"We can't stop here. We have to get out of this building and mingle with the crowd in the Bois."

The apartment was dark and empty. The Free French removed their black outer clothing, discarding the ski masks. With two of the prisoners supporting their wounded countryman, they made it to the front door and out into Avenue Foch and from there to the Bois de Boulogne.

Lacosse gave Loulou her orders. "Take these three men into the crowd. Contact the doctor, tell him to meet us in Rue Benouville. Tell him it's urgent. We'll meet up later. Michelle and Favier, go with Loulou."

Erika shook her head. "I'm with you, Monsieur."

There was no time to argue. Loulou and Favier disappeared into the crowd with three of the prisoners. Lacosse and the fourth prisoner continued to support the injured Jason Jones.

Skirting the crowd, Lacosse took them to a nearby apartment on Rue Benouville. He knocked three times on the door, a woman holding a baby on her hip opened it within seconds, and they went inside.

Lacosse led Jones to a bedroom at the back of the house where he laid the injured man on the bed. The woman reappeared *sans* infant, carrying a basin of water, towels and bandages. Erika and the woman removed Jones's trousers carefully.

Erika found a chair and sat close to Jones's head. He looked grey. His leg was oozing blood. The woman began to clean his wound.

"Jones, listen to me," said Erika. "I am with Special Operations Executive. London sent me to get you out of France..." She paused. Jones made no sign that he had heard her, staring fixedly into space.

"Jones, are you listening? I'm with the SOE. I need you to listen to me."

Jones closed his eyes.

The woman tending to Jones's injury looked up at Erika and shook her head. "He can't hear you, Mademoiselle. He's in a lot of pain. Perhaps later."

Erika stood back and watched the woman at work. "Is there anything I can do?"

"See to my child, perhaps? Her name is Michou."

Erika was aware then of the infant's cries, and went to comfort her. She found the child in the arms of the second prisoner. He was happy to hand the screaming child over to Erika.

She found a bottle of milk, gave it to the child, and settled her in her cot.

When the child was sleeping, Erika and the British airman found easy chairs. The airman introduced himself. "Felix Jones, Flight Lieutenant. Thanks for the rescue."

"Michelle Médard. Glad to be of service," said Erika.

"I'm very grateful. I really thought our number was up in that place when Jerry started shooting at us. Any idea why the Krauts moved us?"

"No, sorry. Most of what they do makes no sense."

"You can say that again." Felix laughed. "We all had the same surname. How strange is that!"

"That is odd. What camp were you in?"

"I was in a transit camp, waiting to be moved to Poland."

"You weren't in a prisoner of war camp?"

Felix shook his head. "My mother was Jewish. I've no idea how the Nazis found out, but I was due to be moved to one of the death camps."

Erika closed here eyes. She needed rest, but Felix wanted to talk.

"You don't sound French, Michelle," he said. "Your English is very good."

"Thanks for the compliment."

"Do you know what's likely to happen next? I'm hoping to get back to England. My future looks bleak otherwise."

"I'm sure you'll be smuggled out. The partisans have already shipped a lot of RAF pilots back home."

#

They spent the night in their armchairs. Felix was snoring within minutes of closing his eyes. Erika was exhausted but every attempt to sleep failed. She finally fell asleep in the early hours and woke at dawn, covered in sweat.

Later that morning there was a triple knock on the apartment door. The woman of the house opened it and Lacosse hurried in, accompanied by a doctor. The doctor placed his bag on a table and examined the SIS man, shining a light in his eyes, asking him various questions in broken English.

"Can you hear me? What is your name?"

Erika watched with interest, but Jones made no replies to any of the doctor's questions. The doctor turned his attention to the wound. The woman assisted him, and Erika could see that she'd done this sort of work before.

Erika left the room. She found Lacosse in a living room smoking an aromatic Gaulois Bleu cigarette. He offered her one and lit it for her. She sat down wearily opposite the Frenchman, sucking the harsh Turkish tobacco smoke deep into her lungs.

"The woman of the house seems well able for medical emergencies," said Erika. "What is her name? And where is her husband?"

"You may call her Madam Y. She is a widow. She studied medicine in the Sorbonne before the war."

"Madam Y? Is that some sort of codename?"

"It is better if you don't know her name. Now tell me why we rescued five airmen. I thought you were after one man."

"To keep the enemy guessing. If we had rescued just one man the Gestapo would have known who the agent was." Erika drew on her cigarette a second time. The tobacco was so loosely packed the cigarette was already half finished. "Have you given any thought to your problem, Monsieur?"

He tossed his cigarette into the hearth and crossed his hands in his lap. "Problem, Mademoiselle?"

"You don't think it strange that the Boches raided that student house when we were there? Or that they picked up so many prisoner airmen recently, moving them from the prisoner of war camps to SD headquarters?"

He scowled at her. "The Gestapo search buildings every day, and the SD move prisoners back and forth between the camps, their headquarters and the Fresnes prison all the time. That is not so strange. What are you suggesting?"

"I'm suggesting that someone from your group has been singing to the SD."

"Singing?"

"Like a canary. Passing information to them." Her cigarette was burning her fingers. She discarded it into the fireplace.

"That is unthinkable," said Lacosse. "No loyal Frenchman would pass information to the enemy."

"You don't think it's strange that every one of the airmen we rescued tonight was called Jones?"

Lacosse shrugged. "Perhaps they identified themselves as Jones in the hope that we would set them free."

"You don't really believe that, do you?" said Erika quietly. "The fact is that within days of giving the name Jones to your men the SD moved every British airman in France with that name to their headquarters for questioning."

"I lost two key men tonight, both close friends," said Lacosse, grimly. "This is no time for wild accusations."

"Yes, and I'm sorry for the loss, but weren't you suspicious when we managed to get into the SD building so easily? And haven't you wondered why they left the door to the top floor unlocked?"

"I agree that was unexpected…"

"And why d'you think the Gestapo took no action until *after* we had freed the prisoners?"

"What are you saying?"

"I'm saying that the Boches waited, hoping we would identify which Jones was the British agent before they started shooting."

Lacosse lit a new cigarette. Erika noticed a tremor in his hands. He offered her the packet, but she declined with a shake of her head.

"I would trust every one of my men with my life. Roger is totally loyal to France. He served in the Foreign Legion. I've known him since the war started. Marcel was best man at my wedding. Favier was one of the first to join the Maquis in Normandy. He lost a brother fighting for *France Combattante* in Algeria before joining our unit of the French Forces of the Interior. No man has done more for the liberation of our country. I have absolute faith in all these men. I would trust every one of them with my life."

"Your trust could be misplaced, Monsieur," said Erika, handing Lacosse the temporary *ausweis* bearing the name Michelle Médard. "Perhaps you could explain how Clanhaus knew my name."

#

The doctor stopped to speak with Erika on his way out.

"Your friend is fortunate. It is a deep wound, but the bullet missed his artery. I have removed it, but really he should be in hospital."

"That's not possible."

"I understand. I have given him a sedative that will dull the pain and should help him to sleep tonight. I shall visit again tomorrow. He needs a lot of rest. Madam will check the wound and refresh the bandages every couple of hours."

"Will he recover?" said Erika.

"Yes, he should make a full recovery, but it will take time. He must not be moved and he should not be allowed to put any weight on that leg."

"How long?" asked Erika.

"Difficult to say, Mademoiselle."

"I need to get him out of France as quickly as I can."

"You're going to have to be patient," said the doctor, without a trace of a smile.

Chapter 38

Bent almost double, Kurt negotiated the slippery channel discharging sewage into a culvert that ran under a track and into the forest. The tunnel was barely tall enough for a child. His boots were sturdy and waterproof, but the soles lacked sufficient grip. Bracing his arms against the slime-coated walls gave him just enough additional purchase to keep from falling into the raw effluent. The ambient light grew dimmer the further he went until he was in darkness, the only remaining light an eerie glow from the slimy walls. The smell was overpowering, and he could hear distant sounds of water splashing.

Coming from an unknown source up ahead, the light began to improve, then 50 metres in, the tunnel opened into a low chamber, two metres high. A 15 cm circular hole in the ceiling suggested a crude toilet. To the side of the chamber was a narrow exit with three steps leading upward. Standing on the top of these steps he found a grille, firmly locked with a rust-encrusted padlock, providing a view into a high egg-shaped chamber with smooth walls cut from solid rock. The purpose of this strange chamber was a mystery.

Another 25 metres through the sewer it opened into a second chamber, this one well lit, 3 metres in height, home to a family of rats. Kurt counted six. Straightening his back, he looked up. Light from a three-quarter moon poured through a metal grille in the ceiling above a rusty iron ladder set into the wall. He climbed the ladder and pushed at the bars of the grille, but it refused to budge. He swore. Before descending, he could see a small inner open-air courtyard.

He pressed on through the narrow channel, and came to another high chamber with a rusty ladder, this one topped by a manhole cover. He climbed the ladder, put his back against the manhole cover and pushed. The cover moved. Applying more pressure, it opened a crack. The room above was in darkness and there were no sounds.

Making sure the manhole cover was secure on his back, he inserted his fingers into the crack and used his hands to slide the cover to the side. He climbed out. He was in an internal corridor containing heavy wooden doors set in massive stone walls. He replaced the manhole cover before trying the first door on the left. It opened to reveal a study equipped with leather armchairs, a broad fireplace, a roll-top desk, and walls covered in bookcases overflowing with books. On a table by the window sat a shortwave receiver/transmitter.

Kurt moved on.

A persistent whiff of sewage followed him wherever he went, and he soon realised the smell was coming from his shoes and the legs of his trousers.

The next room on the left looked like a company boardroom, containing a highly-polished table and 13 chairs, the walls wood-panelled. After that came a drawing room equipped with comfortable furniture.

On the right side of the corridor there was only one door. It opened with a groan to reveal a large room with a vaulted ceiling supported on huge wooden beams. This was a classic banqueting hall equipped with long wooden tables and ornate chairs. Kurt counted 12 arched windows with colourful leaded glass set high in the walls. Beneath each window hung a dark portrait. Kurt ran his eyes over the 12 portraits. The earlier ones were dark. There was a knight on horseback, an elderly man in clerical garb holding a book, probably a bible. Three of the later ones were long-nosed men in aristocratic poses wearing impressive moustaches. The last of these caught Kurt's attention. There was something about the man's bearing, the angle of his head, his piercing eyes and long nose that was unsettling and eerily familiar.

Leaving the great hall, he continued his exploration of the castle. The corridor ended at a wide stone staircase leading to the upper floors. Kurt heard a woman's voice singing, coming from a narrow passageway behind the staircase. He followed the sound and came to an open door. Pressing his body against the wall, he peered inside. This was a kitchen with an elderly cook preparing food.

As he watched, she loaded chopped vegetables into three saucepans on a bench, removed her apron, and said, "That'll do for tonight, girl."

Kurt darted back down the passageway and hid behind the staircase. He waited, but the woman didn't appear. He gave it a few moments before returning to the kitchen door. The room was empty. Running his eyes over the walls, he found a plain wooden door, and behind it a narrow staircase leading downward, spiralling around a stone column.

This was what Kurt had been looking for. Many medieval castles contained dungeons, and this was where he expected to find Gudrun.

Making as little noise as he could, he descended the staircase. But as he rounded a turn of the staircase he came face to face with the old woman.

Her eyes opened wide in terror. She screamed.

Kurt turned and ran back the way he'd come. With luck the screams wouldn't penetrate far within the thick walls of the castle, but he needed to find somewhere to hide – fast.

He reached the bottom of the main staircase. He could still hear the cook screaming behind and below. And there were shouts and sounds of feet hurrying down from the upper floors. He thought about returning to the manhole, re-entering the sewer, but there was no time for that. He ducked into the first room on his left and closed the door behind him.

He found himself back in the great hall, the ancient paintings staring down at him on all sides. Looking around for somewhere to hide, he considered the fireplace. It was wide enough for two or even three men, but hopeless as a hiding place. He checked up the chimney. This was wide enough, but if he tried to climb up there the amount of soot dislodged would certainly give him away.

The room had only one door, and the windows were too high to reach without a ladder. It seemed his only option was to hide underneath one of the tables. Then he spotted a ventilation vent at waist level to the left of the fireplace. He pulled at the cover. It was held in place by four screws. Working as fast as he could, Kurt used the point of Wolfe's knife to undo the screws. He removed the vent cover, and climbed inside. As he pulled the vent cover into place, the door opened, the lights came on.

Kurt had a limited view through the vent, but he could see the bottom half of the door. Three pairs of black knee-high boots entered. One advanced left, the other right. The third pair remained at the door.

The sound of handguns cocking echoed around the hall.

"Show yourself, Müller." The voice was a familiar one. It sent a ripple of apprehension down Kurt's back. Apprehension spiced with revulsion. It was the voice of his archenemy, SS-Sturmbannführer Manfred Necker of the Sicherheitsdienst.

Chapter 39

The safe house in Rue Benouville in Paris was no more than a stone's throw from SD headquarters in Avenue Foch, and yet the fugitives remained undetected. Erika watched at the windows as the Germans rushed about, the Gestapo in Kubelwagens, Wehrmacht soldiers in armed foot patrols, combing the area for the escaped prisoners and their Free French rescuers.

Lacosse brought a photographer to the house. He took pictures of Felix and Jason Jones for their false papers, and left in a hurry.

The doctor visited every couple of days, taking extreme care not to be seen entering or leaving the house.

Erika's apprehension grew with every passing day. By locating Jones and freeing him from the SD she had succeeded in the first two phases of her mission, but unless she could complete phase 3 the whole exercise would be an abject failure. She needed to transport him back to Britain – and soon. It could be only a matter of days before the doctor's comings and goings were spotted, someone betrayed them, or the Gestapo discovered their whereabouts by sheer luck. The thought of what might happen to Madam Y and her small child if they were discovered sent shivers through her whole body. Madam Y and the doctor had shown incredible bravery every day – every hour of every day – that they sheltered and tended to wounded escaping Allied servicemen.

After 4 days, she stopped the doctor as he was preparing to leave. "When will he be ready to move, Doctor?"

The doctor replied, "His wound has stabilized. The healing process has begun, and he's no longer in any danger of necrosis, but I can't see him walking on that leg for at least a month."

Erika was horrified. "A month! You've seen the Gestapo search parties. We could not possibly expect to stay hidden for that long. I doubt if we'll make it beyond the end of this week."

The doctor snapped his bag closed. "I'm sorry, Mademoiselle, all I can do is give you my medical opinion. He would recover much faster in hospital, of course, but since that is not possible I think 30 days is the best we can hope for."

Lacosse arrived later that day with false papers for the Englishmen. Erika told him what the doctor had said. "Somehow, we have to get him out in the next couple of days."

Lacosse shook his head. "I can't see how, if he can't walk or ride a bicycle. It might be better if you left him with us and joined our escape line without him."

"What would that accomplish?"

"Ask him to give you the intelligence information. Isn't that what this is all about?"

Erika's first thought was to deny the existence of any intelligence information, but the expression on Lacosse's face told her that her cover story for Jones was blown. "How did you know Jones was carrying intelligence information?"

Lacosse laughed mirthlessly. "You didn't really think we would swallow that story about the *Croix de Guerre*, did you?"

"Isn't there any way we could move him in Charles's vegetable lorry, perhaps?"

"Let me think about it," he replied.

When Lacosse had gone, Erika went in to talk to Jason.

"I heard you talking to the doc," he said. "What did he say?"

"He said you're on the mend, but it'll be a couple of weeks before we can move you."

"A couple of weeks? He told me a month."

"You do realise that you're the reason I'm here in France? The secret service in London sent me over to rescue you and the information in your head."

"You can prove that?"

She gave him the recognition phrase, "I come from Fenchurch Street."

He smiled. "I never doubted you."

"I've been thinking," she said. "Perhaps you should share your intelligence with me. That way we increase the chances of getting the information back to London."

Jones shook his head. "I don't think so."

142

"Don't you trust me?"

"It's not that, Michelle. It's just that I don't think we should double the chances of the Gestapo beating the information out of us."

Erika couldn't disagree with that. "Fair enough. If the worst comes to the worst and you have no way out, do you have a pill you can take?"

"No. They didn't give me one. Do you have one?"

"No, I don't. But my orders are clear. If you get into an impossible situation and there's no way out, I will have to end it. Do you understand?"

"Yes, I understand. The last resort."

"The last resort. If it comes to that will you pass the intelligence to me?"

Jason replied, "Yes, if it comes to that."

#

Lacosse returned the following day with a plan to move Jason in an ambulance. He had a nurse's uniform for Erika, a driver's uniform for Felix.

Felix's uniform was a little tight. "This war seems to agree with me," he said. "I'm putting on weight."

Erika's uniform was a size too big, but Madam Y thought she could make it fit with a few carefully positioned pins.

"The ambulance will pick you up from the rear entrance first thing tomorrow morning," Lacosse told Erika. "Your cover will be transporting a dementia patient to a sanatorium in Évry. From there you will switch to another ambulance and travel as far as Dijon. The remainder of your journey to the south coast will be organised by the escape line people."

"Why do we need to switch ambulances?" she asked.

"Évry is within the Paris catchment area. Outside Paris the ambulances are different."

"How long will the whole journey take?"

"Three days at most."

"In that case I will need to transmit a signal to London tomorrow. Where can I find a transmitter?"

"Give me the message," said Lacosse. "I'll see that it gets transmitted."

Chapter 40

Jeremy Wichard of the Foreign Office passed the menu back to the waiter. "I'll try the gammon steak."

"Very good, sir, one gammon steak." The waiter made a note on his pad and turned to Claude Dansey. "What about you sir?"

"I don't see the Dover sole anywhere on the menu," said Dansey, demonstrating the insightful skills that had catapulted him to second-in-command at the SIS.

"The Dover sole is off this week, sir. We have monkfish."

"Monkfish. That's like a small shark, isn't it?"

"It's very popular with the members, sir."

"I don't think so." Dansey handed his menu to the waiter. "I'll have the gammon."

Very good, sir, two gammon steaks." The waiter marked his pad. "Would you care to see the wine menu?"

"Bring us a bottle of the Chardonnay," said Dansey.

"As you wish, sir."

Dansey opened his cigarette case and offered them to Wichard. Wichard selected one with care. Dansey took one out, tapped each end skillfully on the silver cigarette case and lit up with a lighter. He handed the lighter to Wichard.

"What's happening with Operation Tabletop?" said Wichard, lighting up. "I heard on the grapevine that the transmission has been received."

"Yes. The trawler is being made ready to sail from Gibraltar."

"So the SOE agent has your man and they're on the move." Wichard smiled his wicked smile. "I thought you said they wouldn't make it back!"

"They're not out of the woods yet, old man," said Dansey.

Chapter 41

Madam Véronique answered a loud knock on the door.

"What are you selling?"

"Open the door. This is the police."

She waved the girls away and opened the door a crack.

"What do you want? We have a special license from the Commissaire de Police."

Two Gestapo men in leather coats crashed through the door and brushed past her.

"We want to speak with one of your girls. Her name is Michelle Médard."

The Madam shrugged. "I'm sorry, Monsieur, I don't know her."

"She goes by the name Angeline."

"Angeline's not here, but we have many girls just as experienced, just as young." Véronique leered at the two men.

"Where may we find this Angeline?"

"As I said, she's not here. If you come back later she should be here."

"Tell us about her. When did she first start working here? Where did she come from?"

"She started this week. I don't know where she came from. She didn't say. She asked for a job, I thought she looked pretty, so I gave her a start. Your colleague, Claus Clanhaus, liked her. He invited her to visit him in Avenue Foch. That's all I know."

"Have you registered her?"

"I took her on for a trial period. If she makes a success of it then I will get her details and have her registered."

"You are obliged under the law to register every one of your employees at once. You have broken the law. You're coming with us."

"I'm sorry. I'll sort it out today, as soon as I see her. Can I get you two gentlemen a drink? I have a bottle of 10-year old schnapps somewhere." She turned toward her drinks cabinet.

The men grabbed Véronique, one on each arm and wheeled her out through the front door to a waiting car.

#

"Tell me what happened," said SS-Hauptsturmführer Polhammer of the SD.

SS-Obersturmführer Spittbendler of the Gestapo had been on the sharp end of Polhammer's legendary temper before, but the SD man's present quiet demeanour was more intimidating than any display of anger. He drew in a breath. "We followed your instructions to the letter, sir. Clanhaus took the doxy to his room. She let a gang of other French terrorists in through a window on the third floor."

"And they killed Clanhaus?"

"I'm afraid so, yes. They stabbed him brutally in the heart."

"The night wasn't a complete waste so," said Polhammer.

"Sir?"

"Never mind. What happened next? Did they free the British spy?"

"We allowed them access to the prisoners. They freed all five of the British airmen from the cells. And my men went into action."

"Meaning what? Did I not make myself clear? Did I not ask you to arrest them all? Did I not forbid gunfire?" Polhammer's voice rose with every beat.

"My men were provoked. They fired, and killed one of the subversives..."

"Didn't I say I especially wanted the prisoners taken alive?" He spoke quietly again, like a volcano between eruptions.

"They escaped onto the roof. We followed them, but they got away."

"Where are they now?"

"They've gone to ground, Herr Hauptsturmführer. One of them is wounded, and judging by the amount of blood loss, the wound is serious. I have men out searching the area. We should have them by morning."

"Your men fired again, Spittbendler? They fired at the prisoners?" Polhammer coloured rapidly.

"They were getting away, sir. We had to do something."

The SD man slapped the top of his desk with trembling hands. "So what you're saying is if he isn't already dead the British spy could be bleeding to death as we speak."

"But on a positive note, we know that the man we're after is definitely one of the five now on the run."

"Unless you shot him." Polhammer leaned back in his seat with a sigh. "What about the doxy from Madam Véronique's salon? What was her name?"

"Angeline, real name Michelle Médard. She escaped with the others."

"You must interrogate Madam Véronique."

"My men are over there now."

When SS-Hauptsturmführer Polhammer was summoned to the fourth floor he found SS-Sturmbannführer Kieffer lying naked on his stomach on a bench, his head on a block of wood, while a muscular Frenchman kneaded his back. His superior's bare buttocks and the folds of flesh around his waist were sights that turned Polhammer's stomach. He could never understand why the Sturmbannführer put himself in such personal danger by subjecting his body to the manipulations of a French masseur. And he was sure that removal of the SS uniform in broad daylight was a blatant breach of military regulations. Of course it was more than his life was worth to report any of this to a higher authority.

"Is that you, Polhammer? Come in. Report." Kieffer's head on the block was facing away from the door.

"Sir," Polhammer clicked his heels. "The operation went according to plan to start with. Madam Véronique's girl helped the Free French to gain access to the building, and they went directly to the fifth floor as expected."

"They freed the British spy?"

"They did, Herr Sturmbannführer, exactly as you predicted. They freed all five of the British airmen."

"So we're no nearer to identifying the British spy? Go on."

"Against my express orders the Gestapo opened fire. Unfortunately, we lost two men, sir."

Kieffer sighed. "More paperwork! Were any of the Free French wounded or captured?"

"The Gestapo shot and killed one of the French subversives and injured one of the airmen. They all escaped."

Kieffer roared, "Tell me they didn't kill the British spy!" He lifted his head from the block. For one dreadful moment Polhammer thought he was going to rise from the bench. A full frontal view of the Sturmbannführer was more than he could stomach.

"No, sir. We suspect that the spy is still at large. The Gestapo are scouring the area. I expect they will have him by the morning."

"We must hope so, Polhammer. I remind you that yours is the head on the block, here, not mine."

Chapter 42

In the castle north of Hamburg, three pairs of boots gathered at the air vent. SS-Sturmbannführer Necker spoke quietly. "You may as well come out, Müller."

Kurt kicked the vent cover. It fell to the floor with a clatter, and he climbed out.

"How did you know where I was?"

Necker barked a laugh. "We could smell you. We followed your stench from the kitchen. Face the wall and raise your hands."

Kurt did so. Necker's men were grey-haired, but they both looked fit. One of them searched him, removing the knife, his passport, Gudrun's photograph and the envelope.

Necker opened the passport. "Kevin O'Reilly, an Irishman. How inventive." He removed the postcard from the envelope. "I see you got my invitation. Welcome to my family home." He pointed to the oldest, darkest portrait on the wall. "May I introduce Brutus, the First Baron van Nechler, Knight of the Teutonic League, who built this castle. The first blocks were laid in 1205 and the castle was completed in 1222." Necker moved on to the third and fourth portraits. "This is the Seventh Baron, the bishop of Holstein, who changed the family name to Necker after a minor scandal. Moving along, here we have the Nineteenth Baron, who distinguished himself in the 30 Years' War and died by the sword in 1640. This last picture is my great, great grandfather, the 36th Baron. When I inherit, I will be the 40th Baron Necker."

Necker was even thinner than Kurt remembered him, tall with short blond hair turning white, the duelling scar on his cheek more pronounced than ever.

"Where are you holding Gudrun?" Kurt said. "I'm here to give myself up in exchange for her."

"All in good time," Necker replied. "The last time we met, you will remember you slipped through my fingers. That was a serious embarrassment for me. I swore then that I would find you and bring you to justice."

Kurt knew he was in deep trouble. Necker had suffered a crushing humiliation at the hands of Kurt and Erika when they had successfully completed their last mission. The SD man had pursued them relentlessly from the far south to the very northern tip of Germany and beyond, but they had escaped his clutches.

"You have me, Necker. You have what you want. You are honour bound to release my fiancée."

"First things first, Herr Müller. You and I have a personal score to settle." Necker ran a finger over his facial scar and nodded to his men. The two henchmen seized Kurt and frogmarched him from the room, through the kitchen and down the stairs. As he suspected, there were dungeons on this lower level. The men opened a door, bundled him into a cell, and closed the door.

The key turned in the lock.

#

The cell had no window, but Kurt could see well enough thanks to a shaft of light streaming in through a square inspection hatch in the door. He stood by the door and called out Gudrun's name. No one answered.

He raised his voice and tried again. "Gudrun, it's Kurt. Where are you? Answer me."

His words echoed around him, but there was no answer.

Kurt turned his back to the door, slid to the floor. Gudrun was not here. Had Necker sent her to Gestapo headquarters in Berlin? Or had he killed her already? How could he tell Anna that her mother would never return? He set his jaw grimly. Necker would pay for Gudrun's abduction and death. All he needed was a half-chance to turn the tables on Necker and his men.

He remained where he was, dozing, until early morning, when he heard footsteps approaching in the corridor outside the cell. Necker's men removed him from the cell and took him up the stairs to a hall deep within the castle. Three full suits of armour stood in corners of the room. The walls were covered in ancient weapons – lances, broadswords, a cutlass, scimitars, axes, hatchets, ancient duelling guns and muskets. Holding pride of place over the mantel was a lethal-looking crossbow and bolt. Kurt realised then how vast the castle was, and how little of it he'd seen. Gudrun could be anywhere. His spirits rose.

SS-Sturmbannführer Necker Lounged against the fireplace in jodhpurs and a loose fitting shirt. He dismissed his men. "We need to talk in private," he said. "We have much to discuss."

"Where are you holding Gudrun?"

"Gudrun is safe. You need not concern yourself about her. You, on the other hand, have fallen into the lion's den."

"What d'you want from me?" said Kurt, edging toward a rack of fencing swords.

"Nothing. I want nothing from you. I invited you here to balance the books. During my long and distinguished career with the Schutzstaffel you are the only man who ever outwitted me. Your continued existence has been an offence to me, an affront, a dishonour. Can you understand that?"

"I am here now. You have me. Release Gudrun. She has no part to play in your personal honour."

Necker shook his head. "You know that will not happen."

"I have information about the Resistance in Germany, information that you could use to restore your good name with your comrades."

Kurt grabbed a sword from the rack and shook it in Necker's face.

"You have chosen a rapier. Good choice," said Necker. He stepped back nimbly, plucked a sword from a wall behind him and adopted a classical fencer's pose. *"En garde!"*

Kurt attempted a similar stance, but before he could blink Necker had thrust forward with his weapon, piercing his right arm. Kurt yelled and stepped back, clutching his bicep, blood seeping through his fingers.

"En garde!" said Necker again, stepping forward, swishing his sword from side to side as if cutting through an invisible cobweb.

Kurt managed to deflect three more thrusts of Necker's sword, retreating backwards each time.

"Come on, Müller, you're not even trying."

"I have no skills with the sword," said Kurt, throwing the rapier to the ground.

"Nevertheless, we shall cross blades. Pick it up."

Kurt retrieved the rapier. Then Necker paused, took a step back and adopted a defensive posture. Kurt tried a flurry of thrusts of his own. Necker deflected each of Kurt's efforts with ease, while backing toward the door. Kurt failed to land a single blow, but Necker continued to back away through the door.

They were in an area open to the sky. Kurt was sure this was the courtyard he'd seen on his way in through the sewer, and yes, there on the ground at the centre was the locked ventilator grille.

He was distracted for a moment and received a second wound in his left upper arm matching the one on the right.

Anger and pain drove Kurt forward, swinging his sword wildly from side to side. Necker stepped back, and then, in a swift movement, hooked his blade around Kurt's rapier, snatching it from his grasp and tossing it to the ground.

Necker laughed. "Pick it up."

Kurt crossed his arms. "This is pointless. I told you, I am no swordsman."

Necker curled his lip. "Pick it up or I'll run you through where you stand."

Kurt picked up his rapier and the match resumed.

With his next lunge forward, Necker caught Kurt on the side of his face. He put a fingertip to his cheek and felt blood. He tasted blood on his lips. Again he was angered and moved forward, stabbing at his opponent. Necker stepped backward, easily avoiding Kurt's clumsy lunges. Out of the corner of his eye Kurt spotted the sewer grille behind Necker and to his left. Taking a step to the left, he increased the ferocity of his attack. Necker turned to face Kurt and took a step backwards. Kurt swung his sword again, Necker took one more step back and his right foot slid between the bars of the grille.

Necker yelped in pain, and shouted, *"Arrêt. Halt!"*

Kurt stepped back. He mopped his wounded cheek with his shirtsleeves. Necker's men appeared. One man ran to Necker's aid, the other advanced toward Kurt, drawing his handgun. Kurt threw his sword to the ground.

Chapter 43

"Take the prisoner below," ordered Necker as the first man helped him from the courtyard.

Kurt was returned to his cell, where he tended to his wounds. The puncture wounds on his arms, though painful, were superficial; the damage to his cheek felt more substantial, but without a mirror he couldn't assess it, and without water he could do little to clean it.

Nothing happened for several hours. Then the two gunmen opened the cell door, grabbed Kurt by the arm, and steered him along the corridor to another cell.

Three times the size of the previous cell, and with a low arched ceiling, this one was bristling with machines and mechanical devices that Kurt recognised as instruments of torture – a table with ropes attached to a ratchetted wheel, a large wagon wheel equipped with manacles, a nasty looking spike hanging from the ceiling on a chain attached to a contraption in a corner, a thumbscrew and mallet on a table.

"This room is my pride and joy," said a voice and Necker emerged from the gloom. "Many of these devices are centuries old. They date from the Middle Ages and the Christian obsessions with witchcraft and heresies. This iron maiden, for example, comes from the Russian imperial court. Before the revolution it was used by royalists to extract confessions from the rebels. After the revolution, the insurrectionists used it to eliminate those same royalists. If you look closely you can still see blood stains on the spikes." He picked up a hinged wooden device with three holes. "This beautiful instrument is a Shrew's Fiddle. The rack is Spanish. It is an exact copy of a type used by the Inquisition. The breaking wheel was used in the Balkans in the eighteenth century. I also have several guillotine blades from the French Revolution, discarded when they became blunt through overuse." He held up a heavy axe. "And this is the axe used to decapitate Charles I of England in 1649."

Necker nodded to his men, who forced Kurt into a wooden chair and manacled his wrists and ankles. One of the men worked a pulley that lowered a rope with a metal hook on the end. The man attached the hook to the underside of the chair between Kurt's legs, the pulley lifted the chair into the air, and Kurt found himself suspended, his feet in the air, his upper body angled downward.

The whole apparatus swiveled and the chair was lowered until the back of Kurt's head was just above a bath of water, his hair touching the surface.

Necker said, "This is the method I prefer. It has produced excellent results in the past. I think you will understand when I demonstrate. I will ask you a number of questions. If you refuse to answer or try to feed me lies, you will be lowered into the water. Are we all ready? Right, here is the first question: How long has Generalmajor Hans Oster been an active member of the Black Orchestra?"

"I know nothing about any orches—," said Kurt. The last word was scrambled as his head was submerged. They winched him out of the water almost immediately. Coughing, he shook water from his nose and mouth.

"You will have gathered that was not the answer I was expecting," said Necker. "Let us try that question again: How long has Hans Oster been a member of the Resistance in Germany?"

"I have no knowledge of Hans Oster's loyalties."

"No? What a pity." Kurt was lowered into the water again, and held under for a little longer. He was raised from the water gasping for air.

"For your information," said Necker, "Herr Generalmajor Oster was suspended from duty several months ago and is currently under house arrest. We have abundant evidence of his treachery to the Fatherland."

Kurt knew Necker was lying. If the Gestapo had proof against Oster he would be in a concentration camp under interrogation. House arrest suggested that they had suspicions, but no definite proof against him.

"Question number two: How long has Hans von Dohnányi been a member of the Black Orchestra?"

"I don't know anyone of—" The water again cut off Kurt's denial.

The time submerged was extended again. When they pulled him out, Kurt coughed and spluttered, struggling to get his breath.

"Question number three: Can you confirm that Admiral Canaris is the leader of the organisation?"

Kurt shook his head and shouted, "Release Gudrun and I will tell you everything you want to know."

"That is noble of you, Kurt. But whether we release your lover or not, you must first answer my questions. You are hardly in a position to make demands. We know that Canaris, Oster, von Dohnányi, and von Neumann have all been plotting against the government and seeking a peace settlement with the British."

"If you already know that, what more do you need from me?"

The dunking that followed was longer than the earlier ones. Kurt's lungs took in some water. Necker waited until Kurt had coughed the water from his lungs and recovered his breath before continuing, "In reality I need nothing from you, Müller. As you so rightly say, there is nothing you can tell me that I do not already know."

Necker nodded to the winchman and Kurt was dunked into the bathtub once more and held underwater for an impossibly long time.

Recovery from that dunking took several minutes. When he could speak again, he repeated his offer. With his eyes closed, he said: "Release Gudrun, prove to me that she is free to return to her daughter in Ireland, and I will tell you what I know of the Black Orchestra."

There was no response.

When he opened his eyes he was alone.

Chapter 44

Erika and Felix waited behind the back door of the safe house in Paris, Erika in her nurse's uniform, Felix dressed as an ambulance driver. Jason sat in a chair nearby.

The ambulance arrived at the rear entrance as dawn was breaking. Erika was relieved when she recognised the driver, Charles the vegetable man looking spruced up in his ambulance driver's uniform, although there was still a slight odour of rotting vegetables about him, and his fingernails were as black as ever.

He greeted her in the Gallic way with a bear hug, kisses on both cheeks and his familiar grin. "Good to see you again, shweetheart," delivered with a Humphrey Bogart lisp.

Charles helped Jason Jones into a wheelchair and pushed him down the garden path to the cream-coloured ambulance. An elderly lady lay on a trolley in the back of the ambulance, clutching a blanket under her nose. Jones was placed on a second trolley that slid neatly into place under the old lady's. A blanket draped over the side and end of the old lady's trolley hid the tall Jones perfectly from view.

"Are you okay under there, Jason?" said Erika.

The injured Jones stuck a hand out from under the blanket and waved.

Erika took her seat on the nurse's station in the back of the ambulance, Felix sat up front beside Charles. Charles started the engine and they moved off.

Fifteen minutes later they ran into a roadblock comprised of a gendarme and an armed Wehrmacht soldier.

"Papers," barked the gendarme.

Charles handed over four sets of papers.

"Madam Duclous, travelling to the sanatorium at Évry?"

"That's right," said Charles.

"Open the back."

"It's not locked," said Charles.

"Open it."

Charles climbed down from the cab, went to the rear and opened the doors. Erika stepped out. The gendarme climbed in and sat down at the nurse's station. The armed soldier sauntered around behind the ambulance to watch. Every muscle in Erika's body tightened at the sight of his Schmeisser automatic machinegun. He stood so close to her she could smell the oil he'd used to lubricate the gun.

The gendarme reached under the blanket and took hold of the old lady's hand. "Madam, what is you name?" he said, raising his voice.

"Is this my stop, conductor?" said Madam Duclous. "I'd like an ice cream, please."

"You're nearly home. You're among friends, Madam," the gendarme said, patting the back of her hand.

He climbed back out of the ambulance. Erika got in and took her station. The gendarme closed the door.

As they were driving away the gendarme turned to the soldier, shook his head and said, "Did you see how big that old lady's hands were?"

The soldier nodded. "Yes, and have you ever seen such hairy knuckles?"

Chapter 45

Kurt was left alone for 30 minutes, coughing up water, his torn cheek stinging and itching beyond endurance.

Necker's man came back and took his place at the winch. Necker followed him into the room, limping noticeably. Standing close, as if conversing with a friend, he said, "Your fortitude does you credit, but I wonder if you realise how close you are to death. A signal from me or an accidental slip of Axel's hand and your life will be extinguished. I doubt if anyone knows where you are. It would be as if you never existed, all memory of you erased."

Kurt said, "I was a member of the Black Orchestra before June 1942, before the death of Reinhard Heydrich."

"You admit that. Good."

"But I have not been in contact with the Resistance since then, and I was never involved at the higher levels. I have no knowledge of the leaders of the movement or what they might be planning."

"So you have nothing useful to tell me. That is a pity." Necker drew his head close to Kurt's. "Have you given any thought to why I brought you here, to Hamburg?"

Kurt shook his head. Whatever Necker's next revelation, he knew it was not going to be good for him.

Necker rubbed his chin thoughtfully. "You were once considered for inclusion in the pinnacle of modern German society, the Schutzstaffel, did anyone tell you?" Kurt said nothing. "But the decision went against you. And do you know why?" Kurt shook his head. "Because you are nothing. I'm sure you think your life has meaning, but in reality you are nothing but the worthless spawn of a lower middleclass local government factotum, barely worth the oxygen you breathe. Your only value to the Fatherland is as a breeder of dull-witted low-level workers, drones, and cannon-fodder."

"I have a lot of valuable information about the Black Orchestra," said Kurt. "Free Gudrun and I will tell you everything."

The glint in Necker's eyes told Kurt that his situation was hopeless.

"You still don't understand, do you? I need nothing from you. Your life is in my hands. I decide when and how you die. Balance has been restored."

Necker and his henchman left him where he was, manacled to the chair, suspended over the bathtub.

Kurt had lost all feeling in his legs. His empty stomach told him it was night-time. He was ravenous and – ironically – mad with thirst. He had never tried sleeping with his head lower than his body, but he slipped in and out of consciousness, his blood pounding in his ears. Snatches of disturbed dreams made him twitch and shake. He emptied his bladder, soaking his clothes above as well as below the waist, and prayed silently that he could retain control of his bowels.

He was overcome with thoughts of his failure to reach Gudrun, the hopelessness of his situation. His continued existence was entirely in the hands of a fanatical madman, and there was every indication that Necker had no plans to keep him alive.

As it had in previous extreme situations, the spirit of his father whispered in his ear. "Fortitude, son," was all it said. "Fortitude," repeated over and over, the voice quieter than he remembered it the last time, as if the spirit of his father had slipped further into the eternal abyss. It felt like the last time he would hear the familiar, comforting voice, and he grieved one last time for his dead father, ridiculous tears rolling down over his ears.

One name that Necker mentioned slipped into his mind – Hans von Dohnányi. He had seen the tall, thin lawyer many times, hurrying in and out of Abwehr headquarters in Berlin, always clutching a briefcase, always with a thunderous expression on his face. Kurt knew that Dohnányi was attached to the Ministry of Justice. The notion that this man might be a member of the Black Orchestra, although stationed in another part of the administration, filled him with hope for the future. Surely, if the influence of the Resistance reached beyond the senior members of the Abwehr they might accomplish something, maybe even the overthrow of the Nazis in government, the end of the war through a negotiated peace with the Allies, or the assassination of Hitler!

#

Necker and his man, Axel, returned in the dead of night. Axel lowered the chair to the floor and released Kurt from the manacles.

Kurt tried to stand, but his legs were useless rubber.

"Get him to his feet," said Necker.

Axel hauled Kurt upright and dragged him forward.

"Give me a minute," said Kurt. "My legs…"

Necker nodded, and Axel dropped Kurt into the chair. Pins and needles raged through Kurt's legs. He flexed his fingers.

"Water, Necker. I need water."

Necker gave a short laugh. Axel dipped a tin cup into the bath and handed it to Kurt. He drank eagerly.

"At least tell me that Gudrun is alive," said Kurt.

Necker shook his head. "The time for talking is at an end. Your lover must remain where she is, and you must resign yourself to the fact that your mission has failed. You will never see her again." He nodded to Axel, turned on his heel, and left.

Again, Axel pulled Kurt to his feet and half-walked, half-dragged him through the door and down a steeply inclined passageway. Axel opened a heavy door and helped Kurt inside a small room. This room was entirely empty, apart from a circular hole cut in the centre of the floor.

Axel walked Kurt to the edge of the hole. Kurt's ankles and feet had not yet recovered fully. Kicking Kurt's feet into the hole, Kurt landed with a thump on his backside on the edge.

"Goodbye, Müller," said Necker's man. Placing a hand in the middle of Kurt's back he pushed Kurt off his perch into the space below. He landed in a crumpled heap. The sound of the heavy door closing echoed around him. Axel was gone.

Kurt looked up. The entry point was out of reach. He looked around him. There was a locked grille to his left and a small hole in the floor leading to the open sewer. He recognised the egg-shaped chamber that he had seen on his way in through the sewer, and he knew what it was, now: a medieval oubliette where unwanted souls could be abandoned, left to starve to death, and erased from living memory.

Part 6 – Escape

Chapter 46

𝖁isible through the hole in the floor, the sewage water oozed by. The hole was no more than 15 cm wide, far too small to get through. He tried kicking at it in the forlorn hope of enlarging it, but the rock was too tough, his boots too soft to make any impression. A lone rat ran by in the sewer, stopped and sniffed the air. Then it stood on its hind legs and looked up at Kurt, its whiskers twitching. Kurt envied the animal. It was free to roam the sewer, the forest outside, the world beyond that. Kurt, on the other hand, was sitting in his own coffin.

Necker was right: Kurt's mission had been a complete failure. Not only had he failed to rescue Gudrun, he hadn't even managed to locate her.

Necker must be holding her in one of the bedrooms on one of the upper floors of the castle.

If she was still alive.

His only hope of escape was to force his way through the padlocked grille in the wall. He examined the bars, looking for the smallest weakness. He found none. He tugged at the padlock. It was badly rusted on the outside, but held as firm as the day it was installed. He applied all his weight to the bars of the grille, pulling and pushing in and out and sideways, without making any impression on them at all. They were too high to land a kick, and he lacked any kind of tool to loosen them. He removed one of his boots and hammered on the bars with that for a while. Nothing changed.

Kurt put his boot back on and tried to get comfortable, although the curvature of the wall at his back made that difficult. The smell from the sewer wasn't as bad here as it had been in the tunnel, but still Kurt needed to keep his mouth covered with his arm to keep from throwing up. He listened with his eyes closed, tuning his hearing to pick up any small sounds above the gurgling and occasional distant splashing sounds of the castle sewage system. Soon he imagined he could hear the squeaking of the rats and even the patter of their feet scurrying about below.

Three hours went by. Kurt's hunger pangs had turned to serious stomach cramps. He had eaten nothing since the overripe fruit that the zookeeper had cadged for him from the monkeys, 39 hours earlier. He began to wonder how long it would take for him to die. Would he die of starvation or thirst or would the foul air kill him first?

He sat with his eyes closed, listening, listening. Then he heard a familiar sound: The banshee squeal of the metal gate at the entrance to the sewer. His eyes sprang open and he strained his ears for any more sounds. Soon he heard rustling, splashing and the unmistakeable sound of boots scraping on the sewer floor. Someone had entered the sewer and was coming closer.

He waited until the sounds were almost below him.

"In here," he said, and Wolfe's head popped up on the other side of the grille.

"Give me a moment," said the zookeeper. He cut the rusty padlock with his bolt cutters. The padlock fell off, but when he pulled at the grille it refused to open.

"Stand back," said Kurt.

Wolfe ducked his head out of the way and Kurt charged the grille with the flat of both palms. It burst open and he climbed out.

They shook hands. "Very glad to see you," said Kurt. "How did you know I needed help?"

"When you didn't come out within 24 hours I thought I'd better go looking for you."

Kurt grabbed the zookeeper's canteen of water, and slaked his thirst.

"How long were you in there?"

"Not long. Overnight. But I thought I was going to die in there."

"What happened to your face? Have you located your missing girl?"

Kurt shook his head. "I only managed to search a small part of the castle before they caught me."

"We'd better get out," said Wolfe.

"You go," said Kurt. "I have to find Gudrun."

Wolfe sighed. "All right. What are we up against?"

"One retired SS man, his cook, and two henchmen with handguns."

"Not so bad. Lead the way."

Kurt brought Wolfe back to the chamber with the manhole cover.

"This is where I got in," he whispered. "Have you brought any weapons?"

"Only these." Wolfe pulled two knives from his pockets. Kurt took one.

Wolfe got to the top of the ladder, lifted the manhole cover and they both climbed out.

Wolfe put on a ski mask. "I can't afford to be recognised."

The kitchen was dark and empty. They crept down the narrow spiral staircase and took a corridor that branched off halfway down. The sound of snoring led them to the cook's bedroom door. Kurt turned the handle quietly and stepped inside. Wolfe stood watch at the door.

Kurt placed his hand over the old woman's mouth. She woke with a start, her eyes wide in fright.

"I mean you no harm," he said. "If you promise not to make a noise I will remove my hand."

She nodded and he removed his hand. She screamed and he put his hand over her mouth again. Wolfe stuck his head round the door for a moment.

Kurt stared at the cook with his most fearsome face. "You promised not to scream. If you do that again I will have to kill you. Do you understand?"

She nodded frantically, and he removed his hand again. She remained silent, pouting. He stood back. "Sit up. I need to ask you some questions."

The cook swung her feet from under the sheet and sat perched on the side of the bed.

"What is your name?"

"Agnetta."

"I'm looking for my girlfriend. Her name is Gudrun. She's somewhere in this castle. Tell me where I can find her."

"I – I don't know. The only people in the castle are me, the Baron, his son Manfred, and his two friends."

"Manfred has her locked up somewhere. You must have taken meals to her, Agnetta."

The cook shook her head. "No, I'm sorry. Are you certain she's in this castle? There are lots of castles around here. Maybe she's in one of those."

Kurt paused for a moment's thought. "Is there somewhere that Manfred could have locked her up without your knowledge?"

"The dungeons down below…"

"She's not down there," said Kurt.

He left the cook trussed up like a Christmas parcel with a bed sock in her mouth, and began a systematic search of the castle.

They found nothing on the ground floor and headed up the stairs.

The first room they came to featured a massive 4-poster bed surrounded by a strange mixture of bulky antiques and elegant modern Bauhaus furniture. Elaborate brocade tapestries covered the walls. An old man in blue striped pyjamas lay in the bed, propped up on pillows. His eyes were closed, but moving behind thin eyelids.

"Baron Necker, are you awake?" said Kurt.

"Is that you, Father?" said the Baron. He opened his eyes to reveal developing cataracts. "I don't want to go swimming, Father. Please don't make me go. Not today, Father."

They moved on.

Necker was asleep in the next room. Wolfe found Necker's clothing on a chair, removed a Luger from a leather holster and tucked it into his belt.

Kurt shook Necker awake. "Where are you holding Gudrun?" he said, holding his knife against Necker's throat.

"How did you get free?" said Necker.

"Answer my question if you want to live. Where can I find Gudrun?"

"You mean you haven't found her yet?" Necker laughed.

"Get up," said Kurt.

Necker got out of the bed. He was dressed in blue flannel pyjamas like his father's, a family crest embroidered on the chest pocket. He slipped his feet into a pair of slippers.

Wolfe waved the gun at him. "Lead on."

Necker went to the door and opened it. "Where are we going?"

"Take me to Gudrun," said Kurt grimly.

"Very well, follow me." Necker stepped into the corridor and shouted, "Axel! To me!"

Wolfe struck him on the head with the pistol and Necker fell to the floor. Further up the corridor two doors opened, Necker's men rushed out, brandishing their weapons.

Chapter 47

Both gunmen fired. Wolfe fired back, twice. One of the men fell. The second man fired again. A bullet whistled past Kurt's left ear and buried itself in the 700-year-old plaster of the wall. Kurt and Wolfe backed into Necker's room, leaving the unconscious Necker lying in the corridor.

Wolfe found a door connecting Necker's room to his father's. They went through into the Baron's room just in time to catch a glimpse of the old Baron leaving by the other door.

Wolfe set off in pursuit.

"Let him go," said Kurt. He strode to the Baron's bedroom door and sneaked a look up the corridor. The wounded gunman was still there, clutching his stomach. Necker and the second gunman had vanished.

Wolfe approached the wounded man with his gun at the ready. The man was in no mood to continue the fight, and Kurt relieved him of his pistol.

Kurt and Wolfe checked each of the remaining rooms on the upper floors, using their guns to blast through any locked doors. Gudrun was in none of them. Kurt ran out of ammunition and threw his gun away.

"I must be nearly out, too," said Wolfe. "We need more fire power."

"Come on," said Kurt. "I know where there are plenty of weapons."

Kurt charged back down the stairs. Wolfe followed. They were stopped at the foot of the staircase by pistol fire. Wolfe returned fire, and they drove forward as far as the door of the weapons room.

Kurt flung open the door and they dived inside. Behind them a volley of bullets from a Schmeisser machine pistol ripped into the heavy wooden door. Kurt slammed the door shut and turned the key.

Wolfe pulled a double-headed axe from the wall and hefted it in his hand. Kurt selected an ancient halberd.

Wolfe said, "Isn't there anything here from this century?"

"I doubt it," said Kurt. "Here, give me a hand."

They tipped a heavy wooden table onto its side in front of the fireplace. Then they collected as many weapons as they could and threw them behind the table – cutlasses, spears, lances, a nasty-looking mace and two ancient wooden shields. Kurt reached up for the crossbow over the mantelpiece

The lock on the door disintegrated under a storm of bullets.

Wolfe and Kurt hunkered down behind their makeshift barricade as Axel charged in, spraying the room with the Schmeisser. They kept their heads down behind the table until the firing stopped. Then Kurt stuck his head up and launched his halberd at Axel. The ancient weapon missed its target, but it distracted the old gunman long enough for Wolfe to take aim and fire his Luger. Axel crumpled to the floor. Necker entered the room, grabbed the Schmeisser, pulled out the ammunition cartridge and reloaded it with a new one. Wolfe took aim at Necker and pulled the trigger again, but his pistol was empty. He threw the empty gun at Necker and ducked behind the table as the Schmeisser opened up again.

Desperate to counter the murderous onslaught, Kurt tossed the double-headed axe over the table followed by a cutlass and a couple of lances. Wolfe surveyed what was left: nothing but a handful of caltrops. He threw those at the advancing SS man.

The caltrops slowed Necker down and distracted him long enough for Kurt to grab a bolt for the crossbow from over the mantelpiece. It took all his strength to draw the string and prime the weapon.

Necker advanced to the table. Kurt and Wolfe took shelter behind two heavy wooden shields as the SS man opened fire again.

The gunfire ceased abruptly. Kurt dropped his shield, loaded the bolt into the crossbow, and stood up. Necker was reloading the Schmeisser. He raised the gun just as Kurt took hurried aim and fired.

The bolt found its target, smashing through Necker's right upper arm. Necker screamed and dropped the Schmeisser. Wolfe jumped over the table and grabbed it.

"I need him alive," said Kurt.

Necker was in agony, the crossbow bolt protruding from his arm, blood soaking into his pyjamas and dripping from the tips of his fingers. He slumped to the floor and passed out.

Kurt checked Necker's elderly gunman. He had been hit in the chest. He was alive, but his pulse was erratic.

Wolfe tore away Necker's sleeve and examined the wound. "His bone is shattered and I think his brachial artery may be severed. He'll need medical attention if he's to survive."

Kurt used a dagger to cut a strip of material from Necker's pyjama sleeve and improvised a tourniquet above the wound. "That should hold it for a while."

"Take his legs," said Kurt, lifting Necker's upper body.

Wolfe picked up Necker's legs. "Where are we going?"

"Into the kitchen."

They carried Necker to the door at the back of the kitchen and down the narrow staircase to the torture chamber.

"What now?" said Wolfe, looking around at the torture instruments.

"Put him in that chair."

Kurt fastened the manacles to Necker's ankles and wrists. He attached the hook to the centre of the chair and sent Wolfe to man the winch.

"Lift him up." Wolfe did so. Necker groaned as the chair rose into the air, his head swinging down below the level of his feet.

Kurt swung the chair over the bath. "Lower him."

"Are you sure about this, Kevin?" said Wolfe.

"I'm sure. Lower him down. Stop just above the water."

Wolfe operated the winch. Necker's blood dripped steadily from his arm into the water.

Kurt moved close to the SS man. "Are you awake? Talk to me, Necker!"

Necker groaned.

"Your arm is badly injured. You are losing blood. Answer my questions and I will get you medical help."

Necker opened his eyes and grimaced from the pain.

"Tell me where you're holding Gudrun."

No answer.

"Where is she? Answer me. If you don't get to a doctor soon you will die."

Necker closed his eyes.

Kurt signalled to Wolfe. "Lower the chair."

"Are you sure about this?" said Wolfe again.

"Lower it!"

Wolfe operated the winch, lowering Necker's head under the water.

"Up. Take him up again."

Wolfe wound the winch wheel and Necker emerged, coughing water.

"Where is she?"

Necker continued coughing.

"Lower him again," said Kurt.

"Kevin—"

"Just do it. He will tell me."

Wolfe lowered Necker's head under the water again. Air bubbles escaped from Necker's nose and mouth.

"That's enough," said Wolfe.

"Okay, wind him out."

Wolfe operated the winch and Necker emerged from the water, his breathing ragged.

"You need to be more careful," said Wolfe. "He's only half-conscious."

"Necker," Kurt shouted. "Look at me."

Necker turned his head and opened one eye.

"The tourniquet on your arm is keeping you alive. Answer me. Tell me where Gudrun is, or I'll remove the tourniquet. You'll die in minutes. Do you understand me?"

Necker remained silent.

"Lower him. Lower him again," said Kurt.

Wolfe locked the winch. "No, not again. He can't take any more."

"Lower him into the water," said Kurt grimly. "One more time should do it. He will tell me."

"Sorry, Kevin. I want no further part of this. Do it yourself."

Necker was ghostly pale, his breathing shallow and laboured. Whether through incapacity or stubbornness, it was clear he was never going to talk.

"Okay, make him as comfortable as you can, but leave him in the chair."

Chapter 48

Kurt returned to the study and broke into the roll top desk. A quick search yielded his Irish passport, the postcard and Gudrun's photograph. He put them in his pocket, pulled up a chair and started on a pile of papers, discarding anything that carried the Wehrmacht stamp.

As he worked he was constantly aware of the radio receiver/transmitter sitting on a table by the window. What was it for? Necker had made it clear that he was no longer an operational member of the SS. Perhaps the apparatus was no more than a souvenir of his active service. Or could he still be using it? Kurt switched the receiver on and watched it warm up. It was set to 2305 kHz, a frequency unfamiliar to Kurt.

He went back to the papers in the desk, the radio receiver humming quietly in the corner of the room.

Wolfe joined him after 30 minutes.

"Found you! I think you'll need to change your clothes before we leave here."

"Why?"

"I can smell you from 20 paces."

Kurt sniffed. "You too! Why don't you see what you can find in the bedrooms upstairs? And check on the cook while you're at it."

Wolfe left the room, and Kurt continued searching through Necker's papers. Necker's cancelled cheques were mostly share dealings, but he found payments of RM 1,000 to one Tobias Thurner for April, May and June. He found nothing else remotely helpful.

He sat back in Necker's chair. There must be something else, some clue to where Gudrun was being held. He began again, examining every scrap of paper on the desk, including the papers carrying the Wehrmacht stamp, this time.

Wolfe returned wearing fresh light grey pants and a military tunic complete with Waffen-SS insignia. He handed Kurt a pair of boots, black slacks and a tunic in a darker grey.

He said, "The two gunmen are dead. The cook's bindings were too tight. I loosened them and changed her gag. She's a lot more comfortable, now."

"Did she see your face?"

Wolfe shook his head. "I kept my mask on."

"What about the old man?"

"The Baron's back in his bed, fast asleep. Have you found anything of value?"

"Nothing." Kurt sprang from the chair and strode to the door. "Come on, Wolfe. I'm going to make Necker talk if it's the last thing I do."

Wolfe followed Kurt through the kitchen and down to the dungeons. "He's in no fit state for more interrogation, Kevin. I doubt if you'll get anything out of him."

Strapped to the chair in the dungeon, Necker's head lolled on his chest. Kurt lifted his chin and shouted at him, "Necker, wake up. Open your eyes!"

"He's not conscious, Kevin."

Kurt scooped a cupful of water from the bath and threw it at Necker's face. Necker groaned.

"He's coming round," said Kurt. "Man the winch. We'll duck him into the bath again."

Wolfe crossed his arms and stood his ground. "He's had enough. You'll kill him if you use the bath again."

"Just do it!" Kurt shouted. "He will tell me where she is. Necker! Open your eyes. Look at me, Necker. Tell me where you've hidden Gudrun."

Wolfe said, "It's hopeless. Look at him. He probably can't recall who you're talking about."

"He will tell me. Wind him up, Wolfe."

Wolfe shrugged and manned the winch. Three quick turns of the wheel and Necker's chair was swinging gently over the bath.

"Necker. Look at me, Manfred. Tell me where Gudrun is and I

will release you. I'll call an ambulance. You've lost a lot of blood. You need a doctor."

Necker opened his eyes, two black pools in a ghostly white landscape. He licked his lips. "Water," he croaked.

Kurt filled the cup again and put it to Necker's lips. Necker sipped.

"You need a doctor," said Kurt. "Tell me where I can find Gudrun and I will release you and send for help."

Necker spoke but Kurt failed to hear.

"Say that again. What did you say, Manfred? I didn't hear you."

"You'll never get away from here," whispered the SS man.

"Let me worry about that. Where is Gudrun?"

Necker closed his eyes.

"Open your eyes. Stay with me."

Necker's eyes remained closed.

"Lower him," said Kurt to Wolfe. "Dip his head into the bath."

"He can't take any more, Kevin. You'll kill him."

"Lower the chair, Wolfe. One more time should do it."

Wolfe lowered the chair and raised it again. Necker's head was submerged for no more than two seconds, but his breathing had stopped.

Kurt swung the chair away from the bath. "Lower it," he said.

Wolfe lowered the chair to the ground and Kurt tilted it forward. He hammered Necker on the back to clear his airway. Necker took a breath. Then he coughed and spat. Several minutes went by before he had recovered enough breath to speak.

"What do you have to say, old man?" said Kurt.

"Gudrun's not here," he wheezed. "She's in England."

Kurt's heart began to thump wildly.

"Where? Where in England?"

Necker's eyes closed again. His head fell onto his chest.

Kurt shouted at him. "Tell me where she is."

Necker was silent and still.

Kurt lifted the SS man's chin. "Open your eyes, Necker."

Wolfe put his fingers to Necker's jugular vein.

"Manfred, talk to me!"

Wolfe removed Kurt's hand and Necker's chin fell back onto his chest. "You'll get no more out of him, Kevin. He's gone."

Kurt checked Necker for a pulse. He found none.

Wolfe said, "It's time we got out of here."

Kurt swore silently. They left the dungeon. Wolfe removed his mask.

As they were passing through the kitchen again, a faint familiar tap-tapping sound reached Kurt's ears. The radio was receiving an incoming signal! Kurt sprinted back to the study, grabbed a pencil, and jotted down the Morse letters as they came in.

…CONFIRM TT

Then a new signal started, but all it contained was:

ENDE

Kurt tore a leg from the chair and smashed the radio with it.

"Fuck it! She's not here. She's in England!"

Over and over he smashed the radio until the chair leg splintered and shattered.

The assault gave him a lot of satisfaction and he was out of breath, but the radio continued to hum contentedly. Only the outer casing was dented. He tore the back off the instrument, ripped out three valves, dropped them on the floor and ground them under his heel. The radio died.

"I think you killed it," said Wolfe.

"Fuck it!" said Kurt. "I have to get back to England."

Chapter 49

The morning routine was always the same. He would remove the handcuffs and allow Gudrun some private time in the bathroom where she could wash in cold water. Her one small luxury was a toothbrush that Toby had bought for her. She brushed her teeth vigorously each morning. She had asked for toothpaste, but he had refused to buy any.

Toby's own teeth were rotting in his mouth, his breath rank. He seemed unaware or unconcerned about that. From the fragments of personal information that he shared with her, Gudrun gathered that Toby had no living family. Perhaps the war had stripped him of everyone that he once cared for. All that remained in his life was a fanatical dedication to someone he called 'The Baron'. Toby was like a half-man, living only for his master, obeying his commands without question.

Toby would supply breakfast and after breakfast they would play cards. He served up two more meals each day, and in between they would play cards. Retiring to bed in the early evening was a blessing.

The only variation in the daily routine was once a week when Toby received his orders from the Baron in Morse code on a short wave radio that he kept in a room downstairs. Gudrun could hear the exchange of signals through the floorboards. Toby never told her what his orders were, but he made it plain that should he receive no orders for two weeks in a row, his instructions were to 'terminate the project'.

"Meaning what?" said Gudrun.

Toby left that question unanswered.

Then one day Toby returned from his radio session wearing a long face.

"What is it, Toby?" she asked.

"There was no response from the Baron," he said. "If there's no response seven days from now I will be obliged to terminate the project."

Gudrun said, "You don't have to, Toby. You could let me go."

"I must follow my orders," he said, and he turned on his heel and left the room.

Chapter 50

Kurt and Wolfe grabbed some bread before leaving the castle and disappearing into the safety of the forest. Wolfe led the way at a trot, back toward the city.

Within 15 minutes the roads on all sides of the forest were swarming with police vehicles and lights.

Kurt said, "The cook must have raised the alarm."

"I don't think so," said Wolfe. "I suspect the old Baron wasn't as demented as he looked."

Wolfe took Kurt to a hide under the exposed roots of an ancient tree. "We used to play in here as kids. It's not waterproof, but it's an excellent hiding place. It's a bit of a tight squeeze, I'm afraid. Funny, I thought it was bigger." There was barely enough room for two grown men.

They remained where they were for a half hour, surrounded by the distant sounds of police activity. They ate the bread.

Wolfe asked Kurt what he intended to do next. "You have been chasing a wild goose, I think."

"I have to get back to England."

"You're sure your girlfriend is there? You believe Necker?"

"I'm certain."

"Do you know where in England?"

"No, but I have a starting point," said Kurt, thinking of the photograph of Gudrun that he'd taken from the dead taxi driver, Erhart – alias Harry Crum – and his house in St Albans.

Wolfe held up a hand for silence. Then Kurt heard the unmistakeable sounds of approaching boots. A police search party, beating the undergrowth, exchanging shouted instructions, passed within 20 metres of their hideout, and moved on.

"That was too close for comfort. We need to get out of the woods," Kurt whispered when the patrol was out of earshot.

"Not yet. If we break cover now they'll find us."

And then Kurt heard a sound that sent electricity tingling over his scalp. "Dogs!"

They ran west at full speed, following forester tracks where there were any, crashing through the brush where there were none. Behind them the baying hounds sounded as close as ever.

They paused for breath.

Kurt gulped air. "Where are we going?"

Wolfe hadn't enough breath to answer. He pointed west and they set off again.

As they broke through the trees a spotter plane flew low over their position. They dived under the shelter of a hedge. Then they were running again, skirting a field of wheat. They left the field and entered a quagmire that clung to their boots, dragging them down, slowing their progress. Kurt could see a wide river ahead, the Elbe, tantalisingly close. The barking dogs and shouts of the soldiers came closer and closer. Finally, they struggled through the marsh to the bank of the river. A barge puttered past. The sound of the dogs was almost upon them.

"What now?" said Kurt.

"Now we swim," said Wolfe. He dived in and Kurt followed.

Kurt was a strong swimmer, but he was hampered by his clothing and boots. The Elbe was wide and deep in the middle, with thin patches of oil on the surface, the water brown with silt stirred up by constant barge traffic. They were 70 metres across before the police patrol spotted them and opened fire. After that they dived and swam most of the rest of the way underwater.

The bank on the far side opened onto flat pastures bordered by rows of spindly trees. Wolfe led the way past a massive rocky outcrop to a farmhouse 2 kilometres from the river. The house was centuries old, with lumpy walls and small windows.

Wolfe opened the door and called out, "Mama, it's me."

A thin, white-haired woman appeared from the back of the house, an elderly sheepdog at her heels.

"This is my mother," said Wolfe. "Mama, this is Kevin."

Kurt shook Frau Wolfe's hand.

"Get out of those wet things," she said.

The sheepdog gave Kurt the once-over, lost interest, and retired to its basket in front of the fire in the living room.

Wolfe showed Kurt to his bedroom where Kurt stripped off his clothes. After a trip to the bathroom with a warm towel he began to feel human again. He examined the scar on his face, cleaning it carefully and applying iodine supplied by Frau Wolfe. Then he shaved, using an old razor of Wolfe's.

His passport had suffered some water damage, the pages damp and curling at the edges. The postcard and photograph were fine, but the envelope was a sodden mess. He tossed it on the fire. Frau Wolfe set about drying his passport, dabbing it with a cloth before placing it in front of the fire on the hearth. Then she hunted through a trunk and pulled out an old suit.

"My father's," said Wolfe.

She held it up against Kurt and nodded.

He dressed and checked his image in a broken mirror. He looked every bit the farmer, but one who'd been in a fight with a bull! He dragged at his hair with his fingers, and she tutted, pushed him into a hard chair at the foot of the table and scraped his hair into a neat parting with a comb.

Kurt looked around. A picture of Adolf Hitler hung crookedly on a wall. The furniture was crude, much of it homemade, a stark contrast to what Kurt had seen in the castle. He examined the family photographs standing in a row amongst the candles on the mantelpiece.

The dog pricked up its ears and barked. Kurt heard a barked response from outside.

Wolfe sprang to the window and looked out. "Kevin, out the back. Mama, hide those wet clothes." He threw the boots into the great pot of soup hanging over the fire.

Kurt ran through the back door. He stopped to pee on the jamb of the barn door and across the floor at the entrance before burying himself deep in the hay.

The search party entered the house. Kurt lay in the hay and listened. He heard the old sheepdog barking at the intruders, the tracker dogs barking back. Then the soldiers came outside to the barn, the dogs barking excitedly, straining at their leashes. The barn doors swung open and the barking stopped. Kurt watched the dogs urinating on the barn door, then running about trying to pick up the lost scent. The exasperated soldiers shouted commands at them.

The searchers poked and prodded the hay with pitchforks, but Kurt was too deeply hidden.

The search party moved on. After 15 minutes Wolfe came into the barn and whistled softly. Kurt rolled out of the hay and returned to the farmhouse.

"I was sure the dogs would find you," said Wolfe.

Kurt told him about the urinating trick that he'd been taught in Abwehr training. Wolfe tossed a log onto the fire and it spat, throwing out sparks. The sheepdog scuttled away to safety. Then Kurt spotted his Irish passport – sitting on the hearth in plain view.

Frau Wolfe served up plates of potatoes and strips of rutabaga. "It's the best I can do."

"Thank you. It's wonderful," said Kurt between mouthfuls.

He asked about the photographs on the mantel. She took them down and showed them to Kurt, one at a time. They were pictures of her three sons, Wolfe's brothers, all at war, two at the Eastern front, one in Italy.

Kurt thanked Frau Wolfe for her hospitality and made ready to leave.

Wolfe said, "Where are you going? You can't leave tonight. Wait until tomorrow."

"I have to get moving. Gudrun needs me…"

"Stay here tonight," said Wolfe. "I have a friend who can help you get back to France in the morning."

#

Kurt hadn't slept in a bed for a month. The mattress was soft, the bedclothes crisp and fresh and he was exhausted. Even so, he had difficulty getting to sleep. Every time he began to drift off the ghastly image of Necker in the torture chair startled him awake.

He had only just managed to get to sleep when Wolfe shook him by the shoulder. "Wake up, Kevin. You'll want to see this."

Even before he'd left the bed he could hear crashes like distant thunder, and flashes of light through the window spraying across the ceiling.

"What is it, a thunderstorm?"

"Take a look."

The sky was criss-crossed with searchlights picking out heavy aircraft for the anti-aircraft guns on the ground. Below, Hamburg was in flames. Wave after wave of Allied bombers swept over the city dropping their lethal cargo. One by one the searchlights went out, but still the bombers kept coming. The flames lit up the sky. Was there anything left of Hamburg to destroy? Surely it was impossible for the city to absorb any more punishment – and yet it continued. Kurt counted the number of bombers in one wave and then counted the number of waves. He estimated over 400 aircraft. This was far more than a conventional air raid; this was an act of sheer wanton annihilation, of bloodlust loosed on a defenceless city.

Kurt tried to imagine what it was like for the people of Hamburg. Londoners could take shelter in their underground rail system; the people of Hamburg had few underground stations, and many of their ancient buildings were made of timber.

Wolfe clenched his fists on the windowsill as they watched. The raid lasted 45 minutes before the bombing came to an end, and the last of the aircraft turned back.

The city was an inferno.

Wolfe threw his clothes on. "I have to see what I can do to help."

"I'm coming with you," said Kurt.

They ran back to the river. Wolfe had a rowing boat. They took an oar each and rowed across the Elbe. Securing the boat of the far side, they ran toward the fires. As they approached the highway Kurt could see kilometre after kilometre of people fleeing the city. This was like the exodus he'd witnessed on the way into the city, but on a colossal scale. It seemed the entire population of the city was on the move.

They made their way through the throng toward the burning city. Kurt saw nothing but sheer terror on the faces of the people. Many carried nothing but their children, stumbling toward an unknown future as the flames consumed their lives.

It was only when Kurt and Wolfe reached the outskirts of the city that the true enormity of the destruction became apparent. The whole city seemed to be burning out of control. A few scattered civil defence teams battled the fires, but it was an impossible task.

On every street they came to they found parallel rows of burning buildings tightly packed together. The few buildings that were not yet ablaze soon would be, as the fire advanced along the streets. On some streets the heat was so intense that even the pavements were blistering and breaking up, the tar in the road surfaces bubbling from the heat. They covered their faces, but still the air scorched Kurt's lungs with every breath and his eyes burned.

They reached the square where Wolfe's apartment had been. There was nothing left. The apartment building was a smoking shell, completely hollowed out by the fire.

Wolfe shouted above the roar of the fires, "Thank God you turned up yesterday, Kevin. If you hadn't I would have spent last night in that. I wouldn't be here now."

They joined a crew manning a fire tender and put their backs into the fire-fighting work, standing shoulder to shoulder with civil defence and municipal police. Even Gestapo officers took their places in the crews, all thoughts of pursuit and capture laid to one side.

They worked their way along one street extinguishing fire after fire, rescuing citizens trapped in basements, pulling the dead and injured from smouldering rubble. By the time the street was safe, the fires under control, the fire-fighters all looked alike, all blackened by soot and ash, and all with blistered hands from handling burning beams and red hot masonry.

"The zoo!" shouted Wolfe. Kurt followed him up the street toward the Stellingen quarter. As they passed a ruined apartment building Kurt heard a faint cry.

"Did you hear that?" he said.

They both stopped and listened. Kurt heard the cry again, muffled and faint, but a definite sound.

Wolfe said, "I hear nothing."

Kurt ran his eyes over what remained of the building. There were walls with blackened holes where the windows had been. The door was gone, blocked by a chaotic jumble of beams and rubble. Access seemed impossible, but Kurt forced his way over rubble, squeezing under smouldering beams.

Wolfe called to him from the street, "Where are you? Can you see anything?"

"I'm inside. It's hell in here."

"Come out, Kevin. It's too dangerous."

Kurt strained his ears and caught the cry again. It was above him somewhere. The remains of a concrete staircase took him up toward the sound. Keeping close to the blackened wall he ascended, one careful step at a time.

Chapter 51

Ħe was halfway up the staircase when part of the façade of the building collapsed inwards and tumbled down with a roar, sending sparks flying upward. He waited, holding his breath until the dust and soot had settled.

Half the staircase had been swept away, but he pressed on, and reached the second floor.

The cries were clearly audible now. They seemed to come from a pile of blankets perched precariously on a remnant of floor at the far side of a gutted room. Kurt climbed across rocky, smouldering joists toward the pile of blankets, testing each with a foot before putting his full weight down. Two of the joists broke away, crashing to the rubble far below.

When he reached the far side of the room he lifted the top blanket and discovered a baby in a cradle, crying, but miraculously untouched by the fire. He lifted the baby out, tucked it into his jacket and began the difficult climb down.

The return journey was every bit as difficult, smouldering beams falling around him, the ruined staircase threatening to give under his weight at each step. He reached the ground floor only to find the way out completely impassable.

"Wolfe, are you there?"

"Where are you, Kevin?"

"I'm close to the entrance, but I can't get out. Can you clear some of the rubble?"

Wolfe shouted for help from the civil defence. A dozen hands wrenched at beams to clear a passage for Kurt through the rubble. The baby continued to scream. As soon as Kurt could see daylight through the hole he passed the baby through. And when the hole was big enough he scrambled through on his hands and knees. He regained his feet and shook the dust from his clothes. A woman, filthy with soot, had pulled out a white breast and the baby was suckling hungrily at it, as her blackened tears fell on its face. She reached out a hand to Kurt – *"Danke... Danke..."*

The building collapsed behind him.

The zoo was gone. Barely a vestige of any of the enclosures remained. Dead animals lay everywhere. A zebra lay screaming, its legs smashed. Capybara ran about in aimless circles. Wolfe sat on a broken wall and wept.

Kurt was sick to his stomach. For the first time since he had discovered the German Resistance movement and joined the Black Orchestra, he questioned whether he was on the right side. Did he really want to be on a side that could inflict this level of punishment on a largely civilian population?

#

As dawn broke they turned their backs on the smoking city and trudged through the fields toward the river. An eerie silence enveloped the scene. They heard no birdsong and saw no birds in the trees. They took the rowing boat back across the river to the Wolfe family farm.

Frau Wolfe put the kettle on while Kurt and Wolfe washed the ash and soot from their bodies, patched up their blistered hands, and put on fresh clothes.

Wolfe told his mother about the city's destruction. He had tears in his eyes when he told her about the loss of the zoo.

"They will rebuild it, Peter," she said.

"Perhaps, but how long will that take?"

"You have the farm," Kurt said.

Frau Wolfe hurried into the kitchen, leaving her son to answer that.

"I have three older brothers, remember," said Wolfe, pointing to the pictures on the mantel. "If any of them survives the war he will be back to claim his inheritance."

An idea was taking shape in Kurt's mind. "Assuming one or more of your brothers survives the war, what will you do?"

Wolfe shrugged. "The plan was to continue with my work in the zoo. Without that I suppose I'll take work on the farm with my brothers."

Kurt said, "I know of a farmer looking for a husband for his unmarried daughter. She will inherit a good-sized farm."

"How big, and what do they farm?"

"Two hectares. Sheep and cattle, I believe. The girl's name is Ingrid."

Wolfe's eyes lit up. "Where is this farm?"

Kurt said, "I need to get back home as quickly as possible. You did say you could help me, Wolfe."

Wolfe replied, "I have a friend called Otto who can take you across the border into France. From there the French Resistance should be able to get you back to Britain."

But that will take forever, thought Kurt. Still, if he could make contact with the Free French again, they might smuggle him across the Channel. A lot of ifs and maybes, but he had no better plan.

Wolfe took Kurt to a tavern in a village not far from the farm. He ordered two glasses of foul-tasting ale. Halfway through their beers, Kurt said, "Where is this friend of yours?"

"He'll be here in a minute. You'll like him. Drink up and I'll order some more."

"I've had enough," said Kurt.

Otto made an appearance soon after that. He had thick lips and protruding ears that made him look like a fish. His bald head and creepy eyes, which seem to swivel independently, added to the impression.

"I hear you want to get into France," he boomed.

"Yes," said Kurt, quietly, hoping to encourage Otto to moderate his volume. They were the only ones in the place, but the innkeeper was within earshot.

"Right," said Otto, "we'll start first thing tomorrow. Do you have a dark suit?"

"No." Kurt was unsure why he needed one.

"I'll bring one." Otto drained his ale and left.

Kurt said to Wolfe, "What's the plan? Why do I need a dark suit?"

"Otto works in a funeral parlour. He sometimes arranges funerals for French people who want to be buried where they were born. He has one planned for tomorrow. You and I will go along as pallbearers."

Kurt asked Wolfe how Otto had avoided conscription.

Wolfe laughed. "There are certain professions the Reich cannot dispense with. Gravedigger is one of them. Also, Otto has certain deficiencies, didn't you notice?"

"I noticed his eyes and his loud voice."

"That's only part of it. There's a lack in Otto. Not enough to have him put away by the Ministry of Health, but just enough to make him unsuitable for the army."

Kurt got to his feet. "I take it these cross-border funerals are used to smuggle materials back and forth. Is there always a body in the coffin?"

"Not always."

Kurt felt a ripple of apprehension at this news, but his apprehension was mixed with pleasurable surprise. If the German and French Resistance movements were working together, perhaps there was hope for humanity after all.

#

The following morning, the funeral party set off. Otto drove the hearse. A second car carried the grieving relatives and a third carried four pallbearers, Kurt and Wolfe among them. They travelled at a good speed despite the bomb craters and burnt out military vehicles on the roads. The sun was high by the time they arrived at the French border and the temperature inside the cars was stifling. All three cars had their windows open. Kurt held his arm out in an attempt to divert cooler air into the car. This was less than successful as the air outside the car was only marginally cooler than inside.

A long line of cars waited in the blistering heat at the border post, but Otto moved over to the left-hand side of the road and drove past them all. He stopped at the border post and presented his papers to the guard. Kurt couldn't hear what was said, but it seemed Otto and the guard began to argue. Then Otto stepped out and moved to the back of the hearse. He opened the back, slid the coffin halfway out on its runners and began to unscrew the lid.

Incensed by what was happening, the grieving family jumped from their car raising a storm of objections. The driver gave vent to his feelings by leaning on the horn. A Wehrmacht soldier armed with a rifle emerged from the border hut and gesticulated at the driver to take his hand from the horn. The driver did so. The soldier then moved around to the rear of the hearse. Otto removed the last screw and opened the lid.

Kurt held his breath. Was there a body in the coffin or was it full of smuggled weapons? He placed his hand on the door handle, ready to make a dash for the safety of the trees, if necessary.

The border guard and the soldier took a quick look inside the coffin and stepped back. Otto closed the lid, replaced the screws, secured the casket, and got back behind the wheel.

The border guard waved them through. "Drive on."

Otto restarted the engine, and the funeral party crossed the border into Occupied France.

Kurt relaxed. Germany was behind him and he was on his way to find and rescue Gudrun, now that he had an idea where she was. A feeling of ease swept over him. But the feeling was short-lived. Ever since the conflagration in Hamburg he had been unsure of his loyalties. When he had first discovered and joined the Black Orchestra he was certain that the Nazis were evil, the Allies a force for good. Now, he wasn't so sure. First, there was the casual killing of van Beuhl in Camp Twenty. Tin-eye Stephens had killed him simply because the man knew Kurt's real name. Second, he had witnessed the bombing of Hamburg. Could the mindless destruction of a medieval city and the deaths of so many civilians be considered a justifiable act of war?

There was something else on his mind, too, something much more personal. He considered himself a moral person. He had never committed an act that he could not justify on his own in-built moral code. Never before now. His obsession with locating Gudrun had driven him to break that code. First he had smashed Necker's arm with a bolt from a crossbow, then he had subjected him to water torture and, when Necker refused to tell him what he wanted to know, he had threatened to untie the tourniquet that was effectively keeping him alive.

And in the end he had done nothing to prevent the SS-man's death. He could have called for an ambulance. The killing was entirely his responsibility. Burned into his memory was the image of Necker's bloodless body tied to that chair. The image made him squirm with guilt and self-loathing. Had he become as evil as the enemy that he reviled?

Chapter 52

In a lonely churchyard on the outskirts of Nancy, Kurt, Wolfe and the other two pallbearers, stepping slowly, carried the coffin from the hearse to the graveside and laid it down gently on the guide ropes. Using the ropes, they lowered the coffin into the grave. Then they stood back, hands clasped in front of them, eyes downcast in respect for the deceased, as the priest read the funeral rites and sprinkled holy water on the coffin.

The grieving relatives, those who had arrived in the funeral cortege and a few others who lived on the French side of the border, stood about in sombre clothing, clutching one another, responding to the priest's words. Someone tossed a single flower onto the coffin. With the final prayer each mourner picked up a handful of clay and dropped it on the coffin before walking away.

Wolfe and Kurt joined the line and shook hands with the grieving relatives before slipping away to a quiet corner of the cemetery.

"Walk into the town," said Wolfe. "It's not far. Look for a café called *Étoile Bleu*. Tell the owner you wish to speak with Gaston."

"I have no French, remember."

"The owner speaks pretty good English."

"Who's this Gaston?" said Kurt.

"Gaston is a code word for the French Resistance. The café owner will contact them for you."

"You've done this before?"

Wolfe nodded. "The graveyard in Nancy is popular with Frenchmen and women who die in Germany and want to be buried on French soil, because it's close to the border. There's an active Resistance cell here for the same reason."

Kurt held out his hand to Wolfe. "Thanks for all your help, my friend."

"Goodbye and good luck, Kevin. Tell Erika to look me up when the war is over. And I hope you find your girlfriend." Wolfe shook Kurt's hand vigorously.

Kurt hurried into the town. *Café Étoile Bleu* was not difficult to find. He sat at a table under an awning, and the café owner came out to take his order.

"I'd like to speak with Gaston," said Kurt.

The owner lowered his head and wiped the table. "You are English?" he whispered.

"Irish."

"What can I get you?" said the owner.

"Café au lait," Kurt replied, and the owner hurried inside the café.

Kurt was sipping his second cup of ersatz coffee when two rough-looking individuals in blue overalls sat down at his table. One of them offered Kurt a packet of French cigarettes. Kurt declined. The other man produced a packet of Lucky Strikes and offered that to Kurt. Again, Kurt declined. The two men exchanged a glance and a shrug.

The café owner scurried out and stood by the table. One of the Frenchmen held out a hand, palm upward and said something that Kurt didn't catch.

"Give him your passport," whispered the café owner.

Kurt did so, and the Frenchmen checked it, one after the other. They handed the passport back and both men stood abruptly.

"Go with them," said the owner. "They will arrange everything."

The two men took Kurt to a country *pension* and checked him in to a room. "*Attendez ici.*" Kurt understood that much: Wait here.

He checked the room. It was sparsely furnished, the bricks of the side of the next building the only view from the window. There was a bathroom with cold running water. Kurt filled the hand basin and tended to the scar on his face.

After 30 minutes he answered a knock on the door. A short man in a smart suit entered and shook Kurt's hand.

"You wish to travel to England?" He spoke in heavily accented English.

"Yes. *Oui, merci*," said Kurt.

"Don't thank me too soon," said the Frenchman. His humourless smile displayed a mouth too wide for his face containing a row of perfect false teeth. He held out his hand and Kurt handed him his passport. The Frenchman took a few moments to flip through the pages.

"We have escape routes through Spain, and a fast route across the Channel. Which would you prefer, Irishman?"

"The faster one across the Channel," Kurt replied.

"You have money?"

Kurt pulled his French money out of his pocket. He had 1,850 Francs and a few sous. He showed it to the Frenchman, who laughed dryly.

"The fee for repatriation to England through Spain is 90,000 Francs. The fee to cross the Channel is 150,000 Francs."

Kurt's heart sank to his boots. He shook his head. "I don't have that kind of money. I thought the Resistance ran escape routes to send British airmen back home."

"You are an airman?"

"No."

"You are British? Your passport tells another story." The Frenchman brushed his hand across the open passport in his hand.

"I am Irish, but I work for British Intelligence."

The Frenchman handed the passport back, stood and moved toward the door. "I would like to help you, Irishman, but what you ask costs money, a lot of money. I will return tomorrow and we will speak again. Think about what you wish to do."

The Frenchman left and Kurt assessed his next move. He had fallen among thieves. The dapper Frenchman was no more than an opportunist criminal making money from desperate people. Surely Wolfe hadn't intended to put him into the hands of criminals?

He handed in his room key at reception, paid the *pension* owner 150 Francs for a single night, and headed back toward the café.

The café owner was closing for the day. Kurt walked up to him and said, "I wish to speak to Gaston."

"*Monsieur?*"

"Gaston. I wish to speak with Gaston," said Kurt.

"You were here earlier today, I think. You spoke with Gaston."

Kurt shook his head. "I have no money. I need to speak with a different Gaston."

The café owner seized Kurt's arm and pulled him inside the café. He locked the door. "Sit. I will use the telephone."

Kurt sat at a table. The café owner disappeared through a bead curtain. He returned with a plate of reconstituted eggs and a carafe of wine. He placed the food before Kurt and poured wine into two glasses.

The owner sat at the table watching Kurt as he ate the eggs. "You must forgive me," he said. "I am a patriot, but there are people who can pay for their passage. I get a small commission... These are difficult times. You understand."

"I understand," said Kurt. The eggs were delicious; he was starving. The wine was the best he had ever tasted.

The owner answered a knock on the outer door of the café and a man slipped inside. He was stocky, wearing worker's overalls and a filthy beret. He sat at the table, and the café owner poured him a glass of wine. Kurt offered him his passport, but the man waved it away.

"I know who you are," he said. "You came from Britain with Michelle Médard, I think."

Kurt said, "Where is Michelle? Has she completed her mission?"

"Michelle is safe. That's all I can say. Did you find your missing girlfriend in Germany?"

The workman and the café owner exchanged a glance.

"The Gestapo are holding her in England. I must get back there as quickly as possible," Kurt replied.

The man sipped his wine, made a face, and plonked the glass firmly on the table. He stood up.

"Come, Irishman. Finish your meal. It's time to start your journey home."

The man gave him a bicycle, a blue beret, and a guide called François.

"The first stage of your journey is to Dijon. Stick close to your guide at all times. Dijon is where the Gestapo have their southern headquarters. The head of the Gestapo there is responsible for capturing dozens of French patriots. His name is Klaus Barbie. Have you heard this name?"

Kurt shook his head.

"Barbie is a cunning and brutal man. A sadist. They call him the Butcher of Lyon. He takes pleasure in torturing his victims. He has killed many of my friends. If you are careful to do everything exactly as François tells you, you will remain safe. Do you understand?"

"I understand. How far is Dijon?"

"It's 200 kilometres. If you keep going without stopping you should get there in about 12 hours."

#

Kurt's was a sturdy woman's bicycle with a wicker basket in front and a canvas cover over the rear wheel to protect a trailing dress or petticoats. It was comfortable enough, causing Kurt to wonder how tall the owner of the bike might be. François's bike was a man's with racing handlebars and two saddlebags slung over the rear wheel.

"We should rest," said Kurt after four hours of non-stop pedalling over hills and through dales.

"You are *fatigué?*" said François.

"No, but the bike is," Kurt replied. Designed for city use, his bike was creaking and groaning under the effort of climbing the hills.

"We will rest after dark."

They pressed on. At 10:30 pm the sun went down over the hills to their left and the stars came out suddenly, shepherding a brilliant half moon.

"We can rest now," said François as they entered a village.

They parked their bikes against a fountain in the centre of the village and slaked their thirst. François produced bread, cheese and wine from his saddlebags, and they shared the meal.

A group of village children approached and watched them silently as they ate. François spoke to them. Kurt was unsure whether they were hungry or simply curious, but when he offered them bread they all ran away like a flock of birds.

They finished the meal quickly, remounted, and cycled on.

Chapter 53

Charles drove the ambulance up a winding driveway and parked at the entrance to the Sanatorium St Jude at Évry, a squat building in peeling cream and duck-egg blue. A second ambulance – this one painted blue and green – stood waiting.

They wheeled Madam Duclous inside and freed the injured Jason Jones from his claustrophobic hiding place. Erika thanked the old lady for her help and she replied, "It was nothing, child."

Charles handed Erika the keys to the second ambulance. "Take the northern route through Montereau. When you get to Dijon, just leave the ambulance anywhere near the railway station." He showed her where to hide the keys in the back. "Didi will take you on the next leg of your journey."

"I don't know Didi. How will I find her?" she asked.

"Didi will find you." He gave Erika a round of enthusiastic Gallic hugs and kisses. "I don't suppose we'll meet again before the end of the war, Michelle. Stay safe."

"You too, Charles."

Charles wished them all luck and headed off back to the centre of Paris in the first ambulance.

Inside the new ambulance, Erika found a driver's uniform. She put it on, concealing the nurse's uniform in a compartment in the back of the vehicle.

Felix drove for the first hour. Erika did the navigating. At Montereau they crossed the Seine for the last time. A couple of kilometres outside the town, they left the main road and Erika took over driving duties.

Six kilometres beyond the village of Tonnerre, they were flagged down by a grey-haired German soldier with an NCO's insignia on his shoulder. Erika thought he must have been in his early sixties.

A Kubelwagen had overturned and lay smouldering in a ditch at the side of the road.

"What kept you?" said the old soldier to Erika. "I've got him out of the wagon, but I was afraid to move him any more."

"You did well," she said. "Is he badly injured?"

"He has no blood injuries, if that's what you mean," said the soldier, "but he may have injured his back."

Erika glanced at Felix. He jumped out of the cab, ran to the back and climbed in.

"Why have we stooped? Are we there?" Jason asked.

"Just sit tight," Felix whispered, pulling out a light stretcher. "There's been a traffic accident."

Erika grabbed a medical kit from the ambulance and followed Felix to the side of the road.

"What happened?" she said, kneeling down beside the injured soldier.

The old man replied, "A terrorist mine exploded under the wagon. I was lucky."

"Keep an eye on the road," she said. "They may come back to finish the job."

The soldier fetched his rifle and stood out on the road.

The injured man was young – 24 or 25 years old at most. He was unconscious, but his eyes were open, glazed. Her rudimentary medical training had not equipped her for this level of injury, but she shone a light into his eyes and noted a sluggish response. She checked his pulse, which was strong and regular. She checked his breathing; there was nothing obstructing his air passage.

Together, she and Felix slid the injured soldier onto the stretcher and carried him into the ambulance.

"We'll take him to Dijon," she said to the old solider. "You should stay here with the wagon. We'll send help from Dijon."

They drove on. The road was straight, lined with thin poplars, spaced evenly apart like prison bars. The temperature in the ambulance soared.

Fifty kilometres down the road, the ambulance began to shake and there were sounds of a struggle in the back. Erika glanced through the window panel.

"Quick – they're fighting."

Felix slammed on the brakes. Erika jumped out and ran to the back. She opened the door to find a bayonet stuck deep in the German soldier's chest and a panting Jason Jones sitting on top of him, his hands and tunic covered in blood.

"He woke up and worked out who I was," said Jason. "Tried to kill me with his bayonet."

Erika and Felix removed the body and dropped it into a ditch by the side of the road. Felix drove on and stopped by a small stream to fetch water for Jason to clean the blood from his hands and tunic.

Jason had aggravated his leg injury. It was oozing blood again. Erika took a few minutes to renew his bandage, tying it as tight as she dared without making the wound worse or causing him unnecessary pain.

#

Dijon was a bustling city, not visibly affected by the war. They arrived in the early evening as offices and shops were closing for the night. Occupying forces were everywhere in evidence and people thronged the streets. Erika spotted a likely parking space within 100 metres of the entrance to the railway station, and pulled over.

Before she could open the door, a black Gestapo staff car drew up beside them, hemming her in. Two men in leather coats stepped out.

One man drew his pistol. "Please step out of the ambulance."

When the second man repeated the order in English for Felix on the other side of the ambulance, Erika knew the game was up.

She stepped from the ambulance and offered her identity card to the Gestapo man. He ignored it, waving his pistol in her face. "Open the back doors."

She opened the doors. Jason was sitting at the nurse's station with a blanket across his legs.

"*Raus!*" shouted the Gestapo man.

Grimacing from the pain, Jason climbed out of the ambulance and stood with Erika. Felix joined them, shepherded by the second Gestapo man with pistol drawn.

The first Gestapo man looked Jason Jones up and down. "Your leg has been injured, no?"

"The terrorists shot him," said Erika. "We are taking him to hospital in Lyon."

"By train? Why not use the ambulance?"

Thinking quickly, she said, "The ambulance is too rough. We hoped the train would provide a smoother ride."

"You are all under arrest," said the second man.

Erika's mind went into freefall. She considered tackling the man, disarming him, driving away in the staff car. She would almost certainly die in the attempt, and if she succeeded, how far would they get? It was hopeless.

A black police wagon drove up and parked behind them, blocking the road. Now, their situation was beyond hopeless. Two uniformed French Milice policemen emerged and conducted body searches of Erika and the two Joneses, watched by a gathering crowd. All their papers were handed over to the Gestapo.

Felix, Jason and Erika were escorted to the back of the wagon and pushed inside. The Gestapo man holstered his pistol. He smiled and said, "Welcome to Dijon."

The wagon doors rattled closed.

Part 7 – The Butcher

Chapter 54

Erika and the two Joneses jounced around in the suffocating heat and semi-darkness as the wagon rattled over the cobblestones.

"What went wrong? How did they find us?" said Felix.

"Someone betrayed us," Erika answered.

"That hardly matters," said Jason. "Our goose is cooked."

"You should make it to the safety of a prisoner of war camp," she said to Felix. "This bunch may be unaware of your background." Felix gave her a grim smile, but made no reply. "And the longer you hold out and tell them nothing, Jason, the longer they will keep you alive."

"I'll feed them a morsel at a time, keep them guessing," said Jason. "At least I have something to trade. What have you got, Michelle?"

"I have nothing," said Erika. "Felix, if you make it back to London after the war, tell them what happened here. Ask to speak to Capitaine Z at SOE, 64 Baker Street. If you mention my name they'll let you in."

"Capitaine Z. Got it," said Felix.

Erika caught no more than a fleeting glimpse of the street as they were bundled into Gestapo headquarters in Dijon, a grey monolithic office block in a street of similar grey office blocks. The only colour to be seen was the red, black and white swastika flying from the flagpole at the front of the building.

They were split up. Erika was placed in a cell on the third floor.

A single light bulb hung from the ceiling. The cell had little air, its one redeeming feature its cool temperature. It was like the inside of an igloo, and would have been a welcome relief after the heat of the day outside under less onerous circumstances.

Two steel hoops close to the ceiling protruded from a harness attached to a wall. Erika had a good idea what they were for. She tried not to think about it.

A damp and filthy mattress on a steel cot was the only furniture, a galvanised bucket the only toilet. She lay on the cot and closed her eyes, but every small movement snagged her limbs painfully on the steel cot, and her body was swamped with adrenalin, foiling every attempt to sleep.

Two hours later, they returned and strapped her to a chair with her hands tied together in her lap. Early morning sunshine poured through the barred window. It was going to be another hot summer day.

They left her there on her own for 30 minutes, and then her interrogator entered alone and stood in front of her.

He spoke to her in perfect English. "My name is Barbie. SS-Hauptsturmführer Nikolaus Barbie. I expect you've heard of me." He smiled proudly. "I am head of the Gestapo in this part of France."

Erika was relieved. He looked like a man she could manage – until she heard his next words. "It is my job to intercept and interrogate terrorists and enemy spies wherever I find them. I have captured and questioned hundreds of members of the so-called Free French forces and countless Maquis terrorists. All that I have questioned have confessed their crimes. Not one has held out against me for more than a few hours. I especially like to break members of the Special Operations Executive sent over by the British to foment rebellion and encourage acts of sabotage against the Greater Germany. You will have heard of the Kommando Order?"

Erika shook her head.

"A recent order from Berlin. Under the order we are obliged to execute all British commandos captured behind enemy lines. I am aware that you are an enemy spy. If I decide that you are a British commando you will be shot."

Barbie paused for effect. Erika said nothing.

"I would not like you to think that I take pleasure in inflicting pain. I do not. I do so only because it is my duty. We are fighting a dirty war. Our enemies bomb our cities, they take thousands of innocent German lives, and they send spies among us to arm and train terrorists to sabotage our railways, blow up our weapon arsenals, kill our soldiers in their beds. What else can we do but defend ourselves against these insidious attacks as best we can? Do you understand?"

Erika made no reply. She was shaking inside, clutching her hands to stop them from trembling. He leaned into her face, cupping her chin in his hand.

"You are a beautiful woman, Michelle. I can only imagine with what perverse pleasure your masters in London chose you for this dangerous work. I will hate to have to disfigure a face as spectacularly beautiful as yours." He stroked her cheek.

Erika was shocked at how young and dashing he was, dressed in his grey uniform, trouser creases like knives, the SS insignia on the collar, the death's head on the brim of his hat, a pistol in a holster on his belt. He held a pair of leather gloves loosely in his left hand. His soft blue eyes sparkled with intensity as he spoke. She hated herself for it, but she was attracted to him. She felt flattered that he was paying so much attention to her, to the exclusion of everyone and everything else. What madness!

"So let me start by telling you what we know. We know that you are a member of the British Special Operations Executive, operating from Baker Street in London. We know that you were sent over to France to recover a British airman called Jones and return him to England. This airman has information that is of strategic importance to the British war effort. We know that you and your terrorist co-conspirators have freed this airman, along with a second airman also called Jones, and brought them both here to Dijon in a stolen ambulance. What I would like you to tell me is which of the two airmen is the one with the intelligence information."

Barbie didn't know which of the airmen to concentrate on! There was another strand of hope in there that Erika seized upon: Barbie was unaware that only one of the Joneses was a real airman. "I really don't know what you're talking about," she said.

"As I said, I have no wish to inflict pain on anyone unnecessarily, but if you refuse to answer this simple question, I will be forced to.

We have two airmen called Jones, one tall, one not so tall. The tall one is a Flying Officer, the shorter one a Flight Lieutenant. Which of the two harbours the strategic information?"

"I don't know," said Erika. "I drive an ambulance. I know nothing of airmen or British spies."

The blow across the face was as painful as it was unexpected.

"Don't think you can make a fool of me, Mademoiselle, let us be clear about that. And I will not be lied to. I ask you once again: Which of the airmen should I interrogate first – the tall one or the short one."

Erika saw a second strand of hope, then, a way to muddy the waters.

She said, "The tall one, of course, the senior man."

Barbie took a step back. He ran his eyes over her body. "The shorter man is the more senior, as you know very well. So which is the spy, the tall one or the more senior one?"

She said, "I'm sorry, you have confused me. Surely the taller man is the Flight Lieutenant."

Barbie replied with infinite patience, "The shorter man is the more senior. So tell me which man is the spy."

"I think it must be the more junior officer, so…"

"Thank you," said Barbie, striding toward the door.

"Unless…"

He turned back. "Unless what?"

"Which is the younger man? I believe the spy may be the younger of the two men."

Barbie closed the door and strode back across the room. He put his gloves on slowly. "You are playing games with me, Mademoiselle. I enjoy games as much as anyone…"

Chapter 55

By daybreak Kurt and his guide, François, were approaching the industrial fringes of a darkened city.

"Is that it?" said Kurt. "Tell me we've arrived."

"Yes, this is Dijon."

"Thank heavens. I don't think I could go much further."

Twelve hours on the bicycle had left Kurt's body a mass of aching bones. He continued to turn the pedals like an automaton. He had lost all feeling in his feet and legs below the knees, but his muscles knew what was required of them and no longer needed any input from his brain.

The heat of the previous day still lingered, another scorching July day in prospect. For a moment the world could have been at peace, Kurt could have been on a cycling holiday with a convivial companion. But then the silence was split by the throaty roar of six aircraft engines, and three Heinkel bombers flew low over them heading south.

"Where are they going?" said Kurt.

His guide replied, "There's an airport at Longvic, six kilometres to the south of the city."

The last part of the road to the city was a gentle gradient. Kurt and François relaxed, letting their bikes freewheel downhill.

François said, "Our contact is called Didi. She will meet us at the railway station and take you to a safe house for refreshments before the next stage of your journey by train to the Spanish border."

"What about you? Will you cycle back to Nancy?"

"Tomorrow, after I've rested."

"François, I want to thank you..." Kurt began, but François held up a hand to interrupt him. A lone cyclist was pedalling up the gradient toward them, bent over the handlebars.

"It's Didi," said François, putting on his brakes. "There must be trouble."

He swung his leg back over the saddle and scooted the bike into the trees. Kurt followed. When Didi reached them she took a moment to gather her breath. She was a small slip of a girl in a summer dress, her bright, intense eyes too watchful for her age, her face pale and drawn. Kurt thought she was no more than 25 years old. She embraced François briefly and they had a rapid conversation before she mounted her bike and turned back for the city, pedalling hard.

François turned a pale face to Kurt. "It's not safe in Dijon. Klaus Barbie's men have captured a group of three. The escape line has been broken."

He stood, indecisive for a moment, then turned his bicycle, mounted it running, and set off fast.

Kurt followed, calling out, "Where are we going?"

"We must cycle around Dijon and make contact with another line man in Lyon," François replied.

"How far is Lyon?"

"About 200 kilometres."

Kurt pulled up.

"What's the matter?" said François, looking back over his shoulder.

"We've just completed 200 kilometres. It took us 12 hours. You want me to do another 200 kilometres, another 12 hours without a break, without food?"

François circled back and drew up beside Kurt. "We have little choice. I've told you, the escape line has been broken. Someone has betrayed us. We are all in mortal danger. Have you not heard of Klaus Barbie, the butcher of Lyon?" His face betrayed his terror.

"I'm sorry, François, but it's madness to continue without food and rest."

François gave this a moment's thought. "You are crazy," he said.

But Kurt stubbornly refused to move. "Find us a place to rest."

He took Kurt to a derelict cottage three kilometres out into the countryside.

"Is this the best you can do?" said Kurt.

François hid the two bicycles in a bramble bush. "No one will look for us here, and there's a village not far down the road where I can buy us some food."

The front door was hanging off its hinges. François lifted it out of the way. Half of the roof was gone, but it felt cooler inside the cottage than outside. The sun had barely risen but already the countryside all around was like an oven.

François left to buy them food. Kurt threw himself down on the bare ground and fell into a dead sleep.

He awoke with a start of terror as François pushed through the door, his pockets loaded with bread and cheese and a bottle of red wine. The bread and cheese were fresh, the wine sweet, but too warm.

After the meal François filled the silence with his life story. He was from a wealthy family with a large, successful vineyard in the Macon area and had enlisted in the French army at the start of the war. He joined the Free French forces after the Germans disbanded the French army.

Kurt told his guide about his quest to rescue Gudrun and return her to her daughter. They discussed their current predicament. Kurt asked what were his chances of making it back to England.

François shrugged. "Who knows? We try to keep the various parts of the escape line in ignorance of each other so that if one part fails the others can stay open, but from what Didi said, the whole line could be lost."

"What happened?"

"Didi was to meet an escape group at the railway station, but when they arrived the Gestapo were waiting for their ambulance. They were arrested and taken to Gestapo headquarters."

"They were in an ambulance?"

"One of the airmen was injured."

Kurt felt something like an electric shock run through his body.

"Airmen? How many airmen were there?"

"Two, and a British SOE agent."

"Do you know the name of the SOE agent?" said Kurt, trying to keep calm.

"No, but I know the British sent her over to find and extract one of the airmen."

Her! Kurt staggered to his feet.

"Why?"

"They say he is a war hero. General de Gaulle is to award him *le Croix de Guerre*."

Erika and the two airmen! It had to be.

"What Free French forces are there in this area?"

"I don't know. Why do you ask?"

"We have to mount a rescue mission."

"What? You're crazy!" said François.

"I mean it. I know who they are, and we have to get them out of there."

François said, "No one has ever escaped from the Gestapo building in Dijon. No one. What you ask is impossible."

"Nothing is impossible. Just tell me how to contact the Free French."

"There's a telephone in the village. I could call someone…"

"Tell your friends that Michelle and the two airmen have been captured," said Kurt. "Tell them they must mount a rescue operation immediately."

François went off to make the call. Kurt cursed his lack of French. Could he rely on François to convey the critical importance of a rescue?

When François returned he said, "The Free French forces know about the capture. They say such a rescue is not possible. It's madness even to suggest it."

This was the outcome Kurt feared. He said, "The intelligence this officer carries is too important. We must rescue him – and the SOE officer – without delay."

François asked, "What is the nature of this intelligence information?"

"I don't know. I only know that it is of supreme importance, and must not fall into enemy hands."

"And if what you ask is not possible?"

"Then the airman must be eliminated. The outcome of the war may depend on it. You'll have to call your contact again."

"No need," said François. "He's agreed to discuss the matter with his colleagues. They will decide what to do."

"How long will that take?" asked Kurt.

François shrugged.

Chapter 56

It was touch and go, but Erika held out against Barbie's first attempts to get her to talk. She was covered in bruises, but she knew that there was worse to come. Barbie was in no hurry; he was enjoying himself too much.

After an hour lying where Barbie had left her, strapped to the chair, on her back with her legs in the air like a stranded tortoise, a Gestapo man with a short crew cut entered. He righted Erika's chair and gave her water to drink.

She thanked him and gulped the water down. "I need to use a toilet," she said.

He untied her straps, but left her hands tied. She stood up and was immediately swamped by dizziness. The Gestapo man gave her his arm to lean on. He took her to a small room containing a toilet and washbasin. No window. And no door.

"Can you untie my hands?" she said.

He shook his head. "You'll manage."

She managed. When she emerged, he took her back to the interrogation room, and set her down on the chair. He didn't replace the straps, but left her hands tied in her lap.

"Rest here," he said, and he left, closing and locking the door.

Erika closed her eyes. The dizziness went wild, taking her to the brink of nausea. She opened her eyes, took a few deep breaths and waited for the room to stop spinning.

The door opened again 15 minutes later. Barbie strode in accompanied by the man with the crew cut.

"Come with me," said Barbie. "I'd like you to see something."

Crew-cut stood by her chair and Erika got to her feet. They took her to the next room along, where Felix Jones was hanging upside down suspended from his ankles, his face bruised and swollen.

"This is Flight Lieutenant Felix Jones," said Barbie. "He has given us very little so far, just name, rank and serial number. He's a fool."

Felix gave her a sheepish upside down smile.

"But a credit to his uniform," said Erika, faintly. She swayed, and the crew-cut Gestapo man pinched her arm hard to hold her upright.

Barbie said, "It would seem a pity to inflict pain on this man if he knows nothing about military intelligence, don't you think?"

They moved on to the next room where Jason Jones was strapped to a wooden table, his injured leg oozing blood.

"Flying Officer Jason Jones here insists that he is the one we are looking for. He wants us to release his colleague. But can we believe him? He could be lying in order to confuse us. What do you say? Michelle, which airman should we concentrate our efforts on? Tell us now and save the innocent man from a lot of pain. Once we are certain we have the right man the other airman will be sent back to his prisoner of war camp."

Erika replied, "I can't help you."

They returned to Erika's room, where Crew-cut put her back in the chair. Her hands were still tied together. Then Erika heard a cry like a cat being strangled. The second cry was a scream of terror and pain, the third a roar of pure pain. She tried to work out where the sounds were coming from; they seemed to echo all around the room.

She cast her gaze about the room as the screams continued and discovered that the sounds were coming from a ventilator grille set high on one wall. The screams continued for over an hour, three or four at a time, interspersed with periods of quiet, driving her close to madness. With her hands tied together, covering her ears was not possible. Each scream cut through her like a knife. She tried to tell herself that they could have been recorded sounds. There was no proof that either man was actually being tortured.

As time passed the screams became fainter. By the end they were no more than groans. Then they stopped altogether.

Drawing breath, she steeled herself for the resumption of the sounds, but there was nothing but silence. With sunlight streaming through the windowpane, the room was like the inside of an oven. She was bathed in sweat.

The door opened and Klaus Barbie strode in, followed by the Gestapo man with the crew cut, or maybe a different one with the same hairstyle. In spite of the heat, Barbie was wearing his leather gloves, and they were saturated in blood.

They took her back to the room next door where Felix Jones was still hanging by his ankles. He was barely recognisable. His face was a bloody pulp, both his eyes closed by swollen cheekbones, blood oozing from his nose and mouth.

"Felix Jones, Flight Lieutenant, RAF, serial number 1123839, is stubbornly refusing to tell us what he knows. Either that or he has nothing of value to tell us."

Erika threw up on the floor. With a look of disgust on his face, Barbie handed her a handkerchief to wipe her mouth. They took her to the next room. Jason Jones lay unconscious, his injured leg still oozing. Erika thought that Barbie hadn't started on him in earnest yet.

"As you can see Flying Officer Jason Jones has a nasty leg wound and is in urgent need of hospital treatment. But he refuses to let me help him. Again, it does seem a pity to punish an innocent airman, if that is what he is. You, Michelle, are in the unique position to free one of these men from further punishment. Just tell me which is the British spy and I will free the other man and send him back to the prisoner of war camp where he came from. I give you my word."

Erika shook her head. "I can't tell you! I don't know!"

They returned her to the room and locked the door.

Barbie had presented her with a puzzle. She could continue to deny that she knew anything. Barbie would torture both men until Jason cracked. She could tell Barbie what he wanted to know, but would he keep his word? And would he believe her? Was there any way she could convince him she was telling the truth? She recalled Capitaine Z's instructions and her discussion with Jason about the 'last resort'. Under no circumstances was Jason Jones to be left alive to give his intelligence to the enemy, but how could she get to him?

An ear-splitting scream reverberated through the room. She leapt to her feet, ran to the door and pounded on it, yelling: "Barbie, Barbie I'm ready to talk."

Almost immediately, the door flew open and Barbie came in.

Erika said, "I've thought over what you said, and I want to help you. It makes no sense to remain silent when I can save one of the airmen from unnecessary punishment."

Barbie slapped his thigh with his gloves. "Sensible girl," he said. "Tell me which airman is the spy."

She said, "Flying Officer Jason Jones is the man you want. Flight Lieutenant Felix Jones is entirely innocent."

"How can I be sure you are telling me the truth?"

"Let me talk to him – I'll prove it to you."

Barbie took her back to the room where Jason lay strapped to the table, his trouser leg split to the crutch, exposing the wound, which was now a blood-soaked mass.

She moved as close as she could to Jason's head and whispered, "Remember what we talked about before, Jason? The last resort?"

"Not so close," said Barbie. "I want to hear what's being said."

Jason blinked his eyes in affirmation.

Erika said to Barbie, "Jason has something he wants to tell you."

Barbie came over, bent down, his ear close to Jason's mouth.

Seizing her opportunity, she pushed Barbie in the back. He lost his balance and fell across Jason's chest. She flipped the leather cover off his holster, whipped out his Luger and pointed it at Jason. But as she pulled the trigger Crew-cut threw himself at her from behind, deflecting the gun downward.

The sound of the gunshot was deafening.

Crew-cut grabbed her hand, rotating her arm until the gun was pointing to the ceiling. It went off again with another ear-splitting crack.

Erika fought to free her arm from the Gestapo man, but Barbie regained his feet and took the gun from her as Crew-cut secured her in a bear hug from behind.

"Thank you, my dear," said Barbie, holstering his weapon. "You have told me all I need to know."

Chapter 57

ℱrançois and Kurt cycled to a tavern in the nearby industrial town of Chenôve, arriving moments before the 10:00 pm curfew. François hammered on the door several times before the tavern owner opened it.

"What is it?" he said, pulling on a woollen jumper.

"Let us in," said François. "Your basement bar is needed for an emergency meeting."

The owner, an old man with a permanent drip on the end of his sickle nose, let them in, and François led Kurt down to the basement.

Loulou and two others joined them quickly. Lacosse and Charles arrived soon afterwards in the vegetable lorry. Loulou and Lacosse embraced, Lacosse adjusted his half-moon glasses and called the meeting to order. He suggested conducting their business in English in order to accommodate Kurt. They all agreed, although there were one or two mumbles of discontent around the table.

One man objected to François's presence, as he was not a member of the *comité*. Lacosse asked him to leave, and he did so without complaint.

"As you all know by now," said Lacosse. "Michelle Médard and the two airmen have been seized by the Gestapo. The Butcher is surely working on them by now. He may already have extracted all the information he needs from them."

"How did they get captured?" asked a muscular man who might have been a heavyweight boxer.

"We don't know yet," said Loulou. "The Gestapo were waiting by the railway station. They knew they were using an ambulance and what time they would arrive."

Sitting close beside Loulou, Lacosse said, "We must assume they were tipped off by someone."

"Someone in the escape line tipped them off?" said Charles quietly.

"Probably. Or someone within our own Free French force, someone closely associated with this *comité*. Possibly someone in this room," Lacosse replied.

A general outburst of indignant French peppered with swear words greeted this statement.

"English, please," said Lacosse, and the hubbub died down. "There will be time enough for recriminations and investigations later. For the moment we need to concentrate our minds on what to do about Mademoiselle Médard and the two airmen."

"What can we do?" said the muscular man. "The Gestapo headquarters in Dijon is every bit as secure as the one in Paris. I doubt that we would get anywhere near the prisoners."

"What, you would just abandon them, leave them there to be tortured?" Kurt was horrified.

"I can't see the value in it myself," said Favier, the diminutive burglar. "I'll be sorry to see Michelle Médard killed, but the British have only themselves to blame. They will keep sending us badly-trained agents. And who cares if we lose the airmen? One less war hero is neither here nor there."

"That's unfair," said Kurt. "She's not badly trained. We've already established that she must have been betrayed by someone on the *comité*."

"The airmen are not what they seem." Lacosse dropped his voice. "One of them is carrying intelligence information which the Boches must not discover."

"You knew this from the beginning?" said the boxer. "Why did you keep this knowledge from us?"

"Can we concentrate on what must be done now?" said Kurt. "We must act quickly. What men and weapons are available to mount a rescue?"

Lacosse responded, "You must be patient, Kevin. No action may be undertaken without the consent of a majority of this *comité*. We will have to see what is possible. Why don't you wait upstairs while we talk about it among ourselves?"

Kurt left the basement. He climbed the stairs and found François playing patience with a pack of dog-eared playing cards. François suggested a game of *Belote*.

"I don't know that game," said Kurt.

François gathered up the cards. "I'll teach you."

Kurt feared that the Free French would turn down his request to mount a rescue operation, or that they would spend so much time discussing it that it would be too late. He resolved to take independent action if he had to, even though such action would be suicidal. He wasn't going to abandon Erika to the Gestapo.

Kurt was dealing the cards for the ninth time when Loulou emerged from the basement. "Come," she said. "The *comité* has reached a decision."

Kurt followed Loulou down the steps to the basement.

Lacosse invited Kurt to sit. "We have considered your request, and we have come to the conclusion that any rescue attempt would be foolhardy. We have very few weapons and the building is too well guarded."

Kurt's heart rate began to rise in anger. "You cannot be serious! Please reconsider—"

Lacosse held up a hand to silence Kurt's outburst. "We do have one chance, one idea that might succeed."

Kurt's heart rate continued to rise – with hope, this time.

"If we can start a sufficiently large fire in the building the Boches will have to evacuate. When they bring their prisoners outside we should be able to seize them by force or remove them in the smoke and confusion."

Kurt thought the plan had a chance of working. "What about the fire brigade? Can they be kept away from the scene?"

"I can arrange that," said Loulou.

Kurt asked how they planned to start the fire.

It was clear that no one around the table had thought the plan through. Charles suggested throwing a Molotov cocktail through the front door.

"Is there another way out of the building?" Kurt said. "We don't want to fry the prisoners."

Lacosse said he thought there might be. Loulou said there must be. "No one builds an office block with only one entrance."

Lacosse pointed out that the ground floor windows could have been used as natural exit points until the Nazis barred them up. There might not be a second exit door.

"We'll have to survey the building," said the boxer.

Kurt hammered his fist on the table and everybody jumped. "There isn't time for that. What we need is to create a lot of smoke in the building, to create an impression of a serious fire, but without risk to anyone's life."

A lively discussion followed. Several suggestions were made about how to make a lot of smoke without a lot of flames. They agreed that they would use a bale of green hay primed with gasoline and a couple of old tyres. Charles would supply the hay bale and the gasoline; François would be ordered to find some old tyres.

Chapter 58

In Gestapo headquarters in Dijon, all was blessed silence at last. Strapped to the chair, Erika slipped in and out of sleep. For hours she had had to listen to the sounds of inhuman torture as Klaus Barbie and his men went to work on Jason Jones's injured leg. She was certain from what she heard that Jason had given Barbie very little if any information in spite of having endured hour after hour of unbelievable pain. The guy was a true hero. At its height the pain rendered him unconscious for short periods – his only saviour. She'd heard Barbie cursing and his men throwing buckets of cold water at the SIS man to revive him.

The abuse came to a halt eventually. The torture could have continued through the night, but it seemed Barbie preferred to do it all himself, and he retired for the night at about 1:00 am, leaving Erika with a promise that it would be his pleasure to interrogate her further in the morning.

Erika ran through her failed attempt to end it for Jason – the 'last resort'. She could have been faster. Had she hesitated a half-second before pulling the trigger? That half-second had been enough to allow Crew-cut to deflect her arm and spoil her aim. She blamed herself for every subsequent moment of agony that Jason had had to endure.

Why had the British SIS not given Jason a suicide pill? That was a puzzle. If it was really so important to keep the intelligence from the Nazis, surely he should have been given one. And why had SOE not given her one? In her present predicament, and with Barbie's sinister promise ringing in her ears, she would have used it.

In a heartbeat.

#

At 2:45 am, 100 meters from Gestapo headquarters in Rue Talant, a shadowy figure climbed a telegraph pole and cut the wires.

Ten minutes after that an old vegetable lorry, with a wooden telephone pole protruding from the back, turned the corner and rumbled up the empty street. It stopped outside the Gestapo building, reversed and accelerated. The end of the pole smashed into the front door of the building, the recoil lifting the lorry a metre into the air. The door flew from its hinges, and the lorry's engine stalled. Less than a minute went by before the lorry was sprayed with machinegun bullets from inside the building. Charles, at the wheel, struggled to restart the engine.

"Leave it," shouted Kurt, and they both jumped from the cab and ran.

They stopped 50 metres from the building.

Kurt removed his ski mask and scratched the scar on his face. "They knew we were coming. We'll have to light it where it is."

Charles nodded grimly. He had survived the bullets, but without his lorry he would be surrendering his livelihood.

Charles ran into the garden of a house and came back with an improvised torch made of dried sticks. He put his ski mask on. "Put yours on, Kevin."

Kurt shook his head. "The wool irritates the scar on my face."

Charles shrugged.

They crept back toward the lorry, keeping close to the buildings out of sight of the windows. They got to within 10 metres before a face appeared at an upstairs window and a shot rang out.

"Light it," said Kurt. Charles lit the torch. Kurt sprinted to the lorry and tossed it in. He ran back to Charles.

There was no sign of fire from the back of the lorry. "It didn't work," said Charles.

Kurt swore in two languages and went in search of a second torch.

Then it suddenly flared up. Inky black smoke billowed out, pouring into the building through the open doorway and up the façade.

They waited five minutes for the Gestapo to come tumbling out of the building with their prisoners, but no one appeared.

"It's not working," said Kurt. "I'm going in."

Charles gripped his arm and held on. "Wait for the others."

The Free French group emerged from a side road and ran down the street, seven of them, all wearing ski masks, armed with handguns and rifles. One carried a British Sten gun. The rescue party charged into the building under cover of the black smoke, discharging their weapons wildly. Kurt saw one Frenchman fall on the steps.

Kurt and Charles followed the Free French into the building. When they'd passed the smoke, they found three Gestapo dead, two in the hallway, one had tripped on the stairs and taken a bullet in the back.

A fierce battle was raging on the staircase, the Free French shooting up the stairs, the Gestapo returning fire with machineguns. The French were outgunned, but they held their ground. Then one German machinegunner was cut down. He screamed and fell through the stairwell. After that the French began to advance up the staircase, matching the fire from above, bullet for bullet.

Kurt conducted a quick search of the ground floor. The rooms were all deserted. He ran after the French to the first floor landing.

The battle had moved on to the second floor. Kurt searched the rooms on the first floor. They were all empty. By the time he reached the second floor the Gestapo had already retreated to the third floor landing under heavy fire, but the French fire was thinning.

Kurt searched the second floor and discovered two half-dead French civilians in chains in two adjoining rooms. He smashed at the padlocks, but they refused to break. "I'll be back," he shouted, but got no response.

He joined the battle on the staircase, but his handgun was next to useless against the withering fire from the Gestapo machineguns. Dashing down the stairs to the ground floor, he seized a Schmeisser and three spare magazines from the dead Gestapo in the stairwell. He returned to the battle. Charles took the weapon and ammunition from him and put the gun to immediate use.

The extra firepower was all the Free French needed, and they began to advance upward, driving the enemy back.

Before they reached the third floor Kurt passed the bodies of a Gestapo on the stairs. He relieved the dead man of his MP28 machinegun and a couple of magazines. They now had more firepower than the enemy, and quickly secured the third floor.

Kurt went in search of Erika. He heard her shouting, kicked in the door and found her strapped to a chair, her face and arms covered in bruises. She had two matching black eyes.

He freed her from her restraints, his heart pounding with excitement. She was pale under the bruises, and had difficulty standing.

"Where did you pop up from?" she said, wide-eyed, struggling to regain her equilibrium.

"I'll tell you later," said Kurt. "Are you seriously hurt? Can you walk?"

"I'm fine. My joints are just a little stiff from sitting in one position for hours. Do you have a gun for me?"

Kurt gave her his handgun.

"Ready?" he said.

"Ready."

Chapter 59

The battle was raging on the top floor. Erika and Kurt passed two dead Frenchmen on the way up. The remainder of the Free French force, their Schmeissers and the Sten gun empty, was fighting a rearguard action with handguns. By the time Kurt and Erika arrived on the scene the Gestapo had regained the advantage. They had advanced to the top of the stairs while the French were retreating slowly, firing off a few isolated shots in reply to the rattling of a lone Schmeisser.

Taking it in turns, Loulou and Lacosse darted out to fire a shot up the stairs in acts of individual bravery. Clearly unhappy, Lacosse argued with her, trying to hold her arm to keep her out of the line of fire, but Loulou would not be restrained. Then Lacosse took a bullet and collapsed, bleeding from a wound in his side. Loulou and Kurt ran to him, dragging him into an alcove, out of the line of fire.

Loulou checked the wound. "It's not too serious," she said, "but we'll have to get you to a doctor as soon as possible."

The firing from above stopped abruptly. Erika's ears were ringing. She wondered if the Schmeisser had run out of ammunition. Kurt fired his handgun. It produced one last shot and died. The response was ten seconds of continuous fire from above. The Gestapo still had plenty of ammunition.

Silence returned. Then a German hand grenade bounced once on the stairs and fell at Lacosse's feet. Kurt picked it up and threw it back. It exploded in the air sending a shock wave back down the staircase.

After that there was no more firing from above. The tide had turned. The French force inched upward again, one step at a time. They met with no resistance.

On the top floor they found two dead Gestapo surrounded by

dozens of spent cartridges, a strong smell of cordite hanging in the air. There was no sign of any living enemy.

Kurt picked up a Schmeisser and replaced the ammunition clip with a fresh one.

The corridor contained a double row of stout wooden doors. Signalling to each other, the French moved along the corridor opening the doors and checking each room carefully. The door to the last room was locked.

Kurt stepped forward, waving the Frenchmen back.

"Barbie," he shouted in German. "Come out. I know you're in there."

There was no answer.

"Come out now Barbie. If you refuse, I will set fire to the building and you will all burn."

Still no answer.

"Come out now. Come out alone and unarmed and we will spare your men."

Framed like that Erika knew the demand was impossible to refuse. To do so would dishonour Barbie in the eyes of his men.

The door swung open and Klaus Barbie emerged, hands on his head. Erika darted forward to relieve the Gestapo chief of his Luger. She tucked it into her belt.

"Close it," said Kurt. Barbie did so. Kurt waved the end of the Schmeisser at him. "Down the stairs. *Schnell!*"

As they started down the stairs Erika shouted in German through the door, "The rest of you stay where you are until someone opens this door."

She led Kurt and Barbie to the interrogation room on the third floor where she had been held. All of the Free French followed, Lacosse supported by the boxer.

"Sit," said Erika.

Barbie grinned at her. She bunched her two fists together and delivered a pile-driver to Barbie's midriff. He gasped and sat down with a thump. Kurt strapped him in, tying his hands to the back of the chair.

Barbie said, "You'll regret it if any harm comes to me."

Favier stepped forward and struck him across the face. "Who told you we were coming?"

Barbie shrugged, still with that grin.

Favier struck him again. "*Cochon*. You knew we were coming. You were prepared for the attack. Tell me who betrayed us."

Barbie shook his head. "I don't know what you're talking about. You're all cowards. Why don't you take off the ski masks and let me see your faces?"

Favier hit Barbie again, with more feeling this time. "Liar! Who betrayed us? Give me his name."

Erika said to Kurt, "This could take some time. We should see to the airmen." To Favier she said, in French, "We'll be back in five or ten minutes. Keep him alive."

Chapter 60

Erika took Kurt to the adjoining room where Felix Jones was hanging by his ankles from a couple of metal hooks. His face was swollen and there was dried blood on his nose and mouth. At first she thought the airman might be dead, but when she touched his face it felt warm. There was no obvious way to release him.

"This is Flight Lieutenant Felix Jones," she told Kurt.

The airman opened an eye. "Michelle, is that you?"

"Yes, Felix. We're going to get you down as soon as we can. I'll get some help."

Felix was not a tall man, but Erika thought he probably weighed close to 100 kg, certainly too much for her to handle.

"I'll wait here, shall I?" croaked Felix with a weak smile.

Kurt went to the door and shouted, "We need help in here."

The muscular Frenchman ran in. Kurt and the Frenchman stood on two chairs, one on either side of Felix, and unhooked his ankles from the restraints.

As they worked, Erika asked, "Where's Gudrun? Tell me you found her."

"No, but I know where she is."

Erika watched as Kurt and the Frenchman lowered Felix carefully to the ground. "Be careful, *attention, doucement*," she said.

She hunkered down beside Felix. "How are you?"

"A little dizzy," Felix replied.

Kurt thanked the Frenchman and he left.

"Can you sit up?" Kurt said to Felix.

Felix made a gallant effort to do so. "Give me a few moments and I'll be fine."

Erika and Kurt helped Felix to a sitting position on the floor and then onto his feet.

"Take your time, Felix," she said.

Felix had been beaten severely about the head, face and chest. His nose was broken, his cheekbones swollen. Erika felt a sharp pang of guilt. She could have left him in Avenue Foch or not taken him in the ambulance. She could have told Barbie that Jason was the one he needed to concentrate on. This was not Felix's fight.

"Does it hurt?" said Erika.

"Only when I laugh. See if you can find my boots."

"You made it to Hamburg?" said Erika, handing Felix's boots to Kurt.

"Yes, but Gudrun wasn't there. She's being held somewhere in England."

"You found Peter Wolfe?"

"I found him."

Kurt laced up Felix's boots for him.

Felix said, "Thanks, old man. I'll be okay. I just need to rest for a minute or two. Go see to Jason."

In the next room, Jason's leg was a bloody mess. A foul smell permeated the room. Erika unbuckled the straps and tried to get him to sit up, but he was too weak.

Standing sentry by the door with the Schmeisser, Kurt watched as Erika drew up a chair and sat beside Jason, cradling the gun in her hands.

"Jason, can you hear me?"

No response.

"If you can hear me, Jason, make a sign."

Jason lifted his forearm.

"Remember what we spoke about before, Jason? The last resort?"

Jason opened his eyes.

She said, "It's time."

He turned his head. There were tears in his eyes. "Listen closely…"

"I'm listening, Jason."

"The German defences north of The Hague…" He gave her the facts in broken sentences. "Promise me you'll get that information back to London."

"I promise," said Erika. "We have to complete the last resort now. Do you understand?"

"I understand. Tell my wife that I love her." He gave Erika an address in Bromley, Kent. "I have a child. I've never seen him or her…"

"I have to do this, Jason. I'm sorry."

"Do it," said Jason. He turned his head away from her.

She cocked the gun, raised it, and pointed it at the back of Jason's head.

Kurt leapt across the room. "Whoa, Erika, what are you doing?" He grabbed her wrist.

"Don't interfere, Kurt. We can't save him. He's too badly injured. And we can't leave him behind."

"So you're going to shoot him?"

"We've discussed it. He knows it's our only option. It's what Jason wants. Now let go of my arm."

Kurt said, "Put the gun away, Erika. I have a better idea."

Part 8 – Rescue

Chapter 61

Erika wrenched her hand away. "What are you talking about, Kurt? Leave us and let me do what must be done."

Jason turned his head. "Please let Michelle do her duty. She mustn't leave me here."

Kurt replied, "We don't have to. We can get you out, Jason, take you back to England with us."

"In God's name, how? Look at him. He won't be able to walk for weeks. He may lose his leg."

Kurt grabbed Erika by the shoulders, stared into her eyes and shook her. "There's an airfield near here. I saw the planes coming in to land. All we have to do is get him to the airfield and steal a plane."

Erika opened her mouth and closed it again.

"Felix is an airman, isn't he?" said Kurt.

"He's a Flight Lieutenant."

"He should be able to fly us home, so."

"How do we get to the airfield?"

"I don't know yet. I'll work something out."

"That's incredibly stupid," she brushed the tears from her face.

"Yes," said Kurt. "But it might just work."

"It might." She grinned.

Kurt ran down the stairs in search of Charles. He found the American by the lorry clutching a bucket of water. The tears in his eyes were not entirely caused by the smoke. He had doused the flames, but his lorry was nothing but a worthless pile of charred, smouldering metal. The air stank of burnt rubber and roasted vegetables.

"Find us some transport," said Kurt.

"Where are we going?"

"To the airfield."

When Erika returned to where Klaus Barbie was being held, she saw a bruised SS man, his chin on his chest, despair in his eyes. The Free French were taking turns to beat and slap him.

The wounded Lacosse had taken command again. He held a hand up to call a halt to the proceedings. "Enough of this barbarity. Do we want to descend to this man's level? Herr Barbie has inflicted huge damage to our people, it is true, and nobody could question our moral right to end his miserable existence. But we must deal with him cleanly and humanely."

Erika said, "You can't kill him."

Lacosse turned on her, his words like bullets. "We don't need your approval. There is not a court in the country that would acquit this man of his crimes. He will get a fair trial and then we will execute him."

"The guillotine is too kind for him," someone shouted.

"Barbie must face a court properly constituted by the French Republic," said Erika. "You will all have to wait until after the war for that."

There was uproar at this. And Barbie muttered, "After the war nothing will have changed. Germany will still rule France."

Favier spat on the floor in front of Barbie. "String him up!"

"You have no voice here, Michelle. You are not French," said Lacosse. "The British have no right to dictate to us what we should and shouldn't do in our own country."

Erika remained calm. "If you kill this man without a proper trial then you will be as evil as he is."

"He is a monster, not a man," said one of the Free French.

"And have you thought of the reprisals?" she said, addressing them all.

There were murmurings at this.

"Barbie is an important member of the SS. If you kill him, the Boches will avenge his death. How many innocent French will die if you kill this one man?"

"There will be reprisals anyway after today," said the boxer.

"Yes, but how many? A hundred? Kill Barbie and that number could be a thousand."

"Ten thousand," said Barbie, his smirk returning.

Two men tore the straps from Barbie and hauled him to his feet. Erika thought they meant to hang him there and then, but they had something different in mind. They seized Barbie's legs and removed his boots. Then they frogmarched him to the room next door, inverted him and, climbing onto two chairs, lifted him into his own torture apparatus, securing his ankles in the metal loops.

Their work produced an ecstatic round of applause.

Erika asked Lacosse, "Did he tell you who betrayed the escape line?"

Lacosse nodded. "Roger the legionnaire."

Erika recalled the tall Frenchman who reminded her of her father. She shuddered and drew a veil over his image in her mind. "Where is Roger now?"

"Wherever he is he won't last the day." Lacosse ran a thumb slowly across his throat.

The Free French rustled up a replacement *camion*, and they carried the injured Lacosse and the freed French prisoners out on makeshift stretchers.

"How is Lacosse?" asked Kurt.

"It's not too serious," said Erika, "but he will need to see a doctor."

Following much hugging and kissing, the Free French force dispersed. Kurt had never received so many kisses before.

Charles reappeared. "There's a Gestapo staff car out the back, but we'll need a key."

Kurt went to the interrogation room and asked the inverted Klaus Barbie where he kept his keys. Barbie swore at him. Kurt climbed onto a chair and shook out Barbie's pockets. He found a bunch of keys and tossed them to Charles.

"I know who you are," Barbie shouted. "You are a dead man, Müller. You'll never get out of France alive."

Chapter 62

Kurt and the boxer linked hands and carried the injured Jason to the front door, just as Charles arrived in a sleek, black Citroën saloon. "Barbie's personal vehicle," Charles said.

They eased Jason onto the back seat. Kurt flung his Schmeisser on the floor before climbing in beside Jason. Felix and Erika piled in, Erika up front with Charles. He grinned at her before accelerating away, heading south.

Before they'd reached the end of Rue Tarant they passed a German truck full of armed troops accompanied by three motorcycles heading back the way they had come. Charles watched them in his rear view mirror.

"Reinforcements?" said Kurt.

Charles replied, "Afraid so. They're moving Bessie out of the way."

"Who's Bessie?" said Erika.

"My lorry – or what's left of her. They're entering the building. They'll be after us in minutes."

"How far is the airfield?"

"It's about four miles," Charles accelerated, weaving around the bomb craters that riddled the surface of the road.

"Isn't there another road we can take?" said Erika.

"They'll all be like this. The airfield has probably taken a pounding, too. We'll be lucky to find anything airworthy."

Felix opened his eyes. "We're heading for an airfield?"

"It's the quickest way home," said Erika.

Kurt spotted a sign on a post that read: 'Longvic 2 km' with an airplane shape on the sign.

"Here come the cavalry," said Charles.

Kurt turned his head to look out the rear window. The three motorcycles were gaining on them.

Charles increased his speed again, skirting the craters, testing the Citroën's suspension close to destruction.

Jason groaned and gritted his teeth.

"Sorry, old man," said Charles. "Hang on. It won't be long now. We're nearly there."

Kurt cocked the Schmeisser.

One of the motorcycles drew level and pointed his gun at Charles. Charles threw the wheel over and the motorbike disappeared into a huge bomb crater.

"One down, two to go," said Erika.

Pivoting in his seat, Kurt pushed the rear window out with the butt of the Schmeisser and opened fire on their pursuers. The two motorcycles zigzagged to avoid the bullets, but they kept coming.

A barbed wire fence on their left marked the boundary of the airfield.

"Keep an eye out for the entrance," said Charles.

"Forget the entrance," Kurt shouted. "Go through the fence."

Charles said, "I don't think we're going fast enough for that."

"Put your foot down," said Erika.

Charles did so and they hurtled toward a giant crater. Just before they reached it Erika grabbed the wheel and wrenched it to the left. On two wheels the car jounced around the edge, through a smaller crater, and ploughed through the perimeter fence. The fence sprang back behind them, wiping out one of the motorcycles.

"Two down," said Erika.

"Make for the hangars," said Kurt.

Three airplanes stood outside the only hangar still standing.

"We'll take one of those," said Erika.

Felix said, "Those are Junkers."

"Can you fly one, Felix?" said Kurt.

"I can fly most things, but I've never flown anything with three engines before."

Kurt made eye contact with Felix for a second. Felix was their only hope; they both knew it.

Charles stopped the car beside one of the planes. All but Jason jumped out. Felix ran to the plane and climbed on board.

The third motorcyclist drove past. He skidded to a halt beside the tower and started up an external ladder, a rifle slung across his back.

Kurt called out to Felix through the door of the plane. "Get a move on, Felix."

Felix jumped out of the plane. "This one's no good. There's not enough fuel in the tanks." He ran to the second plane. The motorcyclist had reached halfway up the ladder. He opened fire at Felix with his rifle. Kurt returned fire, and Felix made it to the second plane safely and climbed aboard.

One of the Junkers' three engines started with a cough and a roar.

Kurt ran for the tower, yelling to Erika and Charles, "Get Jason on board, quick!"

Charles and Erika jumped into the car and Charles drove it over to the second plane. Kurt sprinted to the tower. He ran up the steps and burst into the control room. A shot flew past his left shoulder. He returned fire, spraying the room with bullets. When he took his finger from the trigger and peered through the smoke, there was no one alive in the room, just two dead bodies and a lot of broken glass and damaged equipment.

The plane was moving, all three propellers spinning. Kurt hurtled down the stairs and ran after it. A rifle shot fanned his cheek. He turned and riddled the tower roof with bullets, aiming wildly. The motorcyclist gave a cry and threw up his arms, his rifle fell to the ground and he tumbled after it.

Kurt tossed the gun away and ran for the plane. It was gathering speed. Charles stood at the door. "Come on, Kevin!" he shouted, holding out a hand.

Kurt sprinted alongside the plane, reaching out. Charles grabbed his hand and heaved him in and onto the floor. Kurt got to his feet and took a moment to regain his breath. Charles closed the door.

"I need someone up here," Felix shouted.

Kurt sank into the co-pilot's seat. "What do you want me to do?"

"Strap yourself in and put on the headphones." Felix pointed to the three throttles. "Those are the engines." Then he pointed to three dials on the instrument panel. "Those are the rev counters. I will use the throttles, but I need you to keep an eye on the rev counts of the three engines. When I let go, I want you to make small adjustments to keep them all level. Do you understand?"

"I think so," said Kurt.

Felix throttled up. The plane reached the end of the runway and turned into the wind.

A troop truck careered through the hole in the fence.

"Right. Here we go. Let's see what this baby can do," said Felix, his voice as quiet as if he were reading the menu at his club. He opened all three throttles. The plane advanced down the runway, picking up speed, skirting bomb craters, left and right. The truck kept coming, intending to cut them off. Then it was on the runway, racing toward them.

"We're not going to make it!" said Kurt.

"Keep those rev counters level," Felix replied.

Kurt forced his attention on to the engine rev counters and made a small adjustment.

The plane lumbered into the air, clearing the roof of the truck by a couple of metres. The troops opened fire at them with their rifles. And then they were away, climbing above the airfield to safety.

Felix turned on the radio.

"You'll never make it out of France, Müller!" It was Barbie's voice, screaming, hysterical. "Do you hear me? I'll skin you alive when they bring you back to me..."

Felix turned it off. "Check on our passengers," he said as he executed a turn to the west.

Kurt removed the earphones and straps and went back to the others.

"Everyone all right?" he said.

Charles smiled and waved. Erika was busy improvising a binding for Jason's leg. Jason waved an arm.

Kurt returned to the co-pilot seat and put his straps and earphones back on. "What's the range of this plane?" he asked.

Felix replied, "I don't know, but if we keep an eye on the fuel consumption and the time and if I keep the airspeed constant we can work it out. We have a full tank of fuel."

"What are our chances?" said Kurt.

"Slim to none," Felix replied. "They'll radio ahead and shoot us down."

"I killed everyone in the tower."

Felix glanced across at Kurt. "That might give us a slim chance. There's bound to be lots of traffic in the air. If we stay high enough so that our markings are not visible from the ground we might make it to the coast."

"What about RADAR?"

"That won't be a problem as long as we keep clear of airports," said Felix. "But there's no way we can get through the coastal defences without being spotted."

Chapter 63

ƒelix took the plane to 1,700 metres and levelled off.

He switched the radio on. They heard nothing but static.

Kurt kept an eye on their airspeed. Felix kept it constant at 150 kph. Reading their rate of fuel consumption from the instruments, Kurt calculated the range of the plane: close to 1,000 kilometres. He told Felix.

Felix nodded. "I make it about 875. I wonder how far it is from Dijon to the south coast of England. Any idea?"

"None, sorry."

"Ask our passengers. Charles might know."

"Charles is not a pilot."

"Neither is Jason," said Felix. And when Kurt looked sideways at him, he said, "You don't think I worked that out within 30 minutes of meeting him in Paris?"

Charles said he thought Dijon to London was 750 kilometres as the crow flies. Kurt returned to the cockpit with this estimate.

Felix grunted. "See if you can find a map."

Kurt found a portfolio of maps at the back of the plane. He took a close look at the map of France. It was immediately obvious that they had little room for manoeuvre. They would barely have enough fuel to avoid flying directly over Paris. He took the maps back to the cockpit and told Felix.

"Take the wheel," said Felix, and he released the controls. The plane's nose dipped immediately. Breaking into a sweat, Kurt grabbed the control wheel and pulled it back. The engines roared; the nose of the plane tilted up toward the sky.

"Gently!" said Felix as he brought the plane back to level.

"I know nothing about flying!" said Kurt, gripping the control wheel with trembling hands.

"Don't worry about it. It's just like making love. Treat her gently, make small adjustments, and she'll do everything you want." Felix checked the map. "You're right. We'll just have to take the direct route and hope for the best. If we stay to the west of Paris we should be able to avoid Le Bourget airfield."

To Kurt's relief Felix took the controls again and reset their course somewhere west of northwest. He took Kurt through the co-pilot's responsibilities: Controlling airflow over the engines to regulate engine temperature, manifold pressure, carburettor mixture, fuel flow pressure, lubricant temperature and pressure, and so on.

By the time he'd finished, Kurt's head was spinning. "Is that everything?"

"Well, no, but if you can stay on top of that much we might just stay in the air."

It was a cloudless day. The view from the side window of the cockpit was spectacular. Kilometre after kilometre of countryside rolled by with little or no signs of the War or the Occupation. Only in the vicinity of the larger towns could Kurt see bomb damage and the occasional thin plume of smoke.

Kurt avoided the terrifying vista ahead where there was nothing to see except the nose engine, beyond that a bottomless void stretching all the way to the distant blue sky.

They flew unhindered for 90 minutes.

Charles stuck his head through the cockpit door and said, "When do we get our coffee and biscuits?"

Kurt, who had fallen asleep, woke with a start. He checked the instruments and made a few minor changes to fuel flow and engine cowlings. "You shouldn't have let me sleep, Felix."

Felix replied, "You looked like you needed it."

"Where are we?"

Charles answered, "Just south of Paris."

Kurt looked out the window. Paris appeared in a heat haze in the distance and to their right.

"Better get back to your seat, fasten your belt and tell the others to do the same," said Felix.

Fifteen minutes later a Messerschmitt 109 fighter aircraft came up behind them and positioned itself to their left. The static on the radio was interrupted by a harsh German voice: "Anton Viktor Otto, you are ordered to land. Follow me to Le Bourget."

Kurt translated for Felix, although it wasn't necessary.

Felix had paled visibly. "The game's up. We'll have to do what he says."

"What if we keep going? He can't force us to land, can he?"

"He can shoot us down."

The fighter pilot said, "Follow me to Le Bourget or I will open fire."

Kurt said, "Just keep going. He won't fire."

"This is your last warning. Turn right and follow me to Le Bourget."

Felix looked across at Kurt. "We must comply."

"Trust me," said Kurt. "He won't shoot. They want Jason alive."

They flew on for another three minutes. The fighter peeled away, turned and came back from above them. Kurt heard the rattle of gunfire. Tracers split the air across the nose of the Junkers.

"That was your final warning."

Felix said, "Kurt—?"

"Keep going. He's bluffing."

Staring straight ahead, gripping the control column like a drowning man clinging to a piece of driftwood, Felix maintained level flight.

After a long silence the fighter pilot broke away abruptly, and they were alone again in a vast expanse of blue sky.

Charles appeared at the cockpit door again, grinning. "That was well done. What did you say to him?"

Felix said, "It's too early for celebrations. I'm sure we'll see the Luftwaffe again soon. Better go back to your seat and put on your belt."

They skirted Paris without further incident.

Kurt said, "Are there any other airports ahead?"

"Nothing until we reach the coast."

Felix waited half an hour. Then he cycled the radio through its five frequency settings, sending out a signal each time: "This is Flight Lieutenant Felix Jones. Requesting assistance from any friendly aircraft in the area north of Paris."

They got a response on the third attempt. "Squadron Leader Jack Hazelwood, 504 squadron, here. Where away are you? I don't see you."

Kurt punched the air.

Felix replied, "Heading north from Paris. Returning home in a Junkers 52 Able Victor Oboe. We're about 30 minutes out from Le Havre. Expecting a reception committee."

"Roger," said the squadron leader. "We'll provide cover."

Felix reset the radio frequency to its initial setting.

Mile after mile of farmland rolled by. And then Kurt caught sight of the misty coastline ahead and the sea beyond.

"Any minute now," said Felix.

Seconds later the radio crackled to life with an imperious command in German, "This is Le Havre control. Unidentified aircraft approaching from the south, identify yourself."

"Should we respond?" said Kurt.

Felix shook his head. "The longer we keep them guessing the better."

"Identify yourself. You are entering restricted airspace."

Felix flew on, ignoring the increasingly petulant demands from the airfield for a response.

And then quite suddenly two Messerschmitt 109s, their nose cowls painted yellow, were flying alongside, one on each side. Kurt made eye contact with the pilot on the right. The thunderous look on the fighter pilot's countenance was not encouraging.

The radio crackled to life again. "Return to Le Bourget," in German.

Kurt pressed the communications button on the control column and replied in German, "We are on a special assignment for the Oberkommando der Wehrmacht. We have a senior member of the Kriegsmarine on board. Do not hinder us."

The fighter pilot took a couple of minutes to consider before responding, "We know who you are, Anton Viktor Otto. Follow us to Le Bourget or be destroyed."

"Tell him we don't have enough fuel to go back to Le Bourget," said Felix. "Tell them we'll land at Le Havre."

Kurt pressed the communications button and said, "This is Anton Viktor Otto. We do not have sufficient fuel to return to Le Bourget. We will land at Le Havre."

The fighters hesitated before peeling away and climbing above them.

"Where are they going?" said Kurt.

Felix replied, "They'll watch us from above and follow us down to the airport."

Kurt noticed the altimeter reducing steadily. "Are we landing?"

"We don't have much choice," said Felix. He switched the radio back to the RAF frequency and send out a signal in English: "Coming in at ground. Abbeville high."

The Hurricane responded, "Understood. I have your tail. Good luck."

"Abbeville?" said Kurt.

Felix said, "A crack Luftwaffe fighter wing. The yellow paint on the nose cowling is their signature." He switched the radio back to the German frequency. "Ask the airfield for permission to land."

"Come in Le Havre. This is Anton Viktor Otto requesting permission to land."

Le Havre responded immediately. "Anton Viktor Otto, take runway 3."

"Right, hold on to your hat." Felix took the plane down toward the airport. They descended steadily. Racing along the runway, they reached an altitude of 50 feet, then Felix pushed all three engines to maximum and pulled the control column back. The engines roared. The old plane trundled back into the air. Turning toward the strand, Felix headed out to sea.

Tracers tore through the cockpit. Black smoke poured from the centre engine, obscuring the windshield. Felix cut the fuel supply and shut the engine down. He throttled up the remaining two engines and maintained their slow climb. Then Kurt caught a flash of yellow above them. The Messerschmitt turned and came straight toward them, its cannons firing. The windshield shattered, spraying them both with glass fragments and engine lubricant. Felix screamed. His hands shot to his face. Kurt grabbed the control stick and held on.

And then the Messerschmitts were on the run, Hurricanes on their tails.

"Felix!" Kurt shouted above the roar of inrushing air.

"My eyes!" Felix screamed, "I can't see!"

Chapter 64

"What's our altitude?" said Felix, grabbing the control column again.

"900 and climbing."

"Right. Watch the artificial horizon and tell me when I've levelled off."

Kurt did so.

"Switch back to the RAF frequency."

Kurt switched the radio frequency, and Felix sent out a signal. "Mayday, mayday. This is Able Victor Oboe to Squadron Leader Hazelwood. Requesting escort home. We've lost number two engine and I've been injured."

"I'm with you, Jones. What are your injuries?"

"I'm blind." In a shaking voice, he added, "My co-pilot is a civilian."

"I understand. I suggest Ashford in Kent," said the steady voice of the Squadron Leader. "I'll alert them."

"Roger," said Felix.

"What do I do?" said Kurt.

"You're doing fine. Just watch our altitude. Make sure I keep her level and make sure our air speed doesn't drop below 100."

Felix described the landing procedure in detail. Felix would execute the landing; Kurt would be his eyes. At the end of the lesson, Kurt was less than confident that they would make it down safely. He told Felix how he was feeling.

"It's a doddle. Don't worry about it," said Felix.

They had flown across the water for close to two hours before Kurt saw land ahead and Ashford airfield established contact.

"This is RAF Ashford. Come in Able Victor Oboe."

"This is Able Victor Oboe," Felix replied. "Has Squadron Leader Hazelwood informed you of our situation?"

"Roger. We will be ready for you here. Please adjust your heading to zero-three-five. Wind on the ground is northwest six knots. We have a slight haze. The field is clear for you."

With Kurt reading out their headings, Felix executed a reasonable turn to the right and placed the plane on the required heading.

"Altitude?"

"750 metres."

"Air speed?"

"Just on 100."

"Are we level?"

"Yes."

"We should be reducing altitude."

"We are. We're at 700 and dropping."

"Keep an eye on that. Let me know if it drops too quickly."

"How quickly is too quickly?"

"50 meters every three minutes should be about right."

Kurt said, "Air speed's dropping. It's at 90."

Felix increased power. "Can you see the airfield yet?"

"Air speed 95. And no. I see land, but no airfield."

Soon they were flying over land and descending steadily. Kurt broke out in a sweat as he relayed the instrument readings to Felix.

"I see the airfield!" said Kurt.

"Are we lined up on a runway?"

"Nearly. We need to move a smidgen to the right."

"A smidgen." Felix made a slight adjustment.

"That's perfect," said Kurt.

"Altitude and air speed?"

"300 metres and 70."

Felix increased power.

"Tell me if the nose dips. We need to keep the nose up."

"Right. Altitude 260 metres, air speed 80."

"How far to the runway?"

"About another runway."

"Speed looks good, but you're coming in a little high," said the man on the ground.

Felix extended the flaps. Kurt slid forward in his seat. He had the scary feeling that the plane was about to fall out of the sky.

Felix said, "We need to keep the runway ten centimetres up the windscreen during our approach. Watch that and tell me if I need to go 'up' or 'down'. And keep calling out the airspeed. If it stays at 80 say nothing. If I drift off the correct heading just say 'left' or 'right' and 'stop' when I'm on target."

Kurt said, "seventy-eight."

Felix increased the airspeed.

"Eighty-two. Up. Up! Left! Down. Seventy-nine. Down. Right! Stop. Down…"

"How close are we?" said Felix.

"We've passed the end of the runway."

"How high?"

"Tops of the telegraph poles," said Kurt, gripping the edge of his seat.

Felix squeezed the two throttles back, levelling the nose.

They hit the ground hard, bounced and came down a second time. Felix cut both engines and squeezed the brakes. The plane raced along the runway, skidded to a halt 20 metres from the end of the runway, tipped forward for a moment, and sat back on her undercarriage.

"Congratulations!" said the air traffic controller. "A perfect landing! Welcome home."

A fire tender and an ambulance raced across the grass toward them, followed by several army vehicles. Charles opened the door of the plane and jumped down. He helped Erika from the aircraft.

"There are two injured men in there," he said to the ambulance crew.

The two Joneses were taken away in the ambulance. Erika and Charles were loaded into a military police car and driven to a building in the airfield. Two military policemen took Kurt to a saloon car camouflaged in green and grey.

"Where are we going?" said Kurt.

"Back to your unit," replied one of the MPs.

#

The MPs took Kurt to the Grand Central Hotel, Marylebone, an imposing grey building with endless corridors of linoleum and numbered doors. The air was infused with tobacco smoke and seemed strangely rarefied, as if the hotel had been built on top of a mountain.

"Is this really necessary?" said Kurt.

His escort raised an eyebrow. "You flew in on a German plane."

Kurt spent some time in a washroom where he attempted to remove the aircraft lubricant from his face and hair. Then he and his military escort were kept waiting an infuriating two hours before being interviewed by a grey-faced man in uniform.

"You returned from occupied France in a stolen aeroplane, I'm told. Who else was on board?"

Kurt suppressed a desire to reach across the desk and throttle the man. "We had a member of the Free French forces called Charles – an American…"

"A Free French American?"

"That's right. Also on board we had Jason Jones, a British Intelligence agent who was wounded in the leg, and an SOE agent called Erika Cleasby. Our pilot was called Jones."

"Another Jones?"

"Flight Lieutenant Felix Jones, 617 squadron."

"Tell me about yourself. What were you doing in France?"

Kurt ran through his story again. The military policeman handed over Kurt's passport.

"Did you find your missing girlfriend?" said Grey-face.

"No, she wasn't where I expected to find her."

"I see." Grey-face looked puzzled. He examined the passport carefully. "You claim to be Irish, name of Kevin O'Reilly, and yet your commanding officer, Colonel…" He consulted his notes. "…Colonel Underwood, claims you are German."

Speaking slowly, as if to a child, Kurt said, "I work for British Intelligence. I use several aliases."

Kurt's interrogator scowled at him. "So this passport is a forgery? Would you mind telling me what is your real name and nationality?"

"Kurt Müller. I'm a British Intelligence officer. Please contact Colonel Underwood. He will vouch for me."

"Your nationality?"

"I'm German." Kurt's words were accompanied by a vague feeling of discomfort.

#

It took a while, but eventually Grey-face released Kurt into the custody of his military police escort, who delivered him to SIS headquarters in Whitehall.

Colonel Underwood glowered at him. "Erika tells me she and our agent wouldn't have made it home without your help. I'm grateful for that. But I should throw the book at you. No one under my command has ever gone absent without leave for such a length of time, and no one under my command has ever invaded Germany single-handed before." Kurt opened his mouth to explain. The colonel held up a hand. "No need for explanations. A simple apology will suffice."

"I'm sorry, Colonel. I had to—"

"Just tell me you found your beloved Gudrun."

"Afraid not, sir. She's in England somewhere."

"You don't have an exact location?"

"No, sir, but I think I know how to find her. She's being held by an enemy agent with a radio transmitter. I know the frequency he's using. I can locate him by triangulation as soon as he starts transmitting."

"You'll need help with that, I expect."

"Yes, sir."

The colonel lifted the telephone and dialled a number. "This is Colonel Underwood in Whitehall. One of my men has a rough location for an enemy agent... Yes, he has the radio frequency... He'll need at least three... Thank you, Captain."

He put the telephone down. "That's all arranged. You'll have the use of three direction finder vans for a couple of days."

Chapter 65

Like some sort of gigantic black insect, the GCHQ direction finder van sat crouched in the centre of St Albans close to Harry Crum's lair, the strange antenna on its back rotating slowly.

The van's radio receiver was tuned to 2305 kHz, the frequency used by Necker on his radio in the castle, but they had picked up nothing but static all night. Two more direction finder vans parked at strategic locations to the north and east would enable rapid triangulation of the transmitter's location. If it was ever used again.

The sun hadn't risen yet, but the inside of the van was already hot enough to cook a Sunday roast, so hot that Kurt's headphones stuck to his skin.

"Why don't you take a break, sir?" said the radio operator. "I'll alert you if anything comes in."

Kurt removed his headphones and stepped down from the van. After seven hours cooped up in the stifling heat, choking on the radioman's cigarette smoke, he needed to stretch his legs and get some fresh air.

He felt he was on the last lap of his journey. He would see Gudrun again, soon. The thought was unshakeable and it kept him going, even though it was based on nothing concrete. Some sixth sense was telling him that Gudrun was alive and not far away. Surely today he would put the last piece of the puzzle in place and they would be reunited.

He thought about Wolfe and Ingrid. He had a good feeling about them as well. Theirs was another puzzle close to completion.

Kurt heard the Morse code blips through the metal of the van even before the radio operator's excited shout: "We have it, sir!"

He dived into the van and grabbed his headphones. The radio operator was already in contact with the other two vans. The driver moved it to a new position, and this was followed by more frantic communications between the three radio vans.

The transmission ended.

"He's located to the east of here, sir, about 3 miles."

The three radio locator vans moved east and took up new positions close to the town of Brentwood. They waited, nothing but tension and the hiss of static filling the van. The radioman lit a fresh cigarette. Exactly one hour after the first transmission the radio burst into life again. The message was a short one. Kurt jotted it down, character by character. It was in German and translated as:

CONFIRM TERMINATION TONIGHT TT

The blood drained from his face. "Tell me you have the location."

"We have it, sir." The radioman had drawn four lines on the map, isolating two houses back-to-back near the centre of the town. "He's in one of these two houses, 37 Dunbar Road or 9 Kingswood."

"You can't pin it down to one?" said Kurt.

"Afraid not, sir. A longer transmission would have given us time to get closer and take more directional readings. Should we respond to the signal?"

"No!" Kurt grabbed the map, jumped from the van, and set out on foot toward the centre of the Brentwood.

He soon found Dunbar Road, a double row of terraced houses, all in need of a lick of paint. He knocked on the door of number 36 on the opposite side of the road to number 37. There was evidence of bomb damage. The lintels over both front windows were cracked and the glass had been replaced recently. An elderly woman answered the door.

"Excuse me, Madam, Can you tell me who lives across the road in number 37?"

"Who are you?"

"I'm trying to locate an old friend. His name is Tobias."

She shook her head. "Miriam Fletcher lives in number 37. She's a retired school teacher."

Kurt thanked the woman. He hurried around to Kingswood. A

giant flock of starlings circled above, twisting and turning in incredible feats of coordinated flight. All together, as if on a signal, they flew into a tree, settled, and a chorus of chatterings began.

He knocked on the door of number 41, directly opposite number 9, on the other side of the road. As with the house in Dunbar Road the lintels over both front windows of number 41 were split. The broken panes had not been replaced, but were boarded up.

The door was opened by a young woman, a scarf tied around her hair, an infant clinging to her leg.

"Good morning, Madam. Do you have a couple of minutes to answer a few questions?"

"Who're you?"

"My name's O'Reilly. I'm with the Ministry of Housing."

"Why can't you people leave me alone! You'll get it when I have it." She pushed the door over.

Kurt used his boot to keep the door open. "I'm not here about your rent, Madam. I want to ask some questions."

"I'm a widow. My husband died fighting for this country. Why can't you have a little humanity and leave us be?"

"I want to ask you about your neighbour across the road in number 9."

"What about him?"

"Do you know his name?"

"No, sorry. He keeps himself to himself. Hardly ever comes out."

"How long has he lived there?"

"Coupla months. Three months, maybe. What's this all about?"

"He lives alone, this man?"

"I think so. I've never seen anyone else. Why, what's he done?"

"We're not sure yet."

"Why not knock on his door? Why bother me?" Here eyes opened wide. "You're not really with the housing people, are you?"

Kurt said nothing, but he maintained eye contact.

The door swung open. "I knew it! I knew there was something weird about him. Come in. Come in, mister."

Kurt stepped across the threshold. "What's your name?"

"Daisy Pickering."

Kurt shook her hand. "We're grateful for your help."

He followed her into the front room. Avoiding scattered piles of toys, he made his way to the window and peered through the lace curtains. The house opposite was a two-up two-down just like Mrs Pickering's.

"Does he go to work in the mornings?"

"No. I've never seen him leave. He's in there all the time."

"He must go out for food supplies."

"Once a week on Mondays, usually. He goes to the local shop. I met him in there once or twice and he was very rude. He totally ignored me."

"You tried to strike up a conversation with him?"

"Well, no. But he must know we're neighbours. It's not natural to ignore your neighbours."

Kurt could see no movement in the house. It looked deserted. He thanked Mrs Pickering for her help and left.

He walked briskly the length of road and back again. Most of the houses had empty milk bottles on their doorsteps. Apart from a single empty bottle, the front view of number 9 yielded no new information.

A milkman leading a horse and cart entered the end of the road. Kurt hurried to intercept him.

"I'm trying to locate an old friend," said Kurt. "His name's Tobias Thurner I know he lives on this road somewhere."

The milkman said, "Toby Turner lives at number 9."

Kurt's heartbeat quickened. "That's him! Thank you."

Kurt watched the milkman making his deliveries. When he got to number 9 he left a single bottle of milk on the doorstep and removed the empty.

Kurt waited until the milkman had moved on. Then he slipped into the front garden of the house and took up a position close to the front door but out of sight of the windows. He waited.

The chattering starlings had moved to a tree overlooking number 9.

The door opened, a man emerged and bent to pick up the milk bottle.

Kurt pounced. His first blow to the man's back sent him to the ground. The man swore, "*Scheisse!*" and tried to get up. Kurt struck him again on the back of the neck, but the blow was ineffective and Toby gained his feet.

Wide-eyed, the German agent backed into the house clutching the precious milk bottle to his chest. Kurt followed, grabbing him by the lapels. Determined to hold onto the milk bottle, Toby refused to engage in the fight. Instead, he tried to use his superior weight to push Kurt back out through the door. Kurt buried a fist in Toby's midriff and the German folded. The milk bottle fell and smashed on the floor tiles. Kurt delivered a rabbit punch to the back of Toby's neck as he fell, and the German agent collapsed into the white pool of milk.

"Gudrun, where are you?" Kurt called out.

"Up here, Kurt."

He took the stairs two at a time and found Gudrun in the back bedroom, handcuffed to the head of a brass bed.

They embraced.

"I thought you'd never get here," she said. "What kept you?"

He opened his mouth with no idea how he was going to reply.

"Never mind, Kurt," she said. "Get me out of these handcuffs."

He ran back downstairs to relieve Toby of the handcuff keys, but when he got there the German had gone, his milky footsteps leading through the front door and onto the road.

Chapter 66

Jeremy Wichard stood at his window in the Foreign Office. In the street outside an early morning mist clung to the base of the war memorial like a malevolent cancer. He knew it would dissipate long before the sun appeared above the buildings opposite.

His private secretary opened his door and announced, "Mr Dansey is here, sir."

Claude Dansey of the SIS pushed past her.

"Thank you Yvonne. Get us some coffee, will you?" said Wichard.

Yvonne left, closing the door behind her.

Wichard said, "I missed you at lunch yesterday."

"Sorry, I was unavoidably detained."

"You missed a first rate Angus steak."

"Probably not Angus," said Dansey. "Nothing is ever quite what it seems."

Wichard opened his cigarette case and offered them to Dansey.

Dansey declined. He said, "You've heard about Operation Tabletop?"

"I heard it went tits up." Wichard suppressed a wicked smile. Dansey was an idiot – everyone knew it – but he was a lovable idiot and he played with a straight bat.

Wichard's secretary arrived with a tray of coffee. She put the tray on a table and Wichard waved her out of the room.

Dansey said, "The SOE woman got my agent out, if that's what you mean."

"With a nasty leg wound, I believe."

"The doctors are hoping to save the leg."

Wichard smiled his wicked smile. "And without revealing anything to the Nazis."

"Quite. We'll have to be less subtle next time."

Wichard poured two coffees and handed one to his visitor. "I heard they landed at Ashford in a German aircraft."

"A Junkers 52. The RAF were delighted to get their hands on it."

Wichard nodded. "The operation was not a total loss, so."

Dansey sipped his coffee. "You're going to the briefing?"

"Wouldn't miss it."

"Seriously, old man, I'm going to need all the help I can get. The Prime Minister is spitting nails."

Chapter 67

The kitchen of number 9, Kingswood, Brentwood was equipped with a selection of household tools. Kurt selected a lump hammer, took it upstairs and used it to smash the head of the brass bed.

When Gudrun was free, handcuffs dangling from one wrist, they embraced properly.

"I thought I'd never see Anna again. You know Toby was planning to get rid of me tonight or tomorrow." There were tears in her eyes.

"Toby?"

She nodded. "We never became friends, exactly, but he told me his story. He owed his life to Necker and obeyed him without question. I hope you didn't kill him."

He touched the side of her face. She looked pale, weary. "He's alive and well. He's escaped."

"He promised to make it as painless as possible…" She clutched her face and sobbed.

Kurt held her close. "Did he…? Did he hurt you?"

"Toby was a perfect gentleman."

As they left the house 5,000 starlings rose from a tree and took to the summer air with a flurry of wings.

#

Alerted by the men in the GCHQ van, British Intelligence dispatched a military ambulance and a couple of military policemen in a car to the scene. The policemen removed Gudrun's handcuffs and put her in the ambulance where a young doctor took her temperature and blood pressure. "We'll keep you in hospital overnight as a precaution," he said.

"I feel fine," said Gudrun, but the ambulance driver closed the doors and the ambulance sped away.

Kurt was escorted to the military car. He objected strenuously to the separation, but was transported to Camp Twenty by the two tight-lipped policemen and wheeled into Colonel Stephens's office.

Tin-eye Stephens glared at Kurt through his ever-present monocle. "I hear you uncovered an enemy agent – in Brentwood, of all places."

Kurt replied, "His name is Tobias Thurner. He was operating under the direct orders of a high-ranking SS man called Necker."

"We know all about Manfred Necker," said Tin-eye. "Where is he now, this enemy agent?"

"I knocked him out and rushed up the stairs to rescue my girlfriend. When I went back down to get the keys to her handcuffs he had gone."

The colonel's lip curled in a sneer. "You didn't think to restrain him, tie him up, maybe?"

"No."

Tin-eye frowned. "Why didn't you wait for help before going in? We could have helped with the rescue and we would have been there to take this Thurner into custody."

"I'm sorry, Colonel, I suppose I wasn't thinking straight. I was desperate to get to Gudrun."

Kurt wouldn't admit it, but he would never have involved any branch of the British military in the rescue. They would have charged in with guns blazing, and probably got Gudrun killed.

He supplied a description of the fugitive agent before Colonel Stephens handed him back to his military police escort. They drove him to the SIS building in Broadway where Colonel Underwood was waiting to talk to him.

"How is Gudrun?" asked the colonel.

"The doctor insisted on keeping her in hospital for a night, but I think she's fine. I'd like to take her back to Ireland and maybe spend a few days at home with her."

"Leave? You're looking for leave after nearly five weeks on the lam?"

"You did promise me a few days' leave before all this started. Give me seven days, Colonel. Let me take Gudrun home, spend a few days with Gudrun, Anna and my mother."

"Anna?"

"Gudrun's 10-year-old daughter."

The colonel pointed the chewed end of the pencil at Kurt's head. "I'm sorry, Müller, you're too valuable an asset and too many people in high places know about you. I can't risk it. I'll pay for three nights in a London hotel. That's the best I can do."

Kurt jumped from his chair. "You can't keep me here like some prisoner. I volunteered for service. Surely I'm entitled to leave after all I've been through."

The pencil snapped in the colonel's hands. "Sit down soldier, or I'll lock you up for insubordination."

Kurt resumed his seat.

Colonel Underwood gave Kurt two minutes to calm down before calling Major Faulkner to join them for Kurt's debriefing.

He took them through the whole trip as concisely as he could, revealing as few names as possible.

"This American, the one with the vegetable lorry, what's his name?"

"We called him Charles. He never gave me his surname."

When he described the bombing raid on Hamburg, the colonel and the major reacted as if they were discussing a successful football match.

"I heard about that raid," said the major. "It was very successful. RAF casualties were minimal. I believe we lost just a single aircraft."

"There was an even bigger raid on Hamburg last night," said the colonel. "It was on the news this morning. They say it was the biggest and most successful joint Allied bombing raid of the war. I heard they wiped the city off the map using thousands of incendiaries and over 750 aircraft."

Kurt said nothing.

\#

He took a cab to St Bartholomew's Hospital in Whitechapel Road.

The entrance to the hospital was undamaged, but behind the façade the building had been extensively bombed during the blitz. Whole sections of the hospital had been transformed into massive piles of rubble; other sections were open to the elements. Even within the functioning areas of the hospital exotic fragrances like cement dust and charcoal were mixed in with the usual smells of soap and disinfectant.

Kurt found Jason and Felix in adjacent beds in a ward for wounded servicemen. Felix's eyes were tightly bandaged. Wearing dark glasses, seated by Jason's bed, Erika waved to Kurt. He waved back and took a seat beside Felix.

"Hello, Felix."

Felix held out a hand and Kurt took it. "That sounds like my co-pilot."

"How's your treatment going?"

"Well, I think. The doctors are confident they will be able to save one eye. They're not so sure about the other one, though."

"When will you know?"

"Later today, when they take the bandages off."

"Good luck with that," said Kurt with feeling. "I wanted to thank you. None of us would have made it home without you. We all owe you our lives."

"I owe you even more," said Felix. "You saved my life."

"I couldn't have landed the plane without your exact instructions."

"That's not what I meant," said Felix. "I'm Jewish on my mother's side. The Nazis were planning to send me to Poland to one of the death camps."

Erika was in deep conversation with Jason. Considering how close she'd come to shooting him in the head, Kurt wasn't surprised.

She stood and waved Kurt into the chair.

"No need to leave on my account," he said.

"I'm out of time." She kissed Jason lightly on the cheek and left.

Kurt took Erika's chair and had a short conversation with Jason. The news was not encouraging: his leg was gangrenous and might have to be amputated. The surgeons were considering trying a controversial new treatment from America called HBOT. Jason wasn't sure what HBOT was.

Felix piped in. "Hyperbaric Oxygen Therapy. It involves the use of oxygen under high pressure to recover dead tissue. The treatment is not just controversial, it's downright bloody experimental."

"It may be the only hope I have of saving my leg," said Jason.

A young woman arrived bright-eyed, carrying an infant about 6 months old. Beaming, she hurried to Jason's bedside. "Jason, my love, meet Jason junior."

Kurt slipped away. He found Erika waiting for him in the corridor.

"We need to talk," she said.

They left the hospital and headed south toward the Thames.

"Have you seen Charles since we landed?" he asked.

"He's taking me to a movie tonight in Leicester Square."

Kurt looked at her and raised an eyebrow. "You mean a film?"

"Don't give me that look, Kurt."

He held up both palms. "Did I say anything?"

"No, but I know what you're thinking." She lit a cigarette.

Kurt's only thought was that Charles would need to scrub up if he had serious intentions toward Erika.

"How are your bruises?" he said.

"You tell me." She removed her dark glasses to reveal two faded black eyes. The bruises on her cheekbones were turning yellow.

"Much better," he said.

She put her glasses on again, and they sat side by side on a bench overlooking the river. There was silence between them for two minutes. Then she said, "I asked Jason about his debriefing, and guess what. Nobody's been near him yet."

"I thought he was carrying urgent strategic intelligence vital to the Allied war effort."

"So did I. But he's been back on English soil two and a half days and he's still waiting for someone to collect the vital intelligence information from him."

"Wasn't that why you had to get him out of France? And you were prepared to shoot him rather than allow him to spill the beans to the Germans."

"Those were my orders."

Chapter 68

Kurt and Erika walked along by the river together. It was close to midday, the sun was high and people's spirits were rising. Even the trees had shaken off the dust layer from their leaves. The war wasn't over yet, but the RAF had conquered the skies over England and it seemed unlikely that there would be any more bombing of the capital. Gangs of workmen were removing rubble from the streets in preparation for the years of rebuilding that would follow the end of the war.

Kurt looked across the river. The skyline was fractured with half-demolished buildings, but there were no fires and there were boats moving on the river, two merchant vessels and a Navy minesweeper.

Erika said, "I wondered at the time why Jason was dropped behind enemy lines with no suicide pill. It was almost as if Whitehall wanted him to be caught and interrogated. And sending me to get him out had the singular effect of drawing attention to him, telling the Gestapo that there was a British agent with important information hiding among the prisoners of war."

He said, "But don't forget the Gestapo only knew about it because the Free French had been infiltrated by a Gestapo agent."

"Suppose the SIS knew about that? Suppose they knew that drawing attention to Jones would cause the collaborator to alert the Gestapo and reveal himself…"

"And put Jason in the firing line."

"I think that was the intention all along. If they hadn't sent me across, if I hadn't alerted the Free French to the fact that Jason was important to the Allies, he would have spent the remainder of the war happily in that PoW camp."

"What you're suggesting is monstrous," said Kurt, quietly. "Jason endured incredible agony in order to protect that information. Even Felix was tortured, and he knew nothing. And Barbie beat you."

She touched the side of her face. "He wanted me to tell him which of the Joneses had the information. Thank God it never occurred to him that I might have the information, too."

"You're saying that Whitehall wanted Jason to hold out as long as he could, maybe to die protecting the information, so that the Gestapo would believe it was true. Is that what you're suggesting?"

"Yes, even though the information was bogus. It concerned the German defences along the coast of Holland and Belgium. I suppose if the Gestapo had to take Jason close to death to get the information from him, they would have believed that the Allies were really interested in that part of the coast."

"So it was all a trick designed to misinform and misdirect the enemy? Jason is unaware of this, I hope."

"As far as I can tell, he hasn't worked it out yet."

Kurt accompanied Erika back to the hospital where they found Charles waiting. This was a very different Charles to the man they both knew in France. He was scrubbed clean and dressed in a new clean suit. He had even excavated the soil from his fingernails.

Erika went in search of a bathroom in the hospital to freshen up, leaving Kurt and Charles at the entrance. They embraced in a strange cross between the British and American formal handshake and the French hug and kisses.

"So what are your plans for the remainder of the war?" Kurt asked. "I don't suppose you can return to France."

"I've spoken to the Office of Strategic Services here in London. They may have work for me," Charles replied. "What about you?"

"Oh, I'm permanently joined at the hip to British Intelligence. If you ever need my help, Charles, you know where to find me."

"Likewise, Kevin. My name's Mason, by the way, Chuck Mason."

Kurt grinned. "Hello, Chuck Mason. I'm Kurt, Kurt Müller."

"You're not Irish?"

Kurt shook his head. "I'm German." Again, the words were accompanied by a strong feeling of discomfort, and by the time Chuck and Erika had set off arm-in-arm for the picture house, the feeling had crystalized and sat like a weight on his heart. It was a feeling of deep shame for the abyss that his country had fallen into. The Polish death camps. The gas chambers.

I may not be a Nazi, but I'm German, he thought. This is my shame. But deeper than that lurked another more personal guilt for what he and Wolfe had done to Necker in the castle dungeons.

#

Gudrun was released from hospital. They took a cab to the Fillimore Hotel and checked in. The first thing Gudrun did was to use the hotel telephone to ring home. She rang a neighbour of Kurt's mother who fetched her to take the call. Gudrun told Kurt's mother the good news, and then both she and Kurt spoke to Anna. Anna was delighted to hear their voices, although Kurt had some difficulty explaining why he couldn't go home.

After the call, Gudrun ran a bath.

"Aren't you hungry?" he said.

"Yes, but my bath comes first. It's been a month since my last one. Why don't you see if you can order something from the kitchen? A chicken salad would be nice."

He lifted the telephone and placed an order.

"Food's on the way," he called through the bathroom door. "There was no chicken. I've ordered a salad with a new kind of pressed meat. It's called spam."

"Sounds delicious," Gudrun called back. "We should go out later and see if we can find a present for Anna. We both missed her birthday."

"I know. I tried to get leave, but then your postcard arrived."

There was a knock on the door within minutes.

That was quick, thought Kurt. "The food's here," he said.

He opened the door and caught a momentary glimpse of Toby's ugly face before he was on his back on the floor with the German agent sitting on his chest pummelling him with both fists.

"What's going on?" said Gudrun through the bathroom door.

Kurt used his arms to protect himself from Toby's onslaught. Then he grabbed one of Toby's arms and held on. Toby continued to hit him with his free hand. The fact that Toby was using his fists suggested that he wasn't carrying a weapon. Either that or he wanted the satisfaction of striking Kurt with his bare hands. The blows were ineffective, but Kurt was trapped under the big man's weight.

A knife appeared in Toby's free hand. Kurt grabbed the knife hand with both of his own. It took all his strength to keep the knife at bay. Toby increased the pressure and the knife inched closer to Kurt's chest. In desperation, Kurt twisted Toby's knife hand. The knife flew across the room. Toby went after it.

The bathroom door flew open, and Gudrun emerged wrapped in a towel. As soon as he saw her, Toby forgot about the knife and leapt on her with an indecipherable yell.

Kurt regained his feet to find Gudrun on the floor beside the bed with Toby's hands around her throat, throttling her. He launched himself at Toby, wrapped an arm around his neck and tried to prise him off her. Toby clung on like a limpet mine, a madman whose only reason for living was to strangle the life from Gudrun.

Kurt used his free hand to gouge the German's eyes. Toby screamed and his grip loosened. With Kurt pulling and Gudrun pushing at his chest from below, she managed to wriggle out from under the heavy Nazi, losing her towel in the process.

Toby and Kurt jumped to their feet and wrestled. Toby was bigger and heavier, Kurt lighter and younger. Toby's was wearing heavy boots; Kurt was barefoot.

Kurt tried a couple of punches to Toby's face, but they were too close together, his blows were no more than slaps. Toby replied with a close quarters fist to the stomach that knocked the air from Kurt's lungs and would have caused him to double in two if Toby's grip hadn't been holding him up.

Using the palm of his hand Kurt pushed Toby's face backward and delivered a knee to his groin. Toby yelped. His head dropped. Kurt followed up with a knee to Toby's face.

Toby straightened with a grunt, and stamped with a heavy boot on Kurt's right foot. While Kurt was recovering from that, he wrapped one maw around Kurt's neck and squeezed. Excruciating shards of pain immobilized Kurt. All he could do was hold on to his opponent's arm and try to prise it from him. A wave of dizziness washed over him, threatening to end the contest.

And then Toby let go suddenly, staggered backward and fell to the floor. Gudrun stood over him, stark naked, holding the remains of a pottery vase, her eyes blazing.

Kurt placed a knee in the German's back, immobilizing him. Gudrun cut a rope from the curtains and Kurt used it to tie the German's hands and feet. As he worked, he said, "What's the matter with you, Toby? I thought you would have escaped back to Germany by now."

"I'm bound by a debt of honour," Toby replied. "You wouldn't understand."

"A debt of honour to Manfred Necker?"

"I owe him my life. I didn't want to kill Gudrun, but I gave him my word."

"But Necker is dead," said Kurt.

Toby tried to turn his head to look at Kurt's face. "You lie, but even if that's true, it makes no difference. I am still obliged to keep my word."

Gudrun got dressed. Kurt used the telephone to call for help from the police.

A pair of military policemen arrived quickly and took the Nazi agent into custody.

"Where are they taking him?" asked Gudrun.

"Camp Twenty would be my guess. There's a colonel with a monocle there eager to talk to him."

Chapter 69

The morning after their first night together, they woke late to birdsong and the clatter of London traffic. The summer sun was pouring through the window with enough force to push the curtains apart.

She put a finger on his cheek. "What happened?"

"It's nothing. A duelling scar. Tell me how you ended up in that house. I was sure you were in Hamburg where the postcard was posted."

"Toby found me on the way to pick up Anna from school. He threatened to have her killed if I failed to cooperate. He took me to the ferry. We travelled to England as a couple and onward to the house in Brentwood. Necker was waiting for us there. He gave me a postcard to write. I'm sorry about the postcard, Kurt. I knew it was a trap, but I had to write it. They gave me little choice. They threatened to take Anna."

He squeezed her hand. "I understand, Gudrun."

They made love slowly. Afterwards they lay side by side listening to the sounds of birdsong.

She said, "Couldn't you arrange some proper leave? Your mother worries about you. Anna misses you terribly."

"This is all I could get."

"Three days in a hotel in the middle of a war zone?"

"London's not a war zone, not anymore."

"Isn't it?"

"No. Italy is a war zone. The Far East is a war zone. And Russia."

"What about Germany?"

He propped himself on an elbow and swept a stray strand of hair from her face. "Yes, Germany is a war zone."

He told her about the destruction of Hamburg and the baby that he rescued from the bombed building.

"Something good came from your visit to Hamburg, so," she said, quietly. "If it hadn't been for the postcard you wouldn't have been there when that baby needed you."

Kurt thought about that. If he had been religious he might have believed that rescuing that baby was the point of the whole exercise.

"You're a hero."

He laughed. "I'm no hero. I've had enough, Gudrun. If I could go home to Dublin with you I would. We could get married. I'd never come back here again. Let the Nazis and the Allies fight it out without me."

"What did you say?"

"I've had enough of the war. They don't need my help to annihilate one another."

"Not that. You said something else. Did you propose marriage?"

"Yes, Gudrun, if you'll have me."

"Of course I will, Kurt!" She kissed him full on the lips.

She put her head on his chest. "Anna thinks you're a hero," she whispered.

"I'm not sure I want to be a hero anymore," said Kurt.

THE END

Printed in Great Britain
by Amazon